Highland Alliances

Convenient marriages to save their clan!

Neighboring Scottish clans must form alliances to defeat a dangerous common enemy. New clan leader Ross MacMillan is prepared to enter into a marriage contract to safeguard his people. His brother and sister are under orders to marry strategically, as well. Is there a way for love to flourish amid the battle for land and castles in the Highlands?

Read Ross's story from Terri Brisbin in
The Highlander's Substitute Wife
Available now

Fergus's story from Jenni Fletcher in
The Highlander's Tactical Marriage
Available now

And Elspeth's story from Madeline Martin in
The Highlander's Stolen Bride
On sale April 2022

Author Note

When Harlequin approached Terri Brisbin, Madeline Martin and me with the idea of a Highlander series back in 2020, they gave us carte blanche to come up with whatever story we wanted, which was fantastic in one way and a huge challenge in another. It's not easy coming up with a series when one of you is in the UK, one in New Jersey and the other in Florida but, thanks to Zoom, we managed!

The original concept was inspired by an episode of Neil Oliver's *Blood of the Clans* about Alasdair MacColla (Sir Alexander MacDonald), a controversial figure who led a mercenary army from Ireland in the seventeenth century to reclaim his lands in the west of Scotland, eventually joining the Marquess of Montrose's Royalist campaign in support of Charles I in 1644–45. That's pretty much where the similarity ends, but it gave us the kernel of an idea about an exiled clan leader returning to Scotland to reclaim his former lands, now partly controlled by one family, the MacMillans (two brothers and one sister), forcing them to make marriage alliances in a hurry.

After our first discussion, we were slightly alarmed by the seemingly infinite number of castles we'd come up with, but it all came together over a period of about six months. It's been a real pleasure to collaborate with two authors who have such a knowledge and love of Scottish history and we really hope you enjoy the results. Hopefully, I'll get to meet Terri and Madeline on Scottish soil some day so that we can finally discuss it in person.

JENNI FLETCHER

The Highlander's Tactical Marriage

Recycling programs
for this product may
not exist in your area.

ISBN-13: 978-1-335-40767-2

The Highlander's Tactical Marriage

Copyright © 2022 by Jenni Fletcher

This edition published by arrangement with Harlequin Books S.A.

For questions and comments about the quality of this book,
please contact us at CustomerService@Harlequin.com.

Harlequin Enterprises ULC
22 Adelaide St. West, 41st Floor
Toronto, Ontario M5H 4E3, Canada
www.Harlequin.com

Printed in U.S.A.

Jenni Fletcher was born in the north of Scotland and now lives in Yorkshire with her husband and two children. She wanted to be a writer as a child but became distracted by reading instead, finally getting past her first paragraph thirty years later. She's had more jobs than she can remember but has finally found one she loves. She can be contacted on Twitter, @jenniauthor, or via her Facebook author page.

Books by Jenni Fletcher

Harlequin Historical

Tudor Christmas Tidings
"Secrets of the Queen's Lady"
A Marriage Made in Secret

Highland Alliances

The Highlander's Tactical Marriage

Regency Belles of Bath

An Unconventional Countess
Unexpectedly Wed to the Officer
The Duke's Runaway Bride

Sons of Sigurd

Redeeming Her Viking Warrior

Secrets of a Victorian Household

Miss Amelia's Mistletoe Marquess

Whitby Weddings

The Convenient Felstone Marriage
Captain Amberton's Inherited Bride
The Viscount's Veiled Lady

Visit the Author Profile page
at Harlequin.com for more titles.

For Meggie

Chapter One

Argyll, Scotland—late summer 1360

'Nay, Uncle, you can't mean it. Not him! Anyone but him!'

Coira Barron staggered backwards, feeling as if she'd just been kicked in the stomach. Her nerves had been on edge ever since the summons from her uncle-in-law had arrived the day before, but the reason behind it was even worse than any of the dire possibilities she'd imagined on the eight-hour ride to his fortress. So much worse that she was doing the unthinkable and arguing back. There was no way that such defiance was going to end well, but she couldn't seem to stop herself, the words pouring out of her mouth as if her tongue had a mind of its own. Fergus MacMillan was the last man in Scotland she ever wanted to set eyes on again, let alone marry!

'Please, Uncle, I beg you.' She shook her head so violently that one of her own dark braids escaped from beneath her headdress and hit her in the face. Out of the corner of her eye, she could see various members of Brody's household muttering and tutting with disapproval, not that there was anything new about that, only there *was* something different about it this time, a gloating undercurrent that sent an icy-cold shiver rattling down her spine. She knew that the only reason they still accepted her was because of her son, Gregor, but their antipathy had never been quite so obvious or overwhelming before.

'You'll do as you're told.' Brody MacWhinnie, the fearsome head of his clan, had a voice as cold as the granite outcrop his hall was built on.

'But he must hate me after what I did!'

'Pah.' Brody's shrug implied that whatever her prospective bridegroom might think of her personally was of little importance. 'That was a long time ago.'

'I still doubt he's forgotten,' Coira retorted before lowering her head, sensing she'd gone too far as Brody's pale eyes flashed. Briefly, she thought about prostrating herself on the floor and imploring him to reconsider. Honestly, if he wanted her to crawl around the entire hall on her hands and knees then she was prepared to do it, but hard experience had taught her that Brody MacWhinnie viewed the world from one, and only one, perspective: his own. And once he'd made up his mind, there was nothing anyone could do to change it, least of all a *mere* woman.

'Forgive me, Uncle.' She strove to sound suitably meek and dutiful, the two qualities she knew he valued most in the female sex. 'You just caught me by surprise, that's all, and my understanding is only feeble, not like a man's.' She gritted her teeth at the words, peeking up through her lashes to see if they were having any effect. 'Perhaps you could explain to me why I need to marry at all?'

'Because of the threat from the Campbells! The Mac-Millans and the MacWhinnies need to stand and resist them together.'

'But we can still do that. Surely a marriage isn't necessary? Let me defend Castle Barron!'

'What do *you* know of battle strategy?' Brody's lip curled scornfully. 'It was one thing to let you mind the place for your son while we had peace, but matters are different now. That bastard Alexander Campbell intends to reclaim all of the territory he lost twenty years ago, which means that we need to be ready to defend ourselves. This is war and Fergus MacMillan is one of the fiercest warriors in the Highlands. If anyone can hold Castle Barron, then it's him. I don't want the Campbells' army getting anywhere near my lands.'

So that was the truth of it, Coira thought, dropping her eyes to the floor so that Brody couldn't see them narrowing with contempt. The head of the MacWhinnie clan didn't want the inconvenience of fighting Alexander Campbell or his son Calum himself. Far better to get a MacMillan to do it for him. If that meant sacrificing her in marriage to a man who despised her, then so be it. And *despised* was probably a polite way of putting it…

'But why has *he* accepted this marriage? He'll never be Laird—not when my son's already inherited the title.' She straightened up as a new strategy occurred to her. 'Unless he's planning to push Gregor aside and take his place once the fight with the Campbells is over? MacMillan lands are only a stone's throw from Castle Barron. How do we know that's not really his plan?'

'Because he's already given me his word that it's not.' Her uncle-in-law rose to his feet, a sure sign that he was beginning to lose patience. 'He might be a ruthless son of a bitch on a battlefield, but he's a man of honour, too. More honourable than my nephew was anyway. What the two of you did brought shame on both of our families and there's been bad blood between us and the Mac-Millans ever since. This marriage alliance is a way of finally remedying that.'

'You mean it's already decided?' Coira heard the note of despair in her own voice. Defeat was beginning to feel inevitable.

'Aye. From what I gather, he wasn't best pleased with the idea of marrying you either, but the bargain's struck. He'll have what's left of your dowry as well as Castle Barron for more than ten years until your lad's old enough to take over. As for his reasons, he's doing his duty to his clan. As I expect you to as well.'

'But what if—?'

'Enough!' Brody's voice hardened. 'I refuse to debate my decisions with you, nor any woman.'

'Yes, Uncle.' Coira schooled her features back into submission. If the bargain was already struck, then she was truly wasting her breath. How foolish of her to think that she might be allowed a say in the matter of her own future. Even more foolish to imagine that her uncle-in-law might actually listen.

A fresh bout of bone-rattling horror shuddered through her body, making her limbs shake with a combination of tension and panic. Surreptitiously, she glanced around the hall, acutely aware now of the gloating expressions on the faces surrounding her. No doubt they were all thinking the same thing—that this was her long-awaited comeuppance, no more than a woman with her jaded history deserved.

'I ken you've not been a widow long.' The hard set of Brody's jaw softened infinitesimally. 'But this is what my nephew would have wanted, for Castle Barron to be protected for his son. No matter what.'

'Yes, Uncle.' Coira swallowed miserably. That much was true. Nevin would have given an arm and a leg for his son. Maybe even a hand for his daughter. And not so much as the tip of a finger for her.

'Then the matter's settled. You'll marry Fergus Mac-Millan as soon as he arrives at Castle Barron, likely within the week.'

'Yes, Uncle.'

'And there'll be no running away this time, is that clear?'

'Yes, Uncle.'

'Good.' Brody came to loom over her, so close that she could smell the reek of sour ale on his breath. 'Be an obedient wife, learn to curb that sharp tongue of yours and who knows?' There was a flash of grim humour in his eyes. 'Maybe he won't hate you so much, after all.'

'Yes, Uncle.' She curtsied and turned away, leaving the hall to the sound of mocking laughter.

'What happened?' Grizel, her maid, came rushing across the bailey the moment Coira emerged into daylight, her bouncing, ruby-red curls attracting their usual amount of male attention. 'You look as pale as a ghost.'

'I feel like I've just seen one. Or I'm going to soon. Come on, let's get out of here.'

Coira seized hold of her maid's arm and made straight for their horses. The sooner she escaped the confines of Brody's fortress, the sooner she could vent her feelings. And if she couldn't do it with a cudgel over the MacWhinnie's head, then a good, full-throated scream out in the glen struck her as extremely appealing at that moment. The way she was feeling, she could probably start an avalanche.

'You're starting to worry me.' Grizel threw her a nervous look. 'Surely it wasn't *that* bad?'

'Ha!' Coira shoved her foot into a stirrup, swinging one leg over the back of her palfrey so roughly that the animal shied sideways. 'He's ordered me to marry again.'

'Marry?' Grizel let out a squeak of high-pitched indignation. 'But it's barely six months since Nevin's accident!'

'I know, but he claims it's what Nevin would have wanted.' She made a face, thinking once again that Brody was right. Her husband had always had a dark, twisted kind of humour. Her present situation probably *would* have amused him, just like anything else at her expense.

'Does he have someone in mind?'

'That's the worst part.' Coira beckoned to the half-dozen riders she'd brought along for protection. 'The man he's chosen is Fergus MacMillan.'

'No!' Grizel sounded appropriately horrified. 'Surely not?'

'Surely, yes. And it was all decided two days ago. The only reason he summoned me here was to tell me his decision.' She glared over her shoulder at Brody's hall. 'He probably thinks that I ought to be grateful he bothered telling me face to face at all, the cowardly, self-centred, miserable, old—'

'Shh.' Grizel nudged her horse closer. 'At least wait until we're through the gates.'

'Aye.' Coira sucked in a deep breath and then let it out again slowly, biting back a string of invectives. 'It's just…'

'I know. Fergus MacMillan of all people.'

'Exactly!'

'After you ran away from him.'

'It wasn't quite like that.'

'On the eve of your wedding, too.'

'Aye…' Coira shuffled uncomfortably '…but only because there was no other way. I honestly wished that I could have gone and discussed the matter with him instead, but he wasn't the kind of man you could just talk to.'

'What do you mean?'

'He didn't talk! No more than he had to, anyway, and hardly ever to me. We can't have exchanged more than a few words and most of those were mine. The only thing we had in common was our age.'

'I've heard of his reputation. Is he really so fierce?'

'Aye! He might have been handsome otherwise. Black hair, dark eyes, strong features…' She paused for a moment, remembering how unexpectedly breathless she'd felt at her first sight of him only three days before their wedding, premarital nerves battling a strange sense of excitement. 'But always frowning! All he ever did was stand and scowl at me. Like this.' She clamped her brows together so fiercely that her eyebrows met in the middle. 'No matter what anyone says, it wasn't as if *he* wanted our marriage either. He made that very clear. His pride might have been damaged when I ran away, but that's all.' She tipped her head to one side. 'Although I admit that I could have timed my leaving better.'

'You thought you were doing the right thing.'

'Mmm,' Coira murmured non-committally. In all honesty, she'd never thought *that*, not exactly. No matter how monosyllabic or intimidating she'd found Fergus MacMillan, running away from Sween Castle in the middle of the night to marry Nevin Barron instead had struck her as a poor way of repaying his family's hospitality, even if she *had* only been following her brother's orders. Not that anybody else had ever known that. As far as the rest of the Highlands was concerned, she and Nevin had fallen in love at first sight and risked clan war to be together. Not even Grizel, her one true friend over the past four years, knew the whole truth.

She heaved a sigh of relief as they rode out through the fortress gates and joined the track south, though her spirits refused to lift as they usually did at the sight of the wild heather-and-pine-clad hillsides and snow-capped peaks towering around them. It was still August, but some of the trees in the valleys were already showing hints of red and orange, signalling the impending arrival of autumn.

The thought brought with it a heavy sense of foreboding. Her spring and summer of freedom were well and truly drawing to an end. After Nevin, she'd hoped that she'd never have to marry again, but if it *was* truly necessary then surely Brody could have found somebody else? Somebody kind, ideally with the capacity to smile once in a while? Somebody who might have been a friend and companion. She didn't expect or even want love, not when she had no intention of returning it. She'd tried that once and the experience had scarred her for ever. All she wanted now was a quiet, uneventful life, free from bitterness and rancour and insults. Surely that wasn't so much to ask? Instead it seemed she was destined to follow one bad marriage with another.

What if it was even worse?

Her chest constricted at the thought, as if there were a steel band around her ribcage, squeezing tight. A year ago, she couldn't have imagined a worse husband than Nevin and yet here she was, on her way to marry a man she'd very publicly rejected and humiliated. A man who probably loathed the very thought of her and was doubtless even more angry at the situation than she was. It was like some kind of cruel joke! She might almost have suspected that Brody had planned it on purpose, except that his reasoning was sound. Castle Barron's position on the edge of MacWhinnie territory *did* make it vulnerable to attack and the fact that Gregor was only five years old even more so.

She leaned forward over her saddle, urging her horse into a gallop. At least Fergus was an honourable man, as Brody had said. His reputation preceded him in that regard. Warrior though he was, there had never been rumours of any cruelty or brutality. He wouldn't physically hurt her, of that she was reasonably certain, but there were other ways to cause pain. Which of those would he choose? How long would it be before he sought his revenge? And who outside the confines of Castle Barron would even care? No one, that was who.

'Is there no way to get out of it?' Grizel rode up alongside, her voice sounding as if it were coming from a long way away.

'Short of joining forces with the Campbells and declaring war on all of my neighbours…?' She took a couple of seconds to seriously consider the possibility. 'No. I can't defy Brody and my brother won't do anything to help me. I doubt he'd reply even if I sent word. I'm on my own.'

'Well, then…perhaps Fergus MacMillan won't be so bad?'

'How many warriors are more approachable at twenty-three than they were at seventeen?' Coira snapped before shaking her head apologetically. 'I'm sorry. I shouldn't take my temper out on you.'

'It's all right, I understand. All I'm saying is that the situation might not be as bad as you think. People *can* change and six years is a long time. Neither of you will be the same person now that you were back then.'

'Aye.' Coira smiled half-heartedly. It might have been a long time—she herself had changed more than she'd ever imagined possible and probably not for the better—but she had a feeling that a warrior like Fergus MacMillan would have a much, *much* longer memory.

Chapter Two

One day later

It wasn't enough. Fergus MacMillan lowered his brows, scowling ferociously as Ross, his elder brother, mounted the horse beside him. One hour was all that Ross had offered. One hour with no weapons, just the two of them and their fists to make amends for Ross's decision—demand—that he marry Coira Barron. Which meant one hour to pummel him violently into the ground, nowhere near enough time to vent the amount of rage he was currently feeling, if he could bring himself to do it. Which his clever, conniving brother knew damn well that he couldn't.

Bastard.

'Ready?' Ross caught his eye as he turned towards the gates.

'As I'll ever be.'

'Goodbye, Fergus.' Their younger sister, Elspeth, raised a hand in farewell. 'I hope——' She caught his gaze and faltered, apparently thinking better of saying whatever it was she'd been about to say.

'Aye.' He gave a grunt of acknowledgement before flicking on his reins. 'So do I.'

'That was rude.' It took Ross all of two seconds to catch up with him.

'That wasn't my intention.'

'It's one thing to take your temper out on me, another when it's Elspeth.'

'I *said* that it wasn't my intention.' Fergus rounded on him. 'It's not like she doesn't know me. *And* she agrees with me about this marriage, by the way.'

'I know. She told me.'

'So you can't expect me to smile. Not today of all days.'

'No, but you're looking even more thunderous than usual, which for you is saying something. My offer still stands. One hour, no weapons. We both know you're capable of doing far more damage to me than I am to you.'

'Don't tempt me.'

'Fergus…' Ross's tone shifted. 'I know this isn't easy.'

'Easy?' Fergus curled his hands into fists, sorely tempted to shove his brother off his horse and on to his backside in the dirt. 'You honestly dare use that word after the way she humiliated our family? Humiliated *me*?'

'You were the one who said you didn't want revenge.'

'That doesn't mean I still want to marry her!'

'I know. I'm sorry. If I could think of any other way, I'd take it.'

'Think harder.'

'I've racked my brains, but we need alliances and Castle Barron needs to be well defended. It guards one of the main routes north.'

'So get Brody MacWhinnie to defend it.'

'I can't. Our agreement is still too recent for me to trust him. You know as well as I do there's been trouble on our borders ever since—'

'Since his nephew stole my bride?' Fergus shot him a death glare at the reminder. 'He publicly denounced Nevin, didn't he? What more do you want?'

'Just because he denounced him doesn't mean he was as ignorant of the plan as he claimed. That's why I need you to do this. MacWhinnie might be on our side now, but he's a wily old fox. If he's really threatened, he'll do what's best for him and I can't run the risk of him making a pact with the Campbells against us. At least you get Castle Barron out of it. The place has a fine prospect.'

'It already has a laird. I'll be a custodian at best.'

'The Laird's a five-year-old boy. You'll have more than ten years to manage the place yourself. Not to mention your wife's fortune.'

'What's left of it, you mean. I don't give a damn about her fortune anyway. I never did.'

'Aye.' Ross's expression struck him as far too perceptive all of a sudden. 'I know.'

'So why are you accompanying me?' Fergus shot him another glare, none too subtly changing the subject. 'We both know I'm not going to fight you, no matter how much you deserve it. If you're here to make sure I don't go back on my word, then I'm insulted.'

'Of course not. And I'm not accompanying you, at least not the whole way. I have other business to attend to.'

'What business? Who with?'

There was a noticeable pause before Ross answered, 'At the Abbey.'

'The Abbey?' Fergus drew his mount up short. 'Any particular reason?'

'I want to get Elspeth away from Sween. She needs somewhere safe to stay until Leith MacLachlan returns from Edinburgh and they can be married.'

'You still intend to go through with that, then?'

'Aye. It's a good match.'

'They're not suited. Elspeth's far too high-spirited for a man like him.'

'Sometimes people surprise us.'

'Not MacLachlan.' Fergus pushed a hand through his dark hair. 'You know she's not happy about it either.'

'Aye, but she understands the reasons. I've sworn an oath to protect the clan. That's more important than anything, our own personal inclinations included. Besides, it's not like I'm asking either of you to do anything I'm not prepared to do myself. I'm not exactly thrilled by my own marital prospects, but alliances are necessary if we're to defend our home against the Campbells.' Ross thrust his jaw out, looking every inch the formidable clan leader. 'I know it's a lot to ask, but maybe you ought to give Coira Barron a chance, too?'

'I already did. Six years ago.' Fergus clenched his jaw grimly. 'I don't believe in giving second ones.'

'This is where we part ways.' Ross pulled on his reins where the track forked on either side of a giant, gnarled-looking wych elm. 'Are you sure you won't take any of my men with you?'

'No. I ride alone.' Fergus let his gaze sweep the hills

in the distance. 'With any luck, I'll run into one of the Campbells' war bands and they'll kill me before I ever reach Castle Barron.'

'Fergus…'

'Aye, I know, it's for the clan. If it makes you feel any better, I'll do my best *not* to get killed.'

'That's all I ask.' Ross reached across and gripped his arm. 'For what it's worth, I'm grateful.'

'You should be. Just don't expect any nephews and nieces. I'll wed the woman if I must, but that doesn't mean I want anything to do with her. And that part's not up for discussion. As far as I'm concerned, this is a marriage in name only. I'll shore up the defences and hold the place until the Campbells are defeated, but I'll be leaving as soon as all this is over.'

'And do what?' Ross threw him a surprised look.

'I'll think about that when the time comes. Frankly, I don't care as long as it's not with her.'

'Did you tell Brody all this?'

'Aye.'

'And?'

'He didn't seem to care.'

'Very well.' Ross nodded. 'Then it's understood.'

'Good. Off to the Abbey with you, then. I'll see you…' Fergus lifted an eyebrow. 'When *will* I see you again?'

'Whenever the Campbells force us into another battle, most likely.' Ross glanced over his shoulder as if he expected to see an army following at their heels. 'Send for me if you need me.'

'The same to you.'

'One more thing.' Ross's expression hardened. 'No

matter what you might hear, I need you to stay at Castle Barron until you get word from me and me alone. I'm told that Alexander Campbell has a talent for manipulating people and I won't let him do it to us. I need your word on this, Brother.'

'Then you have it.'

Fergus nodded farewell before directing his horse north-east towards Barron territory. The castle was still another day and a half's ride away. Another day and a half to brood and wonder what kind of woman he was going to find there. The Coira Barron he remembered, Coira Roy as she'd been six years before, had been of average height, slender and slim-hipped, with midnight-black hair and eyes the colour of thistles. Her brother had been head of a small but notorious clan, one with a dubious reputation for shady dealings and cattle theft, but prepared to pay well for an alliance with the more powerful MacMillans, even with a second son, and Fergus had been captivated the moment he'd set eyes on her.

Despite her background, Coira had seemed to him like a princess out of one of Elspeth's stories. He'd been utterly smitten, not just by her looks, but by the keen intelligence that shone from her eyes. Her low voice had sounded to him sweeter than birdsong, her words so thoughtful and observant that he'd found himself literally struck dumb in her company, unable to utter more than a few stilted syllables in response. She'd seemed a hundred times too good for an uncouth, tongue-tied warrior like him, for whom learning had always been a chore—an opinion she'd obviously agreed with since she'd run away the night before the wedding with one of their own guests, Nevin Barron.

Tensions between the clans had escalated rapidly, with one side demanding retribution for the insult and the other loudly proclaiming its ignorance of the lovers' plans, until Fergus himself had stepped in. Little as he'd believed Coira's brother's protestations of ignorance—Brody Mac-Whinnie's had been somewhat more convincing—the fact that she'd left willingly, attested to publicly by several witnesses, had put an end to his infatuation. Tempting as taking revenge on the runaways had been, he'd suffered humiliation enough to last him a lifetime. He'd been prepared to let the matter rest, to serve as a lesson for himself, too, against any further foolishness.

He ought to have known better in the first place. Love, romance and all such tender emotions weren't for the likes of him. He was little more than a pair of fists and an effective sword arm, a fearsome warrior with a pathetically broken heart, one that he'd made sure no one, not even Ross, had known about.

Ever since, and every day for the past six years, he'd done his utmost to forget Coira Barron and yet the blunt truth was that he'd never entirely succeeded. He'd managed to push her to the back of his mind, sometimes for as long as two or three days at a time, but the image of her was always there somewhere, taunting him, ready to remind him of his humiliation and rejection.

Because of *her*, he'd chosen never to marry, despite several opportunities, little thinking that he'd ever be in this position, on his way to wed the one woman he'd never wanted to see or hear from again. Worse, the one woman he could never trust.

A growl tore from his throat at the thought. Maybe he should have told Ross everything, but the thought of articulating his feelings out loud horrified him. It probably wouldn't have made a difference anyway. When it came to protecting the clan, Ross was implacable. In which case, he would just have to be implacable, too. He'd do his duty to the clan and put up with his *wife*, but only for as long as was absolutely necessary. After that, he'd get away from her as quickly and permanently as possible.

That, he told himself, was the most important thing—that this time, he would be the one to leave her and with his heart still intact. He would keep his distance and not let his guard down, not for so much as a second.

Coira Barron, the woman he'd once loved, would never mean anything to him ever again.

Chapter Three

'Are you absolutely certain about this?' Grizel hurried down the keep steps after Coira, her voice laced with panic.

'No.' Coira didn't falter, striding determinedly across the bailey to where her palfrey stood saddled and waiting. 'And, yes. Honestly, I don't know, but I can't sit around waiting any longer or I'll go mad.'

'But why go alone?' Grizel looked as if she wanted to tackle her to the ground and restrain her. 'There's strength in numbers and it's not so much longer to wait. The scouts said he'll be here within the hour.'

'I'd still rather not have an audience. Call me cowardly, but if he's going to shout and condemn and berate me for what I did six years ago then I'd prefer that he did it in private.'

'You're not cowardly at all.' Grizel reached for her hand and squeezed it. 'You're the most courageous person I know and you shouldn't be shouted at. This isn't right. None of this is right.'

'But it will be.' Coira squeezed her hand back, trying to show more certainty than she felt. 'Considering what I did, the least I can do now is look Fergus Mac-Millan in the eye and apologise, and if he doesn't accept that…' She let the words trail away, her stomach feeling hollow at the thought. 'Well then, I'll just have to bear it, but if I meet him on the road then that should be the worst of it over with…hopefully.'

'It's going to rain. I heard thunder a few moments ago.'

'Aye, so did I, but honestly, rain is the least of my worries at the moment.' She shook her head when Grizel looked about to protest some more. 'It's better this way, trust me.'

'If you say so, my lady.'

'I do.' She climbed on to the mounting block and on to her palfrey. 'Now stop worrying and wish me luck. I need as much as I can get.'

'Good luck.'

Coira stiffened her spine as she rode out through the gates, trying to quell the tumult of nerves raging inside her. She wouldn't have thought it possible, but somehow she was managing to feel defiant, apprehensive and overwrought all at the same time, a combination that made her want to simultaneously hit something, ride off in the other direction and collapse in a fit of both tears and hysterical laughter. After three days of unremitting dread, she wasn't sure how much more emotional upheaval she could take, but she had a feeling the end of her tether was within sight and drawing rapidly closer.

All she *did* know was that she couldn't just sit placidly in her solar, doing embroidery and waiting for Fergus MacMillan to ride back into her life. Her head was throbbing with tension, which made it infinitely better to get out and do something, *anything*, else. It wasn't as if she wanted to be railed at, but she reasoned that if she met him face to face on the road and gave him an opportunity to vent his feelings, then at least the worst would be over with and they could start making the best of a bad, or in their case terrible, situation. Since there appeared to be no way of avoiding the marriage then surely the least they could do was come to some kind of understanding? Something that might one day lead to friendship?

It was a small hope. Ridiculously tiny really, but at that moment, it was all that she had. She just had to cross her fingers and trust that her new—*old*—future husband would feel the same way.

The sun had already dipped behind the hills on the second day of his journey, casting the path ahead of Fergus into shadow, by the time his stallion's hooves finally crossed on to Barron land. Castle Barron itself was only a couple of miles further away, its crenellated parapets and grey stone tower already visible in the distance. Ross had been right, the place had a pleasing prospect, standing at the far end of a loch, just above the flat base of the valley where two glens met, but no view was worth such a price. His freedom. His future… If only Ross had let him challenge Alexander Campbell to open combat as he'd wanted instead of dismissing the idea as too risky…then he might have saved both of the precious things he was about to sacrifice.

He lifted his face to the sky, aware of the wind pick-ing up at the same moment as he heard a low roll of thunder rumbling in the distance, as if the weather it-self were in sympathy with his mood. Whichever way he looked at it, his future was bleak. No matter how quickly and efficiently he managed to fulfil his duty to his clan and escape, he was still going to be bound for life to the one woman he most wanted to forget. He wasn't sure who he was more furious with, Ross, Brody or *her*...

He was still brooding when he spied the object of his ire sitting on a chestnut palfrey in the centre of the track ahead, as if she'd been summoned up by his thoughts, her hood pulled back to reveal two coils of gleaming black hair on either side of her head. *Coira.* She was obviously waiting for him, looking as sombre as if she were on her way to the gallows. Another, lon-ger roll of thunder only exacerbated the grimness of the scene. Evidently, the lack of enthusiasm for their marriage was mutual.

He drew rein several paces away, not offering a sin-gle word of greeting as he took a long, hard look at her face. She was not, after all, the woman he remembered. Even considering the fact that she must still be grieving for her husband, she'd aged significantly more than six years. The soft, round cheeks he'd once admired now looked gaunt and pallid, their bloom not so much dulled as utterly spent, while her figure, though still slender, had a new stiffness about it, as if every muscle in her body was rigid with tension. Perhaps they were. She looked as taut as a bowstring. If it hadn't been for her eyes, he might not have recognised her at all, though even those had altered. The spark he'd fallen in love with had well and truly gone out, the bright thistle-blue gleam faded to a lustreless grey.

Her lips moved. He had no idea what she said since the voice that emerged was too quiet, but he was aware of a sudden, intense sense of relief. Now that the moment of reunion was over, he could admit that a small part of him had been afraid he'd take one look at her and be just as hopelessly infatuated as he had the first time. Thankfully, he could say with complete honesty that his emotions were entirely unmoved. He was spared that fresh humiliation at least.

'Coira.' He tipped his head very slightly in acknowledgement, aware of, but hardly caring, how hard his voice sounded. 'Your scouts told you I was on my way, then?'

'My scouts?' She cleared her throat, her voice marginally louder this time. 'You saw them?'

'And heard. One of your men breathes far too loudly.' He nodded towards a hummock behind which two scouts were currently hiding. 'They need better training. I'll see to it.'

For a split second, he thought he saw a flash of anger in her eyes before she blinked and it was extinguished. 'As you wish.'

'Good.' He leaned sideways, looking pointedly around her towards the castle. 'Are you on your way somewhere? Or were you so eager to come and greet me? We never got a chance to say goodbye the last time, as I recall.'

She tilted her chin higher, ignoring the sarcasm. 'I thought it would be useful for us to talk before you arrived.'

'Why?'

'Because I think we have a lot to talk about. Perhaps we could go down to the loch side?' Her gaze darted briefly towards the hummock. 'Away from my scouts.'

Fergus drew his brows together, considering. His first instinct was to refuse just for the sake of it. The fact that she'd ridden out alone suggested a conversation in private was important to her, probably so that she could start offering excuses and explanations for her behaviour six years ago. Excuses and explanations that he had absolutely no desire to listen to. It would be best to make that point clear to her sooner rather than later, but the look on her face made him hesitate. Tension was one thing, but there was a hint of something else, too, a wariness bordering on fear. No matter how much contempt or dislike he might feel for her, he didn't want his own future wife to be afraid of him.

'Will you come?' She sounded more uncertain this time, two spots of colour blazing high on her cheekbones as if they'd just been scoured by the wind.

He rubbed a hand over his jaw, letting the question hover in the air for several seconds before eventually, reluctantly, conceding. 'Aye. I'll come. Lead the way.'

Coira dismounted carefully. Honestly, she had no other choice when her hands were trembling so violently that she could hardly keep a grip on her reins. Her palfrey was becoming skittish, too, probably in response to her nerves, which had just multiplied a hundred times over. She could barely hear for the roaring of blood in her ears.

Despite all that, she was relieved that her initial

meeting with Fergus was over and away from too many prying eyes. Waiting for so long in the cold had been worth that, at least. His scowling demeanour hadn't changed a great deal over the past six years, except to grow even fiercer, but she couldn't deny that he was just as good-looking now as he'd been the first time she'd laid eyes on him. *More* so even, as if he'd grown into the brooding handsomeness that had looked a little severe on a seventeen-year-old. He'd gained weight, too, his shoulders and waist broadening, so that now he struck her as bigger and more imposing than ever. If there had still been elements of the boy about him before, today he was very definitely a man. A more talkative one, apparently, since he'd already uttered several full sentences in under a minute. Age, it seemed, suited him. Unlike *her*, a fact that made their respective positions even worse. She was painfully aware of how wrung-out and haggard her appearance was these days and it was obvious that he'd noticed. The way that his eyes had swept over her so dismissively, as if he'd seen nothing at all to admire, had made her want to bury her face in her hands and hide.

'So...' He stalked down to the shingled beach ahead of her, stopping just above the waterline to fold a pair of large, muscular arms. Those had *definitely* grown over the past six years. 'What is it you wish to talk about? Only you might want to make it quick. There's rain coming.'

She came to a halt in front of him, suddenly glad of the cool breeze blowing off the loch, chilling the sweat that was trickling between her shoulder blades and down her back, pooling at the base of her spine.

Surely the answer to that question was obvious? They had so much to talk about that she had no idea where to start. Somehow she'd hoped—*expected*—that he would do it for her, but since he didn't appear to want to… She took a deep breath and raised her pale eyes to his dark ones, trying not to look like a woman whose nerves weren't so much frayed as in tatters. 'I thought that we should talk about what happened.'

'When?'

'When?' She gasped in surprise. Not once in all the many and varied ways that she'd imagined this conversation going had he ever *not* known what she was talking about. 'Six years ago… The night before our wedding when I—' She bit her tongue, deciding not to finish that particular sentence. 'The point is… What I'm trying to say is that I acted badly and I'm sorry for it. And…' she dug her feet into the shingle and tipped her chin up, bracing herself '…I thought that you might have questions? Accusations?'

'No.'

'None?' She felt her jaw drop open.

'It was a long time ago.'

'But…you must have been angry?'

'Must I?'

She held on to his gaze, beginning to feel oddly disorientated. She hadn't brought him there to defend herself. The blunt truth was that she *had* run away with Nevin, after all, but after the way that she'd humiliated Fergus and all the MacMillan clan, she'd assumed that he'd jump at the opportunity to condemn her. Apparently not.

Instead, his face was a square-jawed, tight-lipped,

emotionless mask, as if they were meeting for the very first time and he didn't feel anything towards her at all. Which maybe he didn't. Maybe she'd built the whole thing up in her imagination for no good reason. Maybe he'd been so against the idea of marrying her six years ago that he'd been secretly relieved when she'd run away? Although, even if that *had* been the case, he must surely have still felt the insult to his family? He must have felt *something*?

She peered closer, but it was impossible to tell anything from his blank expression, and his impenetrability only made him more intimidating. Was he saving up all his accusations and condemnations to publicly denounce her later? Or was this an indicator of how their future would be and he had no intention of *ever* discussing the past with her? She wasn't sure which was worse. Whatever the explanation, however, it was painfully obvious that he didn't want to be there. With her. Somehow that felt like condemnation enough.

'I thought that you might want to...' She ran her tongue over dry lips. 'Call me names perhaps?'

'Names?' He frowned. 'What names?'

Treacherous whore. Fickle harpy. False-hearted bitch.

Those were just a few of the words Nevin had used. And they had been the kinder ones...

'I don't know,' she lied. 'Whatever you wish to call me.'

'Do you think me a boy still? A child who hurls pointless insults?'

'No, of course not. I just thought...' She swallowed

hard. 'I simply thought that if you wished to insult me then it would be better to do it in private.'

'Where your people won't overhear me, you mean?'

'No.' She narrowed her eyes at the hint of contempt in his voice. 'My children.'

There was a momentary pause before his brows clamped even more firmly together. 'Children? I thought you only had a son?'

'A son *and* a daughter. Gregor and Ailis.'

'Brody only mentioned a son.'

He would. She pursed her lips to stop herself from muttering the words aloud. Typical that the head of the MacWhinnie clan wouldn't think to mention a mere girl. 'Ailis is still a babe, not yet a year old. No doubt she slipped his mind.' A faint ray of hope struck her. 'But if my having another child bothers you...'

'Then I might change my mind about our union?' A black eyebrow quirked upwards. 'Apologies, my lady. I would that it were so easy, but I'm here at the order of the head of my clan. It doesn't matter what, or *who*, bothers me.'

'I see.' She twisted her face to one side at the insult, gazing out at the murky green depths of the loch. She'd always liked this beach. She'd come here often for solace during the dark days of her marriage, the sight and sounds of the water soothing her troubled spirit. Now the waves were building as the towering rain clouds moved steadily closer, but she could still see her reflection wavering side by side with Fergus's... She stared at his, slowly absorbing the bitter import of his words.

That was the truth then, just as she'd feared. He was there under duress and against his will, and he had no desire to exchange as much as a few words of greeting with her. He was as terse and taciturn, albeit slightly more communicative, as he'd been six years ago, only this time it wasn't simply a matter of not wanting to marry her. Now he actively despised and resented her, too. It was hopeless. She might as well try to befriend one of the mountains.

'Was that all you wished to talk about?' If anything, his voice sounded even harder than before.

She lifted her head, wondering if she ought to make one last attempt to get through to him, but the glacial look in his eyes, as if he had no interest in anything she might possibly think or say, froze the words in her mouth, turning her very lips numb. She was vaguely surprised that she didn't turn to ice on the spot.

'Yes.' She let her shoulders slump forward deject-edly. 'That's all.'

'Good. Shall we go, then?'

A third roll of thunder agreed.

Chapter Four

The rain began to fall at the precise moment they entered the bailey, little more than a threadbare drizzle at first, but still enough to extinguish Coira's last spark of hope that she and Fergus might come to some kind of amicable understanding. The only positive from their meeting was that at least now it was over with and she knew where she stood. That knowledge made her nerves subside a little, although she was also painfully aware that the murk of the afternoon only drew attention to the crumbling stone walls and general air of dilapidation about Castle Barron, the result of years of neglect coupled with Nevin's refusal to spend money on anything or anyone but himself.

She'd done her best to make repairs over the past few months, but it wasn't easy when Brody had been holding on to what was left of her dowry, not trusting a woman to spend it wisely. Now she couldn't help but wonder what Fergus thought of his new home.

She stole a sideways glance at him as they dismounted, trying to gauge his reaction, but his expression was just the same as before. Give or take the occasional lifting of an eyebrow, she didn't think it had altered once since they'd met.

'My lady?'

She winced at the sound of a voice in her ear. Nevin's head man, now nominally *her* head man, had to be part-cat, he was so good at sneaking around.

'Iver.' She acknowledged him with a cursory glance, noticing the stains on his tunic and catching the whiff of ale on his breath as she did so. 'Fergus, this is Iver. He looks after the guards.' She paused and then couldn't resist adding, '*And* the scouts.'

'Then I'll speak to you and your men first thing in the morning.' Fergus looked the other man up and down appraisingly. 'Be ready an hour after dawn.'

Coira tensed, waiting for Iver to make one of his usual surly comments, but, for once, he only muttered acquiescence.

'Well…' She pushed a strand of damp hair out of her face, irritated to think how differently her head man would have responded if *she'd* been the one giving orders. 'Let's get into the dry, shall we? Then I can start showing you around.'

She marched off towards the keep, leading Fergus up some stone steps and through a guards' room into the antechamber outside the great hall. She'd left clear instructions for the tables to be polished, the floor rushes to be changed and a jug of wine to be waiting beside the fireplace, reasoning that if she couldn't impress him herself then she could at least impress him with her housekeeping, but instead they were greeted with a scene of utter and ear-splitting chaos.

She came to a halt in the hall doorway, frozen in horror. At least half a dozen wooden benches had been tipped on to their sides while a group of kitchen boys ran up and down the space between, jumping over trestle tables and generally looking as if they were enjoying themselves far too much to stop. Meanwhile, two maids stood at one side, gesticulating madly, all to a background din of whistles, high-pitched yaps and shrieking.

'Coira! Thank goodness you're back!' Grizel came running over, almost skidding to a halt and dropping into a curtsy at the sight of Fergus behind. 'I mean, apologies for the uproar, my lady.'

'What's happened?' Coira craned her neck. 'Oh, no, don't tell me—'

'The pup's escaped again!'

'Mama!' Gregor emerged from beneath a table to hurl himself against her legs. 'I'm sorry. I only opened the door for a second, but then Duncan tripped over her and she got scared and ran away.'

'Oh, dear.' She looked across to the stairwell where the aged Duncan was sitting, rubbing his ankle and looking resentful.

'Look!' Gregor pointed. 'She's over there!'

'Right. Wait here.' Coira threw a brief glance at Fergus, inwardly bemoaning the unladylike spectacle she was about to make of herself, before rolling up her sleeves and starting off down the hall. Judging by the way the rushes under the high table were rustling, Gregor was right and the rebellious puppy was busy helping herself to the remains of the midday meal.

'Come here, little one. I'm not going to hurt you… Who's a good dog? It's you, isn't it? Yes, it is…' She crouched down, cooing platitudes as she slid her arms slowly under the table. If she could just lure the beast closer and wrap her hands around its belly… Closer… And closer… Unfortunately, the pup had other ideas, darting away with a playful yelp just as her fingers skimmed its fur.

'Oh, no, you don't!' Coira dived sideways at the same moment, smacking her shoulder hard into the table leg as she grabbed hold of the squirming creature. 'Ow! Got her!' She let out a whoop of combined pain and triumph and then grimaced. Aside from the throbbing ache in her shoulder, her sleeve was now decidedly damp and, if the smell was anything to go by, she didn't want to know what it was she'd just landed in.

'Here.' She tramped back down the hall, passing the still wriggling, floppy-eared creature back to Gregor. 'Keep a closer watch on her this time.'

'Yes, Mama.' Gregor nodded cheerfully, submitting to a vigorous face-licking.

'And perhaps from now on—' She was about to re-monstrate further when she noticed Fergus's dark form looming beside them. For a few moments just then, she'd actually forgotten his presence, which she supposed was one thing to be grateful to the puppy for…

'My apologies.' She looked from him to her son and then back again. 'Fergus, may I present—'

'You must be Gregor.' He spoke over her, crouching down on one knee to bring his face level with that of both boy and hound. 'Is the pup yours?'

'Aye.' Gregor regarded him curiously. 'Mama gave her to me.'

'What's she called?'

'Duffy.'

'That's a good name.'

'Except that she won't come when I call her. She keeps running away.'

'She's young.'

'What if it's because she doesn't really like me?'

'I'm sure it's not that,' Coira interrupted, wincing at her son's choice of words, though thankfully Fergus seemed not to notice the irony. 'Just look at the way she's nibbling your ear. Duffy, stop that!'

'Are you here to marry my mother?' Gregor thrust his lip out, his gaze suspicious suddenly.

'Aye.' Fergus nodded.

'Do I have to call you Father?'

'No.'

'Oh.' The lip wobbled and then drew inwards again. 'What should I call you, then?'

'My name's Fergus. You can use that if you like.' He reached out to smooth a hand over the pup's silken head. 'You know, I had a hound like this when I was a boy. He was a wild, mangy creature, but I wanted to tame him so I used to carry around a pouch filled with scraps of dry meat. Eventually he learned to trust me.'

'Is he here?' Gregor looked around eagerly.

'No, he died a few years ago, but he was a good, old age.' Fergus looked up, his gaze locking briefly with hers before moving on again. 'Your mother met him once.'

'Really? Was he a good dog, Mama?'

'Aye.' Coira smiled at the memory. Now that she thought of it, there *had* been an ancient-looking terrier that used to follow Fergus around. 'Mangy' hardly began to describe the state of its wild, curly hair, not unlike Duffy's, although it had still been a hundred times friendlier than its owner. It had even licked her hand and let her rub its ears.

'Can I have a pouch to keep food in, too?'

'That sounds like a good idea. I'll make you one. In the meantime, perhaps you could take her outside and play?'

'I'll keep an eye on them, my lady.' Grizel put a hand on Gregor's shoulder, steering him tactfully away. 'Excuse us.'

'Thank you.' Coira threw her a grateful smile, even extending it to Fergus after they'd gone. 'And thank you, too. I think Gregor was nervous about meeting you.'

'There was no need to be. He's just a lad.'

'Of course, I didn't mean…' She bit her lip, wondering if everything she said was going to bring on a fresh contraction of his brows because it was beginning to feel inevitable. 'I mean, I'm glad it went well. As for Duffy, she may not have been one of my better ideas.'

'Why not?'

'She's just so unruly.' She lifted her shoulders. 'Gregor was very close to his father and after he died… well, I wanted to make him smile again. I thought that an animal, something to focus his attention on, would make him feel better, but now I'm not sure whether she's helped or not.' She sighed and then cleared her throat, remembering that she was supposed to be showing him the keep. 'Anyway, this is the hall. Obviously it's not quite looking its best. Oh, Duncan…' Out of the corner of her eye, she noticed the old servant hobbling towards the door, aided by one of the kitchen boys. 'Are you all right?'

'Nothing broken, my lady, no thanks to that little cur.'

'Come and sit down by the fire. You don't need to do any more work today. Jamie here will fetch you some ale, too.'

'Thank you, my lady.'

'Right. Now, this way...' She walked towards the stairwell, beckoning to Fergus and vaguely wondering what fresh disaster might befall them next. 'I'll show you to our private rooms.'

'As you wish.'

'This is the solar,' she commented as they reached a door at the top, pushing it open to reveal a cosy, tapestry-clad room containing a daybed, two benches, a small desk in one corner and a giant oak coffer with thistles carved into the lid. 'Through there is where the children sleep.' She pointed towards another door. 'They have their own maid and Grizel, who you just met, sleeps in there, too.'

'The girl with the red hair?'

'Aye.' She threw him a suspicious look before leading him out through the solar and on to a minstrels' gallery. 'And this leads to my—that is, *our*—chamber, but I'll have a bed made up for you out here tonight.'

'No.'

'What?' She spun around, startled. 'What do you mean?'

'I'm not sleeping out here.'

'Then I'll sleep in the children's room.'

'No. We sleep together.'

'Absolutely not.' She wrenched her shoulders back

indignantly. 'We won't be sharing anything until we're married.'

'We will be. Tonight.' He strode past her, opening the door to the bedchamber and tossing his pack of belongings inside without so much as a glance.

'But…that's impossible!' she protested when she was finally able to stop spluttering. 'We can't be married tonight!'

'Why not?'

'Because it's too soon! You saw the hall. It's a mess! And what about a feast? It's too late to prepare anything special.'

'Good.'

'*Good?* Why good?'

'Because there's nothing special about any of this.' His dark eyes captured hers, practically boring into them. 'Our marriage isn't an event to be celebrated. It's merely one to be got over with as quickly as possible and we don't need a tidy hall for that, or a feast either. All we need is a ceremony so that I have the authority to act on your son's behalf.' He advanced a step towards her, his tone glacial again. 'My purpose here is to make sure that your defences can withstand a possible assault by the Campbells and, from what I've seen so far, I've only just arrived in time.'

'Meaning *what* exactly?' She folded her arms, offended. It was the longest speech she'd ever heard him make and now she honestly wished he'd stayed silent.

'Your east wall for a start. It's bulging in places. Half of the stones need tearing down and rebuilding, if not replacing. As for your men, your scouts are incompetent and the leader of your guards is a disgrace.'

Coira dug her top teeth into her bottom lip, unable to deny any of those statements. The east wall *was* in a sorry state, the less said about the scouts the better, and as for Iver…well, he'd been one of Nevin's men for years and she hadn't known how to replace him, no matter how much she'd wanted to. Still, it was hard not to take such comments personally.

'None the less, I'd like at least a day to prepare. Brody only told me about this arrangement a few days ago and—'

'No.' His answer was unequivocal. 'The sooner we're wed, the sooner I can get on with my work. As for waiting, forgive me if I'm not prepared to take the chance on your still being here tomorrow.'

'You don't trust me?' She thrust her chin up at the implication and then immediately regretted it as he took another step closer.

'Why would I?'

She narrowed her eyes, refusing to be cowed even if her knees were feeling somewhat unsteady. 'Because even if this castle didn't belong to my son, I'd hardly attempt to run away with you sleeping right outside my door!'

'I still don't care to make the same mistake twice. Now I presume that you have a priest here?'

'Aye.'

'Then find him.' He started to move away and then stopped, his gaze dropping to the large damp patch on her sleeve. 'On second thoughts, *I'll* find him. You might wish to put on a different gown.'

'Oh, really?' She slid her hands to her hips belligerently. 'Are you sure you want me to go to so much effort? I wouldn't want to be accused of doing anything *special*.'

'Honestly, I don't care.' He turned his back on her. 'Only hurry up before it gets dark.'

Dark, raining and miserable. Those were the words that would describe her wedding night. Coira stared after him and tried not to despair.

Chapter Five

It was over. They were married. The brief marriage ceremony was concluded and she was a new bride once again, the band on her finger glittering like a small golden shackle. But perhaps a hasty wedding had been for the best, Coira thought, looking out over the hall from her seat at the high table. She'd woken up that morning with her nerves already torn to shreds at the thought of seeing Fergus again. If she'd known there was even the faintest chance of being married by nightfall then she might have hidden under the blankets and refused to come out. Instead, she'd met him and wed him within the space of a few short hours. She'd done her duty and got it over with, as he'd so gallantly put it. She was Coira MacMillan now, just as she ought to have been six years ago. Only now everything was a hundred thousand times worse.

She sucked the insides of her cheeks as she cast a sidelong glance at her husband. It unsettled her to be sitting this close to him, but he seemed completely unaffected by her, staring straight ahead with his expression as stern and impenetrable as ever. Just as he'd looked during their wedding. She was starting to wonder if his face could do anything else.

He'd certainly been right about one thing. Their wedding hadn't been remotely special. Just like her first. It had been hard *not* to compare the two events, although between them, it was hard to say which she'd enjoyed the least. She hadn't exactly been forced into giving her consent on either occasion, but she hadn't acted altogether willingly either. Both had been rushed, but at least Nevin had made *some* attempt to woo her after she'd been bundled out of her bed and on to a horse in the middle of the night, declaring his eternal attachment and insisting upon taking their vows immediately upon reaching Castle Barron. He'd said that he couldn't bear the thought of waiting in case it gave the MacMillans a chance to reclaim her and he'd been *so* charming about it. Too charming, she realised now, but at the time it had made a refreshing change to the perpetually scowling Fergus. Nevin had been several years older than her, with an air of attractive maturity, having inherited his title and lands at the age of eighteen, and he'd known how to flatter a woman. She hadn't entirely deluded herself, having overheard enough gossip to guess that her dowry held a far greater appeal than her*self*, but it had felt good to receive a few compliments and she'd thought that Nevin at least would be a husband she could talk to.

And, for a while, he *had* been. For a while, she'd considered that she'd had a lucky escape and married a man she might be able to love. Too young to know better, she'd surrendered herself to him body and soul, yet by contrast his interest in her had seemed to wane with every passing day. Barely a week had gone by before he'd started complaining about the inferiority of her birth. It didn't matter how wealthy her brother was, he'd told her. She should never dare to imagine that a large dowry made her his equal. His own family would never approve of her—an assertion that turned out to be completely true—but their marriage was all Brody's fault for refusing him the money to restore Castle Barron to its former glory in the first place.

Before the end of their first month together, Coira had come to realise that her husband's motivation for running away with her had been twofold: a means of enriching himself while spiting his uncle. By which time, it had been far too late to turn back. From then on, their conversations had been largely one-sided and things had only got gradually, but inexorably, worse.

There had been several occasions since when she'd wondered how different her life might have been if she'd refused to go along with her brother's plans that fateful night. One scream and she could have awakened every man, woman and child in Sween Castle. Then she would have married Fergus as planned and...what? Would her life have been any happier with him? It was a question she'd stopped asking herself after Gregor's birth and yet now, ironically, it seemed she was about to discover the answer anyway.

'My lord, my lady...' Iver stood up from his place at the end of one trestle table, swaying slightly as he raised his goblet, a gesture that was immediately mirrored all around the hall. 'To a long and happy marriage!'

'Thank you, Iver,' Coira answered when her new

husband remained silent, apparently far more interested in the contents of his cup than in anything or anyone around him, least of all her. He hadn't spoken a word throughout the entire hastily arranged feast, as if, having made his feelings clear before the ceremony, he had nothing more to say to her. As if he wanted everyone to know just how reluctant he'd been to wed her, too. Her only consolation was that Grizel had taken Gregor upstairs to bed early so that at least her son didn't have to witness this farce of a celebration. She only wished that she might have gone, too. After two consecutive restless nights, she was thoroughly exhausted. And just thinking about being exhausted made her want to yawn so badly that she had to lift her cup to hide her mouth.

'Tired?'

'What?' She'd become so used to Fergus *not* talking that the sound of his voice made her start so violently that she splashed wine all over the table, narrowly missing her gown. 'Oh…yes. It's been a long day.'

'Go to bed. Get some sleep.'

Her stomach knotted and quavered at the words. It was their wedding night. Little as she was looking forward to it, tradition dictated that they be escorted upstairs and put to bed together. Nevin had wasted no time at all in consummating their marriage and yet her new husband showed no sign of even getting up from the table. He still hadn't as much as turned his head to look at her. And now that she thought of it, he'd just told her to go and *sleep*! Which was both a huge relief in one way and a sharp slap to the face in another.

'What about you?'

'I'll stay here for a while, but you go up.'

'I see.' She picked up her cup again and took a long draught, attempting to swallow the words along with the wine. As much as she wanted to go to bed, her husband's distinct lack of enthusiasm for joining her would make it even more obvious to everyone how little he wanted to be there. How little he was attracted to her, too. As if his severe expression didn't already make the point strongly enough! She didn't even know if he was making a suggestion or giving her an order and she didn't want to draw any more attention to them by finding out. All she *did* know was that if he was trying to publicly insult her then he was definitely succeeding!

'Very well.' She stood up, giving him the barest hint of a curtsy. 'If that's what you want, I'll bid you goodnight.'

'Goodnight.'

She kept her back straight and her chin high as she made her way down the centre of the hall, aware of the volume of noise around her diminishing and being replaced by an embarrassed-sounding hush. She could sense heads swivelling in her direction, too, but she didn't turn to see their expressions. She knew that they would contain either pity or, in Iver's case, mockery and she didn't want to see either. It was curious, but after years of insults from her first husband, she'd assumed that she would be immune to humiliation by now, but apparently not. Well, she'd never let Nevin crush her spirit, at least not completely, and she wouldn't let Fergus do so either. She wasn't about to let him or anyone see just how mortified she felt!

The hall seemed to stretch on for ever, but at last she reached the privacy of the stairwell and ran headlong up the stone steps. Briefly, she considered going to kiss the children goodnight before deciding against it. Grizel would be with them and the last thing she wanted was to have to explain what she was doing on her own on her wedding night. Hopefully by the morning she would be able to put a brave face on things again, but at that precise moment, she was horribly afraid she might cry.

Silently, she made her way through the solar and out on to the minstrels' gallery, keeping herself hidden in the shadows as she stopped to peer down at Fergus. He looked just the same, *of course*, although it struck her suddenly that despite the frequency with which he'd lifted his goblet to his lips that evening, it had only been refilled on a couple of occasions. In fact, the longer she looked at him, the more she had the impression of a man who was surreptitiously taking stock of his surroundings. He certainly wasn't intoxicated, not compared to most of the men in the hall. Which made his behaviour towards her all the more deliberate and hurtful.

She spun away, hurrying into her bedchamber and sinking back against the door, overcome with a feeling of utter wretchedness. Was this some kind of revenge? One of the ways that he intended to punish her for what she'd done six years ago? Or was it simply that he had no interest in bedding her? She knew that she ought to feel relieved and she was, but more than that, she felt weary and careworn and far too young to feel so old.

Despite her earlier comments, she'd actually made an effort with her appearance for the ceremony, putting on her best maroon-coloured velvet gown and cream silk headdress, ornamented with a chain of amber beads. She'd flattered herself that she'd looked reasonably presentable, too, but now a glimpse in her hand mirror told her how delusional she'd been. Her skin looked dull and pasty and her eyes were ringed with purple shadows. It was no wonder that Fergus had no interest in bedding her. Her looks had long since faded, just like Nevin had said.

Slowly, she peeled off her clothes and splashed her face with water before climbing into bed and burrowing her way beneath the blankets. Perhaps this was just the way her second marriage was going to be. And perhaps icy disdain and implied insults were preferable to loudly expressed ones. All things considered, her new husband's behaviour could have been much worse.

In any case, what did it really matter what he thought of her? They were married for one reason and one reason only: to defend Castle Barron against the Campbells. Much as she hated to admit it, Brody had been right when he'd said they stood a much better chance of holding it with Fergus than without. *That* was what had finally reconciled her to this marriage. Her son's inheritance was much more important than anything she might feel. And at least Fergus had been kind to Gregor. She could suffer any number of insults for that.

If only… She gritted her teeth, stopping the thought before she had a chance to find out where it might lead. There was no point in *if only*. This was her marriage bed. Now all she had to do was find a bearable way to lie in it.

Fergus dragged his feet slowly up the stairwell. Despite his earlier insistence, he had no desire whatsoever to share a room, let alone a bed, with his new wife, but sleeping in the hall would have occasioned even more comment and the place had been buzzing enough when he'd left. On reflection, sending Coira upstairs on her own had been a mistake, seeming like a deliberate insult rather than a mere suggestion. *She'd* obviously taken it as such, if the brief, albeit swiftly concealed, flash of mortification on her face had been anything to judge by, although humiliating her in front of her entire household hadn't felt anywhere near as satisfying as he might have expected. The opposite even, as if *he'd* been the one in the wrong.

In his defence, however, he hadn't set out deliberately to humiliate her. After their wedding ceremony, he'd simply wanted some time alone with his thoughts. Standing side by side as they'd said their vows had affected him far more deeply than he'd anticipated, as if he were still a seventeen-year-old youth marrying the woman of his dreams. He'd had to remind himself, *repeatedly*, that she was a different woman now, one to be resented and distrusted, not idealised, and yet knowing that and accepting it were two very different things. And it definitely hadn't helped that she'd been wearing a dark crimson gown, one that brought out the lustrous raven's wing sheen of her black hair and made her lips look tantalisingly red and inviting.

When they'd met earlier by the loch side, he'd thought that he hadn't been remotely attracted to her. He'd been quite clear about his feelings, in fact: anger, resentment, contempt. Now that he'd spent a little time in her company, however, he'd caught several disturbing glimpses of the Coira Roy he remembered, not least in the way her eyes softened, almost seeming to glow, when she looked at her son, making it increasingly difficult to separate the beautiful woman he'd first fallen in love with from the haggard woman he'd been forced to marry today. Worse, it made it harder to hold on to his resentment. Resentment he needed if he was going to retain any shred of sanity...

He drew up short in the solar as someone emerged from the children's room suddenly, hurrying towards the stairwell as if they hadn't expected to meet anyone coming the other way.

'Oh!' It was the maid from the hall earlier, the one with the pretty face and vivid red hair. Grizel, Coira had called her. 'Excuse me. I was just...' She dropped her gaze, though not fast enough to hide her expression of guilt. 'On my way to the kitchens.'

'Now?' He lifted an eyebrow. 'It's late.'

'Aye. Perhaps my errand can wait until morning.' She glanced past him, her brows knitting as if she couldn't understand what he was doing there, before bobbing into a curtsy. 'Goodnight, then.'

'Goodnight.' He inclined his head, waiting for her to retreat before continuing through the solar and across the minstrels' gallery, opening the door to his new bedchamber and closing it softly behind him. The light from the fire was dimming, the previously roaring flames reduced to a dull orange glow, though up close the heat was still scorching enough. He sat down beside it, staring broodingly at the remains of a log for several minutes before removing his plaid, pulling off his boots and going to lie down on top of the covers. Coira was lying on her side, her back towards him, but it was obvious from the stiff set of her body that she was still awake.

He rolled his shoulders, trying to get comfortable, but the heat seeping across the bed between them, warming the entire left side of his body, was distracting. He felt far too aware of her, *everything* about her. The soft sound of her breathing, the mass of hair spread out across her pillow, the subtle scents of lavender and cloves, not to mention the long willowy limbs he'd too frequently fantasised about, even, to his shame, after she'd run away from him. If he closed his eyes, it might be possible to pretend that the past six years had never happened, to hold and touch and caress her in all the ways he'd imagined back then—and he'd imagined a lot.

The idea made his skin prickle and every nerve in his body thrum with suppressed desire, but no matter how much his fingertips might be itching to touch her, he knew that it wouldn't be right. Admittedly, it would make their marriage more binding, but in the end, she was a widow, which made it his word against hers as to whether their union was consummated or not. As long as they gave the appearance of sharing a bed, nobody else would ever know the truth, whatever rumours his recent behaviour might have caused. Besides, even if she submitted to him, it would only be a joining of bodies, not minds, and he wouldn't take her in anger, nor as an act of revenge. No matter what he'd said about their marriage not being special, the memory of the girl she'd once been would always be special to him. He only wished that it wasn't.

He clenched his jaw and rolled on to his right side away from her, the feeling of being in the wrong still haunting him. The blunt truth was that he'd behaved dishonourably in sending her to bed, albeit unintentionally. And as if their whole situation wasn't bad enough, now he had his conscience to contend with as well! No doubt he owed her an apology at some point, but at that moment he wasn't in the mood for talking and she was pretending to be asleep. Tomorrow he might try to find some *small* way to make amends, but first he needed to put her firmly out of his mind and get some sleep.

If only sleep would come so easily.

Chapter Six

'Get up!' Fergus waited two seconds before swinging back the pail of water he'd just personally drawn from the well and tipping the contents all over the slumbering bulk of the castle's head guard.

'What the—?' Iver leapt to his feet with a roar, shaking himself so vigorously that he almost toppled over in the process. He looked and smelled like a large, extremely unkempt dog.

'I told you to be ready an hour after dawn.' Fergus returned his glare unflinchingly. 'Where are your men?'

Iver didn't answer, hunching his shoulders and curling his hands into dripping wet fists as if he were preparing to attack instead. Fergus hardened his gaze. If the man wanted a fight, then he'd be more than happy to oblige, but it would make his life a lot easier if they could simply get started with repairs to the fortifications at once. Now, more than ever, they didn't have time for delays. If the Campbells chose to march north, their army could be outside the castle walls within days.

'I'll go and fetch them.' The rebellious look on Iver's

face faded under Fergus's gimlet stare, replaced by one of sullen anger.

'Good. In that case, I'm going to inspect the east wall. I expect everyone to be gathered in the bailey by the time I return. I don't care how badly their heads hurt.'

He tossed the pail aside, stalking out of the guards' room and up the gatehouse steps to get a better look at the wall, shaking his head at the lack of any visible guards on patrol. He doubted that there were any concealed ones either. If the Campbells had chosen that morning to attack, the inhabitants of Castle Barron wouldn't have stood a chance.

He stopped halfway along the ramparts and drew a hand across his jaw at the sight before him. From this elevated position he could see that a large section in the centre of the wall was curving inwards, like a pustule waiting to pop. It wouldn't take long for a battering ram to find a weak spot. It might not even take that much. A windy day might be enough to send the whole structure collapsing inwards. He certainly wasn't going to risk using the walkway above. Frankly, it was a disaster waiting to happen. They might as well just open the main gates and let the Campbells march on through.

He shook his head, his gaze wandering unconsciously towards the window of Coira's chamber. *His* chamber now, too, he reminded himself, strange as the notion seemed. He wondered if she was still asleep in there, her midnight-black hair splayed across her pillow like a silken blanket. Waking up beside her had been a deeply unsettling experience, a confusing mixture of raging lust and deep-seated antipathy. He'd opened his

eyes to find the pair of them nestled together in the centre of the bed, their faces mere inches apart, breaths and
body heat mingling in a way that had almost caused him
to abandon his resolve of the previous night.

The urge to take her in his arms had been so over-
powering that he'd had to force himself to remember the
depths of his humiliation six years before, then wrench
himself away and pour half a jug of cold water over his
head for good measure. The result was that he'd started
the day in the foulest and most frustrated of moods,
escaping their chamber just as she'd rolled over and
murmured something incomprehensible and yet still
somehow maddeningly enticing in her sleep.

'It's in quite a state, isn't it?'

'Aye.' He turned his head, relieved at the interrup-
tion to his thoughts. An old man was heading along the
ramparts towards him, the entire lower half of his face
and most of his neck hidden by a bushy, grey beard.
Malcolm, if he remembered correctly from the ban-
quet, the castle steward and, fortuitously, the very man
he wanted to speak to, the one responsible for keeping
the walls in good repair.

'I know what you're thinking.' Malcolm anticipated
his question. 'It should never have been allowed to get
this bad. We did our best to patch the worst up, but...'

'But?'

'Money.' The older man cleared his throat awkwardly. 'And manpower. Iver can find endless excuses
for his men not to do any work.'

'Not today, he won't.' Fergus tucked his thumbs into
his belt, looking the steward up and down. He had an
honest face, the half he could see of it anyway. 'What

about the last Laird? This wall's been in a bad way for some time.'

'He wasn't much keen on repairs either. He had other priorities.'

'Is that so?' Fergus lifted an eyebrow. Judging by the tone of the other man's voice, they weren't priorities he approved of.

'Aye. If anyone's held this place together, it's Lady Coira.' Malcolm nodded sagely as if to reinforce his point. 'She's a good lady. A good mother, too. She didn't deserve any of this.'

'*This?*' Fergus bridled, narrowing his gaze fiercely. If the steward thought to chide him for his behaviour the night before then he could think again. 'Meaning *me*?'

'No-o!' His companion looked shocked. 'I meant… That is…'

'What?'

'Forgive me, I meant no offence. Perhaps I should not have spoken.' Malcolm started to back away. 'I have work to attend to, if you'll excuse me?'

'Aye.' Fergus stared after a pair of hastily retreating shoulders, trying to make sense of the conversation. The steward had seemed genuinely shocked by his interpretation, but if 'this' hadn't meant 'him', then what had it meant? More than crumbling stone walls, for certain, but what else hadn't Coira deserved?

He drummed his fingers on the rampart wall, looking over his shoulder at her window again. Maybe her marriage hadn't been quite the bed of roses that he'd imagined. He'd always assumed that she and Nevin had been blissfully happy after their elopement, laughing

about him behind his back and revelling in her lucky
escape, but maybe…

He shook his head, dislodging the thought. It was
probably best not to wonder, or to think about Coira
too much at all. Whether she'd been happy or not with
Nevin Barron was irrelevant. It made no difference to
him either way and, frankly, his time at Castle Barron
would be a lot easier if he stopped wasting his time with
wondering and simply got on with the task at hand. With
any luck, he'd only be there for a few weeks at the most.
After that, he could leave and start trying to forget about
her all over again.

He nodded firmly, reinforcing his intentions to himself, before starting back down the rampart steps. He
had a job to do and it was time to get started. Iver ought
to have gathered the men together by now… Still, the
question persisted, refusing to leave him alone. What
had Malcolm meant? What hadn't Coira deserved? And
what, considering how little of her dowry had been left
after Nevin's death, had all the money been spent on?

'My lady?'
Coira looked up from the collection of coloured
beads she was using to teach Gregor his numbers to
find the leader of her guards standing on the other side
of the table, looking unusually damp. It was still early
in the morning, but the last time she'd peeked outside,
the skies had been bright and clear. Surprisingly so,
given the murk of the previous day.

'Iver?' She tried not to smile at the bedraggled sight
before her. 'Is it raining?'

'No, my lady.' His nostrils flared as a flash of irritation crossed his features. 'I just wondered if I might speak with you for a moment? In private?'

'You may. Here, Gregor, keep practising.' She slid the beads towards her son, indicating for Iver to join her by the fireplace. 'What is it?'

'A serious matter, my lady. I thought you should know what's happening out there.'

'The Campbells?' She pressed a hand to her throat, panic clawing at her insides suddenly.

'No, my lady, it's about your husband.' Iver threw a stealthy look over his shoulder. 'It might not be my place to say anything, but I couldn't remain silent. His behaviour is causing some resentment among the men. You've always been a good lady to serve and I know that you'll listen...' he leaned forward conspiratorially '...especially after the way he treated you last night.'

'Is that so?' Coira allowed herself to relax while she assessed the leader of her guards anew. Coming to complain to her about Fergus was bad enough, reminding her of her humiliation was worse, but appealing to her as an ally was jaw-dropping. After the insolent way that Iver had always behaved towards her, was he really so deluded as to believe that a few insincere compliments were all it would take to get her on side?

Yes, apparently.

'Tell me.' She folded her hands in front of her, feigning concern. 'What exactly has he done?'

'It's the way that he's talking, my lady.' Iver thrust his chest out, obviously under the impression that his dubious charms were working. 'He seems to think that he's in charge of the men's training. That's *my* job.'

'I thought that you were making a start on the east wall this morning?'

'We are, but he's taking small groups aside to test their fighting skills.'

'That sounds like a good idea.'

'My lady?'

'Surely it's important that he knows their abilities?'

'*I* see to their training.' Iver adopted a superior expression, somewhat at odds with his soggy appearance. 'Your first husband was happy to let me do so and I've never had any complaints.'

'Really?' She pursed her lips. Because she distinctly recalled several conversations over the past few months about the *lack* of training that seemed to go on. 'So what is it you wish me to do about it?'

'Speak to him, my lady. Tell him how things work around here. Your son's the Laird. That gives you some authority.'

'Does it? Well, how nice to know that I have *some*.' She lifted her eyebrows. 'I'm teaching my son at the moment, but I intend to take a walk outside shortly. Perhaps I could speak to my husband then, if that would please you?'

'Aye, my lady.' Iver looked smug. 'I knew you'd come round to my way of thinking.'

'Oh, I didn't say that. In fact, I think it's high time we made a few changes around here and it sounds like he's made an excellent start. Now I'll be along soon, but in the meantime I suggest that you change your clothes before you catch a chill. Then you can return to *your* training.'

She smiled sweetly in response to the look of outrage

on Iver's face before he stormed away. *That* conversation had been thoroughly satisfying. Ironically, it had also had the opposite effect to the one he'd intended. Fergus might have insulted her the night before, but Iver had been a thorn in her side for years. The thought of him finally meeting his match made her laugh out loud for the first time in days.

'What's so funny?' Gregor gave her a curious look.

'Oh, I was just thinking about how funny men can be sometimes.'

'I don't think Iver's funny. He tried to kick Duffy the other day.'

'Did he? Well, I hope she took a bite out of his ankle.'

'Mama! You told me not to let her bite anyone!'

'For Iver, I can make an exception.' She leaned over the table and gave him a nudge with her elbow. 'Fortunately, I have a feeling that things are going to be different from now on.'

'Because of Fergus?'

'Aye.' She picked up one of the coloured beads and rolled it thoughtfully between her fingers. Stern-faced and implacable he might be, but perhaps there were a few unforeseen advantages to her new husband, after all.

Chapter Seven

Coira waited a couple of hours, until she couldn't contain her curiosity any longer, before following the sounds of thuds and chiselling towards the eastern side of the bailey. The whole area was a hive of activity, with some men sawing wooden beams, others arranging them into piles and still more using ropes and planks to erect some kind of scaffold. She stopped and stared in amazement. The amount of progress that had been made in one morning was nothing short of incredible.

Surreptitiously, she cast a look around for her husband, finally spying him off to one side, standing in the middle of a half circle of about a dozen soldiers. Despite Iver's comments, there was no obvious atmosphere of resentment. On the contrary, most of the men were watching with interest as he swept a long wooden stick from the ground up to waist height, stopped it in mid-air, twisted to the side and then jabbed forward, apparently engaged in some kind of demonstration.

As she watched, impressed despite herself by both the precision and speed of his movements, he lifted the stick over one shoulder and swivelled about, turning his head so that he was looking straight in her direction. Quickly, she jerked her own back around, returning her attention to the wall. The last thing she wanted was for him to see her watching. Or worse, to think that she'd come outside to see him! A stone wall was far more interesting. Probably a great deal more communicative, too. Now, with any luck, he'd simply carry on with whatever it was he was doing and leave her alone to inspect the building work in peace.

'Coira?'

She closed her eyes and groaned inwardly, surprised and dismayed by the speed with which Fergus must have crossed the bailey to reach her. And since he'd made his lack of interest in talking to her obvious the day before, the only possible reason he'd approached her was to issue more orders, to exert his husbandly authority and reprimand her for being there. Just the idea of it made her curl her fingernails into her palms. At least this morning he couldn't send her to bed again like a child, but wasn't she allowed to walk around the bailey without his permission now? As if this wasn't her own home? Well, last night she might have fallen into old, oppressed habits, the ones she'd learned around Nevin, allowing herself to be cowed in order to avoid a worse scene, but those days were over. She didn't care how many of her men were watching. Public humiliation or not, she had no intention of being sent anywhere this time without a fight!

'What do—?' Fergus started to say something else.

'I'm allowed to look, aren't I?' She spun around, al-

most shouting the words, taken aback by her own vehemence.

'Of course.' Except for the slight lift of one eyebrow, his own expression remained unperturbed. 'I was just going to ask what you thought.'

'What I thought...?' She stared at him, blinking a few times at the question. *Not* a reprimand or order then. 'About...?'

'Our building work.' He lifted an arm, pointing as if there might be some doubt about which building work he was referring to.

'Oh...' She looked from him to the wall and then back again, feeling her cheeks heat at the misunderstanding. 'It looks like it's going well.'

'Aye. We're making props.'

'Props?'

'To hold the stones up. We can't take the risk of knocking the whole section down and rebuilding it right now, not when we don't know who's watching, so we're going to prop it up from the inside. Hopefully we can push some of the bigger stones back into place so that the weak point won't be too obvious either.'

'I see.' She blinked one more time for good measure. 'That sounds like a good plan. I wish I'd thought of it myself.'

'Then you approve?'

She glanced at the wall again, stalling for time as she tried to work out what was going on. It was impossible not to be suspicious of the sudden change in his demeanour. Yesterday he hadn't wanted to talk to her at all and now he was asking for her opinion and approval? Judging by his expression, however, he was in earnest.

If he'd been any other man, she might have thought he was making an effort and trying to make amends for the way he'd acted the night before... Even his frown looked marginally less severe today, his brows barely clenched at all. There was a whole finger's width between them.

'I approve very much.' She nodded and started to move away, deciding to go and think about his behaviour elsewhere. No doubt Ailis and Gregor would be getting hungry by now. Children at least were consistent in their behaviour.

'Sorry about the noise.' Fergus reached a hand out, catching her arm gently just above the wrist, as if he didn't want her to leave. 'I hope that it isn't disturbing you too much?'

'No-o.' She glanced down in surprise. And now he was apologising? Not to mention touching her. It was the mere lightest of touches and yet as unexpected as if he'd just hauled her into his arms... She waited for him to pull away, but his fingers only flexed, warming the skin beneath and causing an unexpected, but vaguely familiar, tingling sensation in her abdomen. It was strange, like the ghost of a memory, one that she'd almost forgotten had ever existed and yet she *had* felt it before...a long time ago and with him, too, that first time they'd met when she'd been breathless at the mere sight of him. She cleared her throat in confusion, pushing both the feeling and memory aside. 'It doesn't matter anyway. It needs to be done.'

'It does.' He met her gaze and then released her abruptly, stepping back with a slightly unfocused look in his eyes as if even he didn't quite understand what he'd just been doing.

'So…' She found herself clearing her throat again. 'I see that you're training the men?'

'Aye.' His voice had a husky edge, too. 'They're not in bad shape, but they could be better. I need every man to be at his fighting best if we're to defeat the Campbells.'

'Will it really come to that, do you think?'

'Maybe, maybe not, but we need to be ready, just in case.' He looked past her towards the keep. 'I noticed Iver paid you a visit earlier.'

'He did, although I think he intended it to be a secret.'

'That explains why he can't train scouts.' He gave a grunt of derision. 'I suspected it was only a matter of time before he complained to you, but he was even faster than I expected.'

'Iver isn't a man to suffer in silence.'

'I know his type. Is it me he objects to or taking orders in general?'

'Both. He seemed to think that I might be sympathetic to his plight.'

'Is that why you came out here?' The gap between his brows narrowed. 'To take issue with me?'

'No. If anything, I came to thank you. Iver's a lazy, incompetent bully. He always has been. He'll make trouble for you if he can.'

'I can handle him.'

'By tipping him into the loch?'

A flicker of something like amusement passed over his face, softening his features for the briefest of moments. 'It was only a bucket of water. He needed waking up.'

'Ah.' Her lips curved at the image. 'Well then… thank you.'

'You're welcome.' He bowed his head. 'Coira, about last night…'

'What about it?' She stiffened, tensing at the reminder.

'I shouldn't have told you to go to bed. Or I should have gone with you. It was badly done of me.'

'Oh.' She scrunched her mouth up, surprised by the admission. In six years, Nevin had never apologised for anything. The words were so unfamiliar, it was hard to know how to respond… 'Well, I hope extracting a little revenge made you feel better.'

'It wasn't revenge.' His jaw clenched visibly.

'No?' She couldn't keep the scepticism out of her voice. 'Then what was it?'

'A mistake. I had a lot on my mind and I wanted time to think, but I ought to have considered the way it would look to others. I meant no insult, but I'm sorry anyway.'

'I see.' She swallowed, still struggling to catch up with the direction their conversation had taken. What had happened to the hard-faced, glacial-eyed warrior she'd married? One night's sleep and he seemed, if not a whole different man, then a distinctly less cold-blooded one. 'Then I accept your apology. Did you get all of your thinking done?'

'No.' For some reason the question made his brows contract all over again. 'Not yet.'

'Fergus hasn't come to visit me,' Gregor complained, pouting as Coira tucked the blankets up under his chin.

'He's been very busy repairing the wall.'

'But he promised to come and tell me how it was going!'

'He did? When?'

'When I was outside playing with Duffy. He said that he'd help me to train her, too.' Gregor beamed and then sighed. 'Only he didn't say when.'

'There's a lot of important work to be done.'

'Because we're going to be attacked?'

'What?' She stilled abruptly. 'Who told you that?'

'No one.' Gregor's expression turned sheepish. 'I overheard some of the men talking about it. About someone called Campbell, too.'

'Well, hopefully it won't come to anything, but even if it does, there's no need for you to worry. We have strong walls and fierce warriors.'

'And Fergus. He'll protect us, won't he?'

'He'll do his best.'

'Fergus!' Gregor sprang up again, dislodging all of her carefully tucked blankets as the man in question appeared in the doorway. 'You came!'

'I said that I would.' Her husband tipped his head towards her, his expression guarded. 'If your mother doesn't think it's too late for that report?'

'I wouldn't dare. Here.' She stood up, offering him the stool by the bed as she perched on the edge of the mattress instead.

'Is the wall finished?' Gregor asked eagerly.

'Not quite.' Fergus's lips gave the merest hint of a twitch. 'We're making good progress, but it'll take until the end of the week at least. It's well guarded, however. You needn't have any fears about that.' He looked around the room. 'Where's Duffy?'

'Over there.' Gregor pointed towards a mound of blankets on the floor. 'She likes to burrow underneath so you can only see her nose. Mama almost tripped over her the first time.'

'Did she?' He turned his gaze towards her questioningly.

'Unfortunately, yes.' Coira tucked a strand of loose hair back beneath her headdress, feeling self-conscious under his scrutiny, even more so when his gaze followed the movement. 'She gave me the fright of my life.'

'Mama was just about to tell me a story, too.'

'What about?'

'Well…' She immediately forgot every story she'd ever known. 'I hadn't quite decided yet.'

'Tell him the one about the kelpies.' Gregor grinned as he looked between them. 'That's my favourite.'

'I'm sure Fergus has more important things to do than listen to me tell a stor—' She paused mid-sentence at the sound of a soft cry. Thank goodness for Ailis. 'In any case, it sounds like your sister needs me.'

'Urgh.' Gregor rolled his eyes. 'She always needs you. I'm tired of sharing a room with a girl.'

'Then perhaps you'd prefer to sleep in the hall along with everyone else?' Coira gave him a chiding look, pushing the curtain that divided the chamber aside and bending over her daughter's cot. Ailis's eyes were wide open, her small, rosebud lips pursing and unpursing gently as she made soft burbling noises in the back of her throat.

'Do *you* have a sister?' she heard Gregor ask Fergus behind her.

'Aye. She's even noisier than yours.'

'Really? Did you ever have to share a room with her?'

'No, but I shared with my brother.'

'I wish *I* had a brother.'

'You'll like your sister more when she's older and you're able to play together. Trust me, you'll be friends then.'

Coira stifled a snort as she lifted Ailis into her arms and rubbed her hands in a circular pattern over her back. *Friends?* It wasn't exactly the word she would have chosen to describe her relationship with her own brother. It had been five years since she'd last set eyes on Niall. Or had any communication for that matter. He hadn't even sent a message of condolence after Nevin's death.

'What's your sister called?' Gregor seemed to have an inexhaustible supply of questions.

'Elspeth.'

'Does she look like you?'

'No, fortunately for her. She's a beauty.'

'Like Mama?'

'Don't be foolish!' Coira whirled about, hastening back through to join them. 'It's time to go to sleep, Gregor.'

'What about my story?'

'I'll tell you about the kelpies tomorrow, but right now, I need to tend to your sister. Now lie down and Grizel will be along soon.'

'All right. Goodnight, Mama.'

'Goodnight.' She leaned down, clasping Ailis tight as she pressed a kiss to Gregor's forehead.

'Goodnight, Fergus.'

'Goodnight, lad.'

Coira watched her husband out of the corner of her

eye as they stepped out into the solar. If she hadn't witnessed the scene with her own eyes, she might never have believed it. Not only had he been thoughtful enough to come and tell Gregor what was going on in the bailey, but he hadn't frowned at him once.

'That was very kind of you.' She offered a tentative smile.

'He's a good lad. *And* he's the Laird. It's only right to keep him informed of our progress.'

'I agree. Are you hungry?' She decided to keep the conversation to practicalities. Now that they were away from Gregor, his manner was becoming gruffer again by the second.

'I've had a bite to eat, but I'm too tired for more.' He rubbed a hand around the back of his neck. 'I'm ready for bed.'

'Of course. I need to feed Ailis, but I'll try not to disturb you when I come in. Sleep well.'

He acknowledged the words with a nod, though to her surprise he didn't move on, turning his attention to her daughter instead. 'She's a bonny lass.'

'I think so.'

'She looks like you.'

'Oh.' She opened her eyes wide, startled by the indirect compliment. 'So I've been told.'

'Both of them do, although Gregor... He has Nevin's fair hair.' He frowned again, as if his own words had disturbed him. 'Your maid, Grizel... She takes care of the children?'

'A lot of the time, aye. Only I like to tuck them into bed.' Coira peered up at him from beneath her lashes, vaguely disquieted by the question. A lot of men were

interested in her pretty young maid, but she'd hoped that
her new husband wouldn't be among them, no matter
how little interest he might have in his bride. She didn't
think she could bear the same situation she and Grizel
had gone through with Nevin, not again.

'Do you think her trustworthy?'

'Grizel? Completely. Why?'

'Curiosity, that's all.' He glanced in the direction
of the minstrels' gallery as if he wasn't sure whether
to leave her or not. 'By the way, I spoke to your steward earlier.'

'Malcolm?' She smiled, relieved at the change in
subject. 'You can trust him, too. He's the most honest
man I know.'

'He seems to think you've been hard-treated.'

She felt her expression freeze, alarmed by the way
his eyes were focused intently on her face as if he were
watching for her reaction. 'Did he?'

'Aye. It was strange. At first I thought he was talking
about me and our marriage, but afterwards it struck me
that he was referring to something else. Something in
the past, perhaps? With your first husband.'

She pretended to be distracted by Ailis, bouncing
her up and down in her arms as if she had no idea what
he was talking about. She never spoke about Nevin if
she could help it and she definitely didn't want to talk
about how miserable her marriage had been with Fergus of all people. He might not openly gloat, but he was
hardly likely to be sympathetic either and she still had
some pride left.

'What does the past matter?' she answered at last,
making a funny face at Ailis. '*You're* my husband now.'

'So I am.' There was a long, drawn-out pause before he finally took a step towards their bedchamber. 'Goodnight then, Coira.'

'Goodnight, Fergus.'

Chapter Eight

Fergus stood with his feet apart, arms folded and eyes narrowed, letting his gaze roam all over the battlements for a full minute before slowly nodding his head in approval, earning himself an array of proud smiles and relieved cheers.

'You've done a good job.' He looked around, acknowledging each of the men in turn. 'If that doesn't earn a rest for the remainder of the day then I don't know what does, but be ready tomorrow at dawn. We have a lot more training to do.'

There was another brief cheer before the men dispersed, leaving him alone with Malcolm.

'Something wrong?' Fergus quirked an eyebrow. The old man was regarding the wall with an expression of bemusement.

'Not at all. I can just hardly believe the improvement and all in one week.'

'Aye.' Fergus heaved a sigh of satisfaction. Perhaps he'd pushed the men a little too hard, but it had certainly been worth it. The work had been a useful distraction for him, too, wearing him out enough to keep his mind away from other subjects. Subjects he shouldn't be interested in, but still found himself asking questions about… 'It's not perfect, but it's better. I'd like to see the Campbells get through that.'

'If it's all the same to you, I'd rather not.' Malcolm shuddered. 'I'm still hoping they choose another place to attack, not that I wish ill on anyone else.'

'I know what you mean.' Fergus lifted his gaze, looking out over the top of the wall at the rugged, untamed beauty of the landscape beyond. There was a faint dusting of snow on the tallest of the peaks that day, making them look even more majestic, like silent sentinels sending a warning that autumn was upon them and winter would follow soon. 'It would be a shame to spoil this place with bloodshed.'

'You're beginning to like it here, then?' Malcolm's gaze turned a little too inquisitive.

'Well enough.' He jerked his head towards the keep. 'Come and share some ale with me. There are other matters we need to discuss. Have you made a full inventory of our provisions, as I asked?'

'Aye. We have enough food for a sennight, but any longer and we'll be in trouble.'

'In that case, we should…' Fergus paused, glancing over his shoulder at the sound of an excited shout. Gregor was charging about with Duffy on the opposite side of the bailey, watched over by Grizel and one of the younger guards who'd just stopped to talk with them. Judging by his mane of shaggy blond hair, it was Euan, one of the hardest workers and a promising young warrior. 'Actually, give me an hour. There's another matter I need to attend to first.'

'Take as long as you need.'

He placed a hand on Malcolm's shoulder, acknowledging the smile that was just about visible through his beard, before starting across the bailey towards his stepson. A drink would have to wait. Before that, he had a promise to keep and a wilful puppy to train.

'How do you do it, Grizel?' Coira looked up from where she was folding freshly laundered linens into heaps on the bed, smiling as her maid appeared in the doorway.

'Do what, my lady?'

'Look so fresh?' She put her hands on her lower back and stretched. 'We've both been up since dawn, yet you still look as if you've just woken up.'

'I'm sure that's not true.' Grizel shook her head modestly. 'Besides, you already look a lot better than you did a week ago. Not that you looked bad, of course,' she added hastily.

'If I looked half as bad as I felt then, I certainly did.' Coira laughed, although she'd noticed the recent change in her appearance, too. It was obviously due to relief. Despite a rough start, the first week of her second marriage had gone far better than she'd ever dared to expect. It was still obvious that Fergus didn't like her or want to be there, but at least he wasn't taking it out on anyone any longer, least of all her. The furrow between his brows might be deeply ingrained and his manner only a touch above freezing, but after their wedding night there had been no more insults, implied or otherwise. She'd caught him staring at her oddly a few times, no doubt silently resenting her, but that was all.

'I'm relieved for you, my lady.' Grizel seemed to

read her thoughts. 'He's certainly a very different man
from Nevin.' Her lips curved. 'And more handsome
than you said.'

'I suppose so.' Coira felt her cheeks flush. Fergus
was handsome, despite all the frowning and a nose that
looked like it had been broken at least twice, and yet
even if he hadn't been... Handsome wasn't quite the
right word. Nevin had been handsome, but Fergus was
more attractive than that. There was a raw masculinity
about him, an air of command combined with a lack
of artifice that struck her as far more potent than mere
good looks. 'But it's not like that. We aren't... That is,
we haven't...you know.'

'You haven't?' Grizel opened her eyes wide.

'No.'

'But you sleep in the same bed?'

'Aye, although we rarely go to bed at the same time.'
She closed the coffer lid to hide her expression. One of
them would usually be fast asleep by the time the other
came to bed and Fergus was always gone by the time
she awoke in the morning. She rarely saw him during
the day either. He was always busy, with a seemingly
limitless supply of energy, the complete opposite to her
first husband in that regard. Nevin could have happily
slept all day, whereas the only time Fergus seemed to
sit still was at mealtimes.

'We're being civil to each other.' She nodded firmly.
'It's not friendship, but it's good enough.'

'But it's a good sign. Perhaps there's a chance that
you might come to care for each other one day?'

'*No!*' She said the word more harshly than she'd intended. 'That is, I could never feel that way about a man

again, not after Nevin. That kind of love is for naive maidens and deluded fools and things are much better as they are. I hope that Fergus and I can grow to be friends, but that's all.'

Grizel pursed her lips, looking as if she wanted to say something else before opening another of the coffers, digging down to the bottom and pulling out a yellow gown. 'Maybe you should wear this tonight? The colour suits you so well. You'll look like sunshine.'

Coira reached out, smoothing her fingers gently along the collar. It was embroidered in gold thread with an intricate pattern of tiny flowers and leaves, entwined with a few bees for good measure. Briefly she wondered what Fergus would think of it. The gown was one of her favourites and it really did suit her, made of finely spun wool with a blue tasselled belt to match, but it was far too good for a simple dinner. 'It's tempting, but it might look strange to wear something so fine for no reason.'

'But there *is* a reason!' Grizel beamed, thrusting the gown further into her arms. 'Tonight's meal is a celebration.'

'It is?' She wrinkled her brow in confusion. 'Why?'

'Because the wall's finished. Or safely propped up anyway.'

'How do you know?'

'Because one of the guards told me. And I saw it. I was outside earlier with Gregor and Duffy.' Grizel chuckled. 'It was quite a sight when your husband came to play with them.'

'*Play?*' Coira felt her lips part in surprise. 'Fergus was *playing*?'

'Aye. He was teaching the pup all sorts of tricks,

or trying to anyway. She's quite a challenge! You should have seen it, my lady, Gregor and I were both in stitches.'

'Maybe next time.' She forced a smile, stifling a pang of jealousy at the thought of her attractive young maid laughing with Fergus, never mind playing. Briefly, she wondered whether the same thing would have happened if she'd been there. It seemed unlikely. No matter how civil they were being to each other, she and Fergus were a long way from *playing* together. There was a palpable air of tension whenever they were alone.

'My lady?' Grizel gave her a quizzical look. 'Is something the matter?'

'No.' She shook her head guiltily. It was hardly her maid's fault that she was so pretty. 'I was just thinking.'

'About wearing the dress?'

'I'm really not sure about it.'

'But the men are already celebrating. You wouldn't want them to think you weren't pleased with their work, would you?' Grizel gave her a playful look. 'Besides, if you dress up then I have an excuse to as well. And all the other maids. *Please?*'

'Oh, all right, if you insist. For you. But *only* for you.' Coira smiled wanly. She still thought it was going to look odd, but she supposed it was a *kind* of celebration. As for Fergus's opinion…well, he'd already made it abundantly obvious what he thought of her appearance so she was determined not to care. In all likelihood, he wouldn't even notice.

'We'll need to make arrangements for the people in the village, too, in case they need to come here for safety.' Fergus drummed his fingers on the tabletop as he and Malcolm shared a jug of ale in the hall. The men around them were in high spirits, the one exception being Iver, who was ensconced in a corner, glowering at anyone foolish enough to venture near, not that many did. 'It's unlikely the Campbells will lay siege to us, but it's still possible. We need to be in a position to withstand them, if necessary.'

'For how long?'

'Hopefully no more than a fortnight. That should be long enough for Ross or Brody MacWhinnie to find out what's happening and gather enough men to come to our aid.'

'Very well.' Malcolm nodded. 'I'll see what can be done in the morning.'

'Good.' Fergus picked up his tankard, took a long gulp and then froze at the sight of Coira in the hall doorway. She was dressed in a long, yellow gown that contrasted perfectly with her black hair, although only a little of that was visible beneath a cream silk headdress, held in place with a narrow, yellow filet.

To his increasing annoyance, she appeared to have been shedding years all week, as if she were slowly but surely turning back into the girl he'd first met. Now she looked breathtakingly, infuriatingly, perfectly lovely. Almost as lovely as the first time he'd set eyes on her. She also seemed to be looking everywhere except at him.

'Well…' Malcolm pushed his bench none too subtly back from the table. 'If it's all the same to you, I have some errands to attend to before the meal. You'll excuse me?'

'Aye.' Fergus nodded, scowling into his tankard as Coira made her way to join Gregor on a bench beside the hearth. The polite thing to do would be to join them, but the fact that he even wanted to bothered him. Just like it bothered him that she was so elegant and graceful and obviously well liked in the castle, completely unlike the heartbreaking, treacherous villainess of his imagination. He'd kept himself busy all week in an attempt not to think about what that might mean, but he'd still found himself looking for her far too often, turning his head every time he caught a glimpse of black hair or smelled the faint aroma of lavender. His resentment was waning far too much, too quickly for comfort. So much so that he could hardly pretend indifference to her any longer. Now he knew that if he had any sense at all then he would ignore her and stay seated where he was. Joining her would be a terrible idea...and yet at some point during the last minute he'd already got to his feet and was walking towards her.

'She looks tired.' He crouched down beside Gregor when he reached the fireplace, gesturing towards the puppy who was curled up in a ball with her small chin across her paws and her eyes half-open. 'It might be too loud in here for her.'

'Should I take her upstairs?' Gregor looked at his mother, whose posture, Fergus noticed, had stiffened visibly the moment she'd seen him.

'That might be a good idea.' Her voice sounded tense, too. 'I'll send some food up to your room.'

'Will you come and tell me a story later?'

'Of course.' She smiled, glancing at Fergus as her son scooped the yawning hound into his arms and trotted away. 'I heard that you were playing outside with them today. Gregor says she's a fast learner, although Grizel has a different opinion.'

'She's coming along,' he answered non-committally, gesturing towards the empty spot on the bench beside her. 'May I join you?'

'You want to sit with me?'

'Aye.' If he wasn't mistaken, he actually heard air hiss between her teeth in surprise. 'Unless you'd prefer that I didn't?'

'It's not that. I just didn't think…' She faltered, seemingly unable to finish the sentence and so pressing her lips together and nodding instead.

'Thank you…' He sat down an arm's length away, suddenly unable to think of a single subject of conversation.

'I heard that the wall's finished.' Thankfully, she thought of something for him. 'I took a walk outside before I came here to see for myself. It looks good.'

'So do you.'

'M-me?' She sounded startled.

'Aye. Look good, I mean. You do. Not like a wall… obviously.' He wanted to cut his own tongue out. 'Just good. Nice. In that gown.'

'Oh…thank you.' She glanced down, her cheeks flushing a dusky shade of pink. 'Grizel told me that tonight was a celebration, as much as it can be at the moment anyway, so I thought…just a small effort.' She folded and then unfolded her hands in her lap. 'I'm glad that you like it.'

'I do. It's very…yellow.' He winced, wishing that he'd thought to bring his tankard of ale across the room with him. That might have made this conversation a little easier. He was behaving the same way he had six years ago, like a tongue-tied youth! Although, even if he *had* been able to think of anything coherent to say, his throat felt oddly constricted. Somehow just sitting beside her, not even in very close proximity, was doing strange things to his brain, making it impossible to concentrate.

Absently, he let his gaze drift along the line of her jaw to the tip of her chin and then lower, down the slender column of her throat to the base of her neck where he could see the tiny flutter of her pulse beneath the skin. It looked so small, so tremulous, tempting him to reach out and touch it, to press his lips against it even. He wondered what her skin would feel like...

He tore his gaze away, clearing his throat as a shiver of desire coursed through his body. 'But you're right, we ought to celebrate. The men deserve an evening's rest after all their hard work. There are still plenty of guards outside though, don't worry.'

'I'm not worried.' She seemed faintly surprised by her own admission. 'It's strange, but I'm really not. It makes a pleasant change.'

'Not to worry?'

'Aye.' She nodded, her expression turning thoughtful though her hands still fidgeted in her lap. 'You know, I thought I was doing a reasonable job, looking after the castle for Gregor by myself, even though there was always so much to do and so many things to think about. Now I see that I should have done a lot more.'

'You shouldn't be so hard on yourself. You've done a lot of good work here.' He jerked his head in Iver's direction. 'And you had him to contend with.'

She made a sound of derision. 'That's true. I've lost count of the number of times I've wanted to throw him from the ramparts. Or at least hang him there by his feet.'

'Just say the word.'

She twisted her face towards him, her features softening into a conspiratorial smile, and he felt a sudden lurch in his chest, like a surge of long-pent-up emotion, accompanied by an uneasy feeling, as if the hairs on the back of his neck were all standing up together. It was downright alarming how much he liked seeing her smile. Her eyes didn't even look dull grey any more. The spark that he'd thought had gone out had somehow rekindled and they were the colour of thistles once again, unique and bright and enticing.

Maybe his first instinct had been right and coming to sit with her had been a terrible idea, after all. The more time he spent with her, the more he found himself liking her, and the more he liked her, the more it reminded him of the first time they'd met and of how foolishly infatuated and trusting he'd been...

'I should go and check on the guards.' He got to his feet abruptly.

'Now? What about the meal?' Her smile dropped away, replaced by a look of confusion. 'The food will be here soon. It's beef.'

'I won't be long. Don't wait for me.'

He marched away before she could say anything else, walking fast to calm the sensation of panic building inside him. He needed to get away. More than that, he needed to remember what it was that she'd done and how much she'd hurt and humiliated him all those years ago. He had to remember that she'd looked him in the eye, promised to marry him and then run away with another man. He had to keep on reminding himself that she wasn't a woman to be trusted, no matter what she might seem like now. Otherwise, he was in danger of making the same mistake, not to mention an even bigger fool of himself, all over again.

Chapter Nine

Fergus rammed his shield forward, forcing his quarry to retreat several paces, before jabbing his wooden sword under the rim and swiping viciously sideways.

'I yield!' His opponent, Euan, reeled over, raising his hands in submission.

'Not bad.' Fergus stepped back at once. 'But you put too much energy into your attack. It wears you out so you end up making mistakes all the sooner.' He swept his sword around in a circle, taking in his whole audience. 'Patience is one of the most important qualities a warrior can learn. Bide your time until you find the right moment to strike and you'll make worthy adversaries.' He twisted his head abruptly, levelling a fierce glare in Iver's direction as the guard muttered something under his breath. 'You have something to add?'

'No.' Iver shuffled his feet.

'Yet you said something.' Fergus clenched his jaw. The situation with the guards was beginning to grate on his nerves. He'd found most of the younger ones enthusiastic and eager to learn, as if they'd been held

back from doing so before, but Iver remained a dis-
ruptive presence among some of the elder men who'd
fallen into lazy habits. It amazed him that such a man
could have been tolerated as leader of the guards for
so long. Ten years, according to Malcolm. Ten years in
which he'd obviously done as little work while causing
as much ill will as possible.

He tapped his sword on the ground, considering for
several seconds before turning on his heel and beckoning for Iver to follow. 'Come with me. The rest of you
keep practising.'

'Where are we going?' Iver's voice trembled nervously as Fergus marched them out of the bailey and
on to the track to the village beyond.

He didn't answer, stalking a little way further before veering off the track and into a cluster of trees beside the loch, out of sight of the castle. The sky on the
far side of the water looked threatening again, swol-
len with rain clouds as if a giant grey wave was rolling steadily towards them, but it didn't matter. Not yet
anyway. Another storm was brewing, but what he had
to do wouldn't take long.

He turned around finally, removing his sword belt
and tossing it into a heap of pine needles at his feet.
'Hit me.'

The other man's jaw dropped, as if he'd just seen one
of the mythical beasts some people claimed lived at the
bottom of the loch. 'What?'

'Hit me. As hard as you can.'

'I don't want to fight you.'

'Yet you wish to challenge my authority?'

Iver's expression hardened. 'Training the men was my job.'

'*Was.* Not any more.' Fergus placed his feet apart, bracing himself. 'So this is my offer. You strike the first blow. *And* the second. Even the third if you think that you'll need it. I won't flinch and I won't hit back.'

'And then?'

'Then it's my turn and we both fight.' He shrugged. 'But strike me properly the first time and I shouldn't be able to put up much resistance.'

'So...three times?'

'Aye. Last man standing takes charge of the guards.' Fergus spread his arms out in invitation, noting the gleam of vengeful anticipation on the other man's face. He'd used this trick several times before and it had never once failed. This time it took a few seconds, but just as he'd expected, the other man's fist swung up.

He didn't flinch.

'What on earth happened?' There was a heavy thud followed by a splash as Coira dropped the jug she was carrying on to the floor of the bedchamber. 'You're bleeding!'

'It's just a scratch.' Fergus looked up from a stool by the fireplace, pressing a wet cloth to his cheek to hide the swell of the bruise underneath.

'It's *much* more than that!' She abandoned both the jug and its contents as she hurried across the room towards him, her brow puckering as she bent to take a closer look. 'And you're soaking wet!'

'I got caught in the rain.'

'I can see that. Who did this to you?'

'It doesn't matter. He won't do it again.'

She pulled back slightly, lifting an eyebrow. 'Iver?'

'Aye. He needed to understand a few things.'

'Then I hope it was highly educational. Here, let me do that.' She took the cloth from his hand, dipping it into the bowl of water at his side before pressing it gently back to his cheek. 'Was it really necessary to fight him?'

'Maybe not, but I don't have the time to be subtle. The Campbells could be here any day now and I need the men to follow my commands, not to make trouble.'

'Well, I'm not saying that I approve, but if it *had* to be someone…' She pressed her lips together. 'How badly is he hurt?'

'It looks worse than it is. I was making a point, not trying to break any limbs. We might need all the able-bodied men we can get, although they could still do with more training. Not that I can do much in this weather.' He glowered in the direction of the window shutters. 'This storm's not going anywhere for a while.'

'Well, scowling won't do anything about it.'

'I'm not scowling.'

'You don't think so?'

'Not even close.' He peered up at her from under his brows and then pressed them hard together. '*This* is a scowl.'

'Oh!' A surprised-sounding laugh escaped her. 'I stand corrected. That's very fierce.'

'It's the one I save for proper storms. Or snow.'

'Then I'm surprised it ever dares to rain at all.' Her lips curved. 'Still, knowing that could be helpful. I won't bother to look outside in the mornings to check the weather any more. I'll just look at your face. Speaking of which…is there any more damage?' She pulled the cloth away from his cheek and curled her fingers beneath his chin, turning his face from one side to the other.

Fergus stiffened, wrapping his hands quickly beneath the stool and gripping it tight, stunned by the unexpected touch of her fingers against his skin, their warmth seeping into his jaw and making his heartbeat accelerate until he could feel his pulse throbbing along every vein. He had no idea what his expression was doing now. He was only aware of the full, red curve of her lips as she drew her tongue across them in concentration, turning his own mouth dry.

Desperately, he fought to stifle a groan, willing the pounding of blood in his ears to subside as raw desire coursed through him. He felt his lips start to move and yet no words seemed to come out. He didn't seem able to make any coherent sounds at all. If the tightness in his chest was anything to go by, his heart was attempting to claw its way up his throat. Either that or batter its way out of his chest. Alarmingly, he had a feeling it was succeeding, too. Another few seconds and he wouldn't be able to resist curling an arm around her waist and pulling her down into his lap.

'Don't.' He finally forced a word out, though it sounded more like a growl as he wrenched his jaw away from her fingers, shocked by the violence of his reaction to a simple touch. His body was reacting to her in a way that it hadn't reacted to any woman for a long time, to any woman in fact since…*her*. 'I told you, it's just a scratch.'

* * *

Coira dropped to her haunches in front of the fire-place. She'd touched Fergus instinctively, the way she might have touched Gregor if he'd cut his face, but the moment her fingertips had grazed his skin she'd known it had been a mistake. His whole body had tensed and gone motionless, his jaw turning to granite, just as it had when he'd walked away from her so abruptly in the hall the previous evening, as if he hadn't been able to bear sitting beside her any longer.

This time, however, there had been an arrested, un-focused look in his eyes, too, as if he'd been genuinely shocked by her touch. He could hardly have made it any more obvious that he didn't want her to touch him and yet, for some reason, she still hadn't let go. She hadn't wanted to. On the contrary, she'd been tempted to go further, to slide her fingers along the hard con-tours and rough bristles of his chin and then on, into the thick, dark sweep of his hair. It looked so soft to the touch. Thick and lustrous, falling all the way to his shoulders...

She'd been so caught up in the idea that she hadn't pulled her hand away when she should have, leaving it up to *him* to remove *her*.

'I'm sorry.' She pressed her lips together, red spots of humiliation burning across her cheekbones as she stared at the flames leaping in the fireplace.

'Why?' He shifted on his stool, his voice even gruffer than usual, with a new, guttural note she hadn't heard there before. 'You didn't hit me.'

'No, but...' She sucked in a deep breath and then let it out slowly again. Why *was* she apologising? For touching him? No, it was for a lot more than that: for what she'd done in the past and the position they were in now, for their marriage and all the things he'd already said he didn't want to talk about...

She half closed her eyes, listening to the heavy patter of rain on the roof above. It seemed to be getting heavier, exacerbating the atmosphere of tension in the room. And yet just a few moments ago she and Fergus had been almost relaxed in each other's company, even teasing one another like the friends she'd hoped they might one day become. Teasing a man had been a whole new experience, unfamiliar and yet enjoyable, too, with an added sense of intimacy that she hadn't expected. Maybe that was the real reason she'd touched him. Because she'd liked it. Because despite herself, she'd wanted more. Because a part of her had wanted to see where it would lead...

'I'm sorry for this whole situation.' She spoke softly into the silence. Even if he didn't want to hear the words, she needed to say them. 'I know you don't want to be here.'

There was a long pause before he answered, pushing a hand through his hair before releasing his breath on a sigh as if he were tired. 'That's not your fault either. Our union was Brody and my brother's idea.'

'I'm still sorry. I tried to talk him out of it.'

'Brody?'

'Aye. I told him how much you must resent me. With good reason,' she added hastily, 'but he wouldn't listen. He just said it was for the good of the clan.' She put her hands on her knees and pushed herself to her feet, hoping that he'd mistake the red in her cheeks for heat from the fire. 'So, yes, I'm truly sorry. It's not fair that you've been forced to marry me now after I ran away with Nevin six years ago. I know that you didn't want to marry me, not even back then.'

His head jerked backwards slightly. 'What do you mean?'

'I just know that you never liked me that way.'

'Who told you that?'

'You did.' She blinked at the newly ferocious tone of his voice. 'Or at least your face did. You always looked so stern. And you never wanted to talk to me. I thought...' She paused as his eyes flashed with anger. 'That is, I assumed it was because you didn't really want to marry me.'

'It wasn't because—' He stopped and muttered an oath, dropping his gaze to the floor as if he were searching for words there. 'I've never been good at speaking to people.'

'You don't have to defend yourself. I'm not complain—'

'I *liked* you.'

'What?' She felt her breath hitch.

'I liked you,' he repeated, his gaze still fixed on the floor. 'I wanted to marry you. As for smiling... It's not my way.'

'You *wanted* to marry me?' She gasped the words out, unable to breathe properly all of a sudden. There seemed to be less air in the room. Or maybe there was too much. Either way, it made her feel winded. Slowly, she pressed a hand to her stomach, looking around for a chair to sit on and finding a coffer instead.

Putting a hand behind her to steady herself, she

perched on the edge, her thoughts reeling as she tried to comprehend what he'd just told her. He'd liked her? He'd wanted to marry her? If he was telling the truth, then it cast her running away, her marriage, the entirety of the past six years, into a completely different light. Was it possible? *Could* she have misjudged him so badly? It had never once occurred to her that his severe demeanour might have been a cover for something else. Shyness? But then she'd been so young and naive and he'd been so big and looming, so ferocious-looking... Men like that couldn't be shy, could they? But if he *had* been, then she'd made an even bigger mistake than she'd realised, running away from an honourable man into the arms of a dishonourable one. From a man who'd actually wanted to marry her to a man who'd only wanted her brother's money. From a man she might have stood a chance of being happy with to a man who'd made her utterly miserable, who'd taken her heart and innocence and trampled all over them, who'd made it impossible for her to care for anyone in that way ever again...

She shook her head, feeling as though all her memories from that time were shifting and remoulding themselves into new shapes in her mind. Only a sharp crack of lightning, followed by a low roll of thunder outside, finally brought her back to the moment.

'I had no idea. If I'd known—'

'Then it wouldn't have made any difference.' Fergus raised his head finally, his eyes fierce and accusing, like smouldering coals. 'I wasn't the one that you wanted, was I?'

'But I didn't...' She stopped, biting her tongue. 'It wasn't like that.'

'Then what was it? They told me that you left with Nevin Barron willingly. You were seen riding away together.'

'Ye-es.'

A humourless sound emerged from his lips. 'Then it was a love match, wasn't it? That's why you abandoned our wedding?'

She swallowed hard, suddenly eager to get away and arrange her spinning, confused thoughts into some kind of order. For a moment it had been on the tip of her tongue to defend herself, to say that her marriage to Nevin had had nothing to do with love, but it was impossible to do so without telling Fergus the whole truth and betraying her brother. And if she did that then there was a chance that Fergus might still seek revenge, even after all this time. No matter how scheming, avaricious and underhand Niall had been, no doubt still was, she couldn't risk that. Her marriage had brought about enough suffering as it was.

'It's so long ago now,' she answered at last, aware of the silence between them stretching on for too long. 'It's hard to remember what I felt back then.' She lurched to her feet before he could respond, hurrying towards the door and jumping over the fallen jug in her haste to escape. 'Now I have a meal to attend to.'

Chapter Ten

Coira stretched as she rolled on to her side, roused by movement on the other side of the bed. Her mind had still been whirling when she'd lain down the night before and yet somehow she'd fallen asleep the very instant her head had touched the pillow. She'd slept surprisingly well, too, not even noticing when Fergus had come to join her. Now, as she opened her eyes to find him already up and out of bed again, she felt as if the relationship between them had altered, as if he were a subtly different man from the one whose injury she'd tended.

He'd liked her. Somehow those words had shifted the ground beneath her feet, giving her a glimpse of the man behind the scowl, turning him from a forbidding warrior into a husband with hidden depths. A husband who was nowhere near as fearsome as first, or even second, appearances suggested.

Of course he hadn't said in what way he'd liked her, nor how much, and just because he'd liked her six years ago didn't mean that he still did—in fact, he definitely didn't—but none of that mattered. The knowledge that he *had* made her hopeful that one day, perhaps, they might learn to be friends, after all. Companions to share a calm, stable life together. Just as long as he didn't ask her any more questions about Nevin and she didn't touch his jaw.

It was a pleasant, heartening thought, even though, at that precise moment, her possible future *friend* was also half-naked, washing his torso with a cloth beside the window.

She pushed herself up on her elbows, her mind going blank as she stared, mesmerised, at the ripple of muscles in his back. It was the first time that she'd ever seen him without clothing and despite the swelling of a large yellow bruise just beneath his ribcage, the sight was extremely impressive. Stirring even, making her feel as if her insides were buzzing. Nevin had never once made her feel that way. She was wide awake in a matter of seconds.

'Good morning.'

She coughed the words out and he turned around at once, presenting her with an even more impressive view of a well-toned chest, corded with muscle and covered with a faint dusting of black hair, tapering down to a trim, solid waist.

'My apologies. I didn't mean to wake you.' He nodded his head in greeting, regarding her with his usual sternness, though his gaze lingered briefly on one of her shoulders, exposed by the open neck of her nightgown. She'd been in such a hurry the previous evening, she obviously hadn't tied the laces properly.

'It doesn't matter. I ought to be getting up anyway.'

She tugged her gown back over her shoulder, though she kept her eyes fixed firmly on him. Somehow she found it impossible to tear them away. His torso was so solid it looked as if it had been sculpted from wood. A strong Scots pine... As for his stomach, there were more muscles there than she'd ever seen in one place. She couldn't help but wonder if they felt as hard as they looked... And just thinking about touching them caused a fresh bout of buzzing, accompanied by a warm, churning sensation, like a whirlpool swirling inside her.

Quickly, she dragged her gaze up to his face, licking her suddenly parched lips as waves of heat prickled across her skin. She had absolutely no idea what was happening to her body, but she sincerely hoped he couldn't tell the effect he was having on her. A mere week ago, she hadn't even expected to like him, let alone find him attractive!

'Your cheek looks better already.' She thought it necessary to say *something*.

'My cheek?' He gave her a quizzical look before reaching, to her intense disappointment, for an undershirt. 'Oh, aye, I'd forgotten about that.'

'There's a nasty bruise on your back, too.' She permitted herself one last glance downwards before he covered himself.

'I've had worse.'

'I have some balm that might help, if you like? It's around here somewhere if you want me to rub it in for you?'

He made a burbling sound, his expression looking oddly conflicted before he shook his head. 'No need... Thank you.'

She pulled herself up to a seated position, drawing her knees up to her chest and studying the ceiling as he pulled on the rest of his clothes. 'So what are your plans for today? Rebuilding the keep, maybe?'

'Not this morning.' He came to stand in front of her, waiting until she looked at him again before suddenly, unexpectedly, winking. 'Maybe this afternoon.'

She stared back at him in surprise. His voice was as gruff as ever, but for the first time, there was a definite twinkle in his eye. *A joke?* The last thing she'd ever expected to hear was Fergus MacMillan making a joke! Somehow she felt it in the very pit of her stomach.

'Well, that's all right then,' she answered in kind. 'Just mind that you're not late for dinner.'

'Noted, my lady.' He gave a mock bow. 'Actually, I'm going to the village. I need to tell the people there what to do if the Campbells decide to head this way.' He paused. 'I'm sure you've discussed it with them already, but I should probably introduce myself, as well.'

'I have, but mayhap I should accompany you?' She lifted a shoulder, unintentionally causing her nightgown to slide down again. 'Then I could introduce you properly.'

There was a heavy silence, accompanied by another frown, as if he wasn't sure how to respond. It went on for so long that she thought he was surely about to refuse and was on the point of pre-empting him by retracting her offer when he nodded jerkily. 'All right. I was going to take Euan, but that's a better idea. It's what people will expect.' He nodded again, as if he were confirming the decision to himself, his gaze sliding back to her bare shoulder before locking on her face. 'You *should* come, but you'll need to hurry.'

Coira leapt out of bed the moment Fergus departed the chamber, pulling on the first gown she could lay her hands on before opening the window shutters and breathing in the fresh air. After the storm, the sky was positively gleaming. Bright and blue and cloudless, lifting her spirits and making her keen to get outside. The fact that Fergus hadn't objected to her company was progress, too. The chilly demeanour he'd worn for the past week was thawing considerably. It still wasn't exactly warm, but like the sky that morning, it was definitely an improvement. One step closer to friendship…

Quickly, she darted into the children's room to kiss Gregor and Ailis awake, helping herself to a spoonful of the porridge that Grizel had fetched for their breakfast, before hurrying on down the stairwell.

'That was quick.' Fergus looked impressed as she stepped outside, pinning an amber brooch to her shoulder to hold her fur-lined cloak in place.

'You told me to hurry.'

'Aye, but saying that never works on my sister.'

'Oh…' She lifted her arms out, suddenly afraid of seeming a little too eager for his company. 'Well, here I am.'

'Here you are.' He looked her up and down, his gaze inscrutable. 'Have you eaten? I don't want you missing a meal.'

'A little porridge, but I'm not very hungry. Besides, I'm sure we'll be offered refreshments in the village.'

'As you wish. I'd suggest that we take the lad, too,

but there are matters we need to discuss that I don't want him overhearing.'

'If you mean about the Campbells, then Gregor already knows.' She made a face. 'He has a habit of listening to conversations he shouldn't.'

'Smart lad. Still, I don't want to scare him.' He gestured towards the gates. 'I thought that we'd go on foot, if that's acceptable to you?'

'Of course. It's a beautiful morning.'

She squinted up at the sky as they started to walk. Rays of orange sunshine were gilding the tops of the mountains in the distance and reflecting off the surface of the loch, making it shine like a golden mirror. There had been so many grey days recently when the hills had made her feel trapped and depressed, as if she were hemmed in with no hope of escape, but today the weather brought out the best in their surroundings, elevating her mood and making her feel optimistic about the future even despite the looming threat from the Campbells.

As they left the castle, she stole a stealthy glance at her companion, an image of his hard-muscled body flashing before her mind's eye. He'd barely scowled at all so far that morning, as if the sunshine was bringing out the best in him, too. Unfortunately, he was also setting a pace that would make a horse baulk.

'Could we slow down a little?' she panted when they were halfway to the village. 'My legs are a little shorter than yours.'

'Oh…aye.' He glanced down at her skirts and she almost tripped over. On reflection, it was probably better not to talk about her legs. Or any other part of her body for that matter. Friends didn't talk about such things. The flicker of interest she thought she'd just seen in his gaze was probably her imagination, too. A man like him would hardly be interested in *her* legs.

'So...' She sought for another subject to talk about. 'Other than the east wall, what do you think of Castle Barron? Can we withstand a siege?'

'For a while, but that's not what worries me the most.'

'No?'

'No, it's the man we're likely to be fighting. Alexander Campbell is cunning and ruthless. There's no telling what he's capable of.'

'I remember hearing stories about him when I was a girl.' She paused. 'Was he really so brutal back then?'

'Aye.'

'Oh.' She decided not to ask for specifics. 'People always said it was a good day for Scotland when he was finally chased away from his lands.'

'It was. Unfortunately, now he's back to try to reclaim them. He's one of the most dangerous warriors I've ever come across.'

'What about his son? Calum, isn't it?'

'I didn't meet him on the battlefield, but no doubt he's the same.'

Coira drew her cloak closer around her, feeling a sudden, sharp nip in the air as she thought back to her interview with Brody. She'd asked him to let her defend Castle Barron for Gregor, but it was becoming more and more obvious that she'd been somewhat overambitious. Now, contrary to what she'd expected, it felt good to have someone else here to share the burden. And not just someone, but Fergus, another dangerous warrior. Just walking beside him made her feel so much safer.

'Campbell killed my uncle in battle.' His voice broke into her thoughts abruptly.

'What?' She whipped her head around.

'It was during the summer. We underestimated him. Badly. It won't happen again.'

'I'm sorry. I'd heard that your uncle had died, but I had no idea how it happened.' She felt a twinge of guilt. 'I should have asked.'

'I thought that Brody might have told you.' He turned to look down at her as she made a scornful sound. 'He doesn't tell you things?'

'Sometimes, but not often. He doesn't have a very high opinion of women.'

Fergus was silent for a moment, as if he were taking the words in. 'You know, Ross said that when he approached him with the idea of an alliance between our clans, it was Brody who suggested you.'

'Really?' She drew her brows together. Oddly enough, she hadn't thought to ask whose idea it had originally been. 'I didn't know that. All Brody told me was that he wanted the alliance, partly to make amends for what happened...*before*, and partly because he wanted to make sure Castle Barron was well protected for Gregor.'

'He could have sent men to defend it himself.' His gaze turned oddly intense. 'It strikes me as a strange thing to do to his nephew's widow, especially considering how recently you were widowed. He can't have expected either of us to be pleased, given our history.'

She pursed her lips, unable to answer. What could

she say except that Brody didn't care a fig about how she might feel or whom she was married to as long as his own interests were protected? Her marriage to Nevin had been humiliating enough without admitting how much his family resented her, as well.

'What about your brother?'

'What?' She felt a jolt of panic at the question.

'Your brother. Didn't he have any opinion on the matter?'

'I don't know.' She spoke slowly, choosing her words with care. 'I haven't spoken to Niall in a while.'

'How long is a while?'

'Four or five years, perhaps.'

'You're not close, then?'

'No-o.' She felt herself starting to squirm under his scrutiny. 'But that's only natural. He's nine years older than me and our parents died when we were young so he was never quite like a brother.'

'You'd say he was more like a father, then?'

'Aye, I suppose so.'

'Yet he had no opinion about you getting married again? Especially to me?'

She swallowed, feeling as though she'd just been tricked. 'No.'

'I see.'

'What about *your* brother?' She tried to divert his attention.

'What about him?'

'Why did *he* agree to our marriage? He knew what happened six years ago, too.'

'True enough.' A muscle clenched in his jaw. 'However, Ross believes that defending our land outweighs everything else. He's right, but...'

'But you were still angry with him?'

'Furious.'

'I suppose that our marriage does make amends in a way.' She lifted her shoulders when he turned to look at her again. 'For the insult to your family, I mean. I truly regretted that, more than I can say. Nevin told me there was nearly violence afterwards.'

'There was, but surely he must have expected that? He can't have thought that you and he could just run away and no one would object?'

'I don't know what he thought.'

'That was the part I never understood.' He shook his head disparagingly. 'If he'd wanted you so badly, he could have challenged me. Openly and honourably. Instead, he abandoned his uncle and clansmen to face the consequences of his actions.'

'Aye.' She couldn't refute that. She'd been terrified about what would happen, but Nevin had barely seemed to care. 'What was it that stopped the bloodshed? He never told me that part.'

There was a momentary pause before he answered, 'I did.'

'You?'

'Aye. Brody vowed that he'd had no idea about his nephew's intentions and I believed him. It didn't seem right that he should pay for someone else's behaviour, so I told my uncle to let the matter rest.'

'Oh...I assumed... Actually, I don't know what I assumed. I never knew what happened exactly, but I never imagined... That was good of you,' she concluded. 'But what about my brother? You could say that I abandoned him to face the consequences, too.'

'Aye, I could, and he certainly had a lot more to say in his defence than Brody.' He stopped walking abruptly. 'Are you going to ask me if I believed him?'

She hesitated, curiosity finally outweighing caution. 'Did you?'

'No.'

'Why not?'

'Because it struck me as unlikely that Nevin could have got away from Sween Castle without help. And because your brother's not as good a liar as he thinks he is.'

She felt her lips part. 'Yet you let him go anyway? Why?'

'Because there was no point in punishing him.'

'You could have made an example of him.'

'Would it have brought you back?'

'No.' She lifted a hand, drawing her cloak tighter around her throat. 'It was too late. Nevin and I were married as soon as we reached Castle Barron.'

'Exactly. Your brother might have helped you to flee, but you still chose Nevin.' He started walking again. 'So it was over regardless. All I wanted to do was put it behind me.'

'Oh.' Coira closed her eyes, feeling her heart plummet. For one breath-stopping moment, she'd thought that he'd guessed at the truth, at the scheme that her brother and Nevin had concocted between them and dragged her into at the very last minute, but instead, he'd guessed at only half of it. He thought that her brother had been a mere accomplice, helping them to escape rather than arranging the whole thing, which meant that deep down he still blamed her. Just like everyone else did. And there was nothing she could say to correct him.

It shouldn't have mattered so much, but it did. So much for hoping for friendship.

Fergus studied the track beneath his feet, walking a little way ahead as they approached the village. Despite his resolve not to take any interest in his new wife, he seemed unable to stop asking questions. When Ross had first told him about the proposed marriage, he'd been too angry to pay attention to the fact that the choice of bride had been Brody's. Strategically it had made sense, yet the more he thought about it now, the stranger it seemed, as if the head of the MacWhinnie clan hadn't cared how his nephew's widow might feel about the arrangement.

As far as he knew, Nevin had reconciled with his uncle several years before his death so why would there still be a rift with Coira? Thinking back to his meeting with Brody, Fergus realised now that there had been no warmth in his voice when he'd spoken of her, let alone any care for her future happiness. On the contrary, there had been a satisfied, vengeful, even relieved gleam in the other man's eyes when they'd finally agreed terms, as if he'd gained more than an ally to defend his lands... As if he'd *wanted* to hurt her. As if he'd wanted and expected Fergus to do it for him.

Even more surprising was the way that Coira had spoken about her brother, as if they were also estranged. It would have made sense if she'd betrayed his wishes by running away with Nevin, but if her brother had helped them to escape, as he'd always suspected and she'd implicitly just admitted, then why would she have fallen out with him later?

He had a feeling that he was missing something, probably because he was still unsettled by their conversation the previous night. He'd never intended to tell her the truth about how he'd felt about her six years ago, but the intimacy of the situation, with her leaning over him beside the fireplace, tending to the cut on his face with the sound of rolling thunder and rain pattering on the roof outside, had undermined his control. For a fleeting moment of weakness, he'd wanted her to know how he'd felt, to know how much her leaving had hurt him, too. The words had simply come out before he could stop them.

He frowned at the memory. It had been the briefest of lapses, but it should never have happened. He'd said too much, given too much away. It had been a mistake. Just like letting her join him on this trip to the village today was a mistake. It would have been far better to ignore her again, to make it clear that no matter what he'd felt in the past, that was all over and done with for good. Even if the fact that she hadn't guessed how much he'd liked her—apparently hadn't realised he'd liked her at all!— made him feel slightly better about her running away. Maybe in retrospect, he might have been somewhat at fault, too. Maybe he ought to have made a greater effort to talk to her. And maybe if she hadn't mentioned her legs earlier then he'd be able to stop glancing at them!

'Here we are.' He slowed down, waiting for her to catch up as they approached the first hut in the village.

'Aye.' She looked and sounded preoccupied. 'I'll introduce you to Lyall. He's the blacksmith and unofficial leader.'

'Good.' He nodded before taking hold of her elbow. 'Then let's go and tell people who I am.'

His meeting with the villagers had gone surprisingly well, Fergus reflected, as he and Coira made their way back to the castle a few hours later. Given the haste of their marriage, he'd expected some suspicion and resentment on her behalf, but instead they'd all seemed genuinely pleased to meet him. Of course, if they'd been forewarned of the danger from the Campbells then perhaps they'd reasoned it made sense for him to be there, but still, the warmth of their welcome had taken him aback. He and Coira had made a good pair, too, working together to allay fears while explaining what to do in the event of an enemy army's approach. Everyone had seemed to like and to trust her, so much that, despite his initial reservations, he'd been secretly glad she'd been there.

Even if she'd been looking annoyingly pretty.

Once again, however, something had bothered him. Something that he'd pondered all the way back to the castle and wasn't quite able to put his finger on...until he suddenly did.

'Nobody mentioned him.' He reached a hand out impulsively, holding Coira back as she started to climb the keep steps.

'What? Who?' He felt her muscles tense beneath his fingertips.

He paused deliberately, keeping his eyes fixed on

her face so that he wouldn't miss her expression as he said the name. 'Nevin.'

'Oh.' Her chin jerked slightly, as if she were resisting the impulse to twist away. 'They were probably just being tactful.'

'Perhaps, but it was still strange. Considering that he was the Laird here for almost ten years, I would have expected somebody to mention him at least once.'

'I suppose so.' She opened her eyes wide, though he had the distinct impression she was feigning surprise. Her expression struck him as a little too guarded. 'But perhaps they did and you missed it.'

'Perhaps.'

He watched her go, left with the distinct impression that there was something, possibly some*things*, about Nevin Barron that people weren't telling him, before turning on his heel and heading in the opposite direction. It had been a busy morning, but there was still a lot more to do, a visit to the armoury behind the kitchens for a start. He'd given the place a brief inspection when he'd first arrived, pleased to see a reasonable number of weapons, and in pristine condition, too, but it wouldn't hurt to check again. Maybe then he could keep his mind off his wife!

He strode purposefully up to the door, surprised to find it slightly ajar, peering suspiciously into the gloom as he pushed it open the rest of the way.

'Oh!' There was a rustling sound in one corner, accompanied by a small, but very female, exclamation.

'Grizel?' Fergus lifted an eyebrow, his gaze travelling from his wife's maid to his most promising young warrior as they sprang apart, hastily adjusting their clothing. 'And Euan. This may not be the time or the place.'

'Forgive me. *Us.*' The maid cast her eyes downwards, her cheeks flaming almost the same vibrant shade as her hair. 'I know we shouldn't be in here. It's just hard to find anywhere that we can be alone together.'

'Really?' He raised his eyebrow even higher. 'In that case, perhaps you ought to come to a more formal arrangement?'

'We want to.' Euan lifted his chin, obviously stung by the implied accusation. 'We want to be married, only Lady Coira…' He glanced towards Grizel, his voice trailing away.

'What about Lady Coira?' Fergus narrowed his gaze.

'She wouldn't approve.' Grizel shook her head miserably.

'She might approve of it more than this behaviour.'

'She won't.' Euan spoke again. 'She says that marriage is—'

'Shh!' Grizel gave him a sharp nudge in the ribs. 'Don't you dare!'

'He has a right to know!'

'Not when I told you that in confidence!'

'It's all right.' Fergus held a hand up. As much as he wanted to know whatever it was Euan apparently thought he had a right to know, he couldn't help but take pity on the embarrassed maid. Every patch of visible skin was a luminous shade of red. Besides, what did it really matter to him what his wife said about marriage? It wasn't as if it would change his own plans. She could say what she liked…

'As far as I'm concerned, this meeting never happened. I think that you should trust Coira enough to understand your feelings for one another, but it's up to you. Only in future, perhaps you might try to find somewhere a little less dangerous.' He jerked his head towards a collection of vicious-looking spears and then stepped aside, gesturing for them to go past him. 'Who knows what damage you might do to yourselves in here?'

'Yes…thank you.' Grizel hurried away. 'It won't happen again.'

'Won't it?' He looked questioningly at Euan, who only grinned.

'Not in here anyway.'

Chapter Eleven

'My lady? Excuse the intrusion, but you have a guest.'

'A guest?' Coira looked around at the sound of her steward's voice. She and Grizel were lounging on a daybed in the solar, laughing as Ailis squirmed on her stomach and Gregor rolled around on the floor with Duffy.

She was in a surprisingly good mood that morning. With the wall finished, Fergus had ridden out with a small group of men to investigate the surrounding glens, but he'd almost—*almost*—smiled at her as he'd left. Or at least the contraction of his brows had eased slightly. The sight had caused a warm, tingling feeling in her chest, the same one that occurred whenever she thought about watching him dress. Something she'd done again that morning, feigning sleep while she'd lain on her side and peered at him through her lashes. The sight had been just as impressive and enjoyable as the first time, although it had also left her feeling somewhat confused and overheated. Not to mention guilty, as if she'd been doing something she shouldn't, but hadn't been able to resist.

'Who is it?'

'Your husband's—' Malcolm coughed. 'That is, your former husband's cousin, my lady.'

'Kendrick?'

'Aye. He's waiting below in the hall.'

'Very well, I'll be down in a moment.' She glanced at Grizel. 'Would you mind watching the children for a wee while?'

'Of course not. We're comfortable here, aren't we, Gregor?'

'Thank you.' She threw her maid a grateful smile as she clambered off the bed, smoothing her hands over the front of her gown before descending the stairwell. As Nevin's cousin and close friend, Kendrick had visited Castle Barron many times over the years and, in contrast to the rest of his family, had always been kind to her.

It had been somewhat unsettling at first, that a man so close in appearance to her husband, with the same corn-blond hair and piercing blue eyes, had been so kind when Nevin hadn't been, as if they were two very different sides of one coin, but over time, she'd come to regard him as a friend. He'd witnessed first-hand the contempt with which Nevin had treated her and yet he'd taken her side and even defended her on occasion. She'd overheard them arguing once in the solar. The exact words had been muffled, but she'd heard her name often enough to know that she'd been the subject. She'd been grateful to him for that and his visits usually cheered her, but today she found she wasn't quite so pleased with the idea of seeing him again.

'Kendrick. It's been a while.' She put on a smile as

she entered the hall, surprised when instead of returning the greeting, he marched straight towards her, a hard, confrontational expression on his face.

'Is it true?'

'What?' She almost took a step backwards, alarmed by his vehemence. She'd never seen him look at or heard him speak so harshly to her before. 'Is what true?'

'That you're wed to Fergus MacMillan? I heard a rumour, but I couldn't believe it so I rode straight here to find out. Tell me it's not true!'

She dropped her gaze, struck with a piercing stab of guilt. Kendrick knew how unhappy Nevin had made her, but no doubt he still thought her remarrying so soon a terrible insult to his cousin. 'Aye. It's true.'

'Why?'

'Because I had no choice. Your father commanded it.'

'My father?' He twisted his face to one side, his jaw clenching so tightly she could see the muscles straining in his neck. 'He shouldn't have done so. He ought to have had more respect, for you and for Nevin.'

'I admit I was surprised, too, at first, but he had his reasons. He knew that I couldn't defend Castle Barron from the Campbells on my own. Come.' She touched his shoulder gently, leading him towards a bench by the fireplace while gesturing for a servant to fetch some wine. 'I'm just sorry that you had to discover the truth through gossip. I'd hoped to tell you myself.'

'I wish that I'd been here.' Kendrick sat down heavily, shaking his head as if he still couldn't believe it. 'I've been away, collecting rents from our lands to the south, but if I'd known, I would have done something. I would have stopped the wedding.'

'What? How?' She gave a start, taken aback both by the suggestion and her own unexpected resistance to the idea.

'I would have spoken to my father, for a start.'

'I doubt that it would have done any good. He'd already made up his mind by the time he summoned me.'

'I still would have tried.' He raked a hand through his hair. 'I hate that I wasn't here to protect you from this. You deserve so much better.'

'Thank you, Kendrick.' She felt genuinely touched by the words. 'You've always been so kind to me, but it's done. I'm married and in truth…' she swallowed, feeling her cheeks flush as she spoke '…I'm content.'

'With Fergus MacMillan?' A flash of anger passed over his face. 'The man's a brute! Everyone knows that.'

'No, he's not.' She stiffened defensively. 'I know he has a stern and fearsome reputation, but if people think that then they're wrong. He's not remotely a brute.'

'Is that so?' Kendrick jumped back to his feet, staring down at her with a new kind of intensity.

'Aye. He's a good man. He's been very kind to Gregor.'

'Kind?' Kendrick's whole face contorted as he repeated the word in a tone of contempt. 'And has he been *kind* to you, too? Don't tell me you care for him?'

She opened and then closed her mouth, baulking at the question. She hadn't thought of Fergus in terms of *caring* before. Her overriding emotions in regard to him had been ones of relief and surprise and…well, whatever it was she felt when she watched him dress. She wasn't sure she had a name for that yet…

'I think of him as a friend,' she said instead, lifting

her chin and then catching her breath at her own choice of word. That was how she thought of Kendrick, too, she realised, as a friend, and yet her feelings towards the two of them were completely different. She'd never been remotely curious about what Kendrick looked like naked, for a start. She'd never felt the slightest tingling sensation when he was close by either. In which case... she blinked in consternation...what did that say about her burgeoning friendship with Fergus?

Something she was definitely feeling at that precise moment, however, was irritation. No matter how kind Kendrick might have been to her in the past, whatever feelings she might or might not have for Fergus were her own business.

'Coira?' His eyes narrowed accusingly.

'It's not like that.'

'Good. Because if I thought for one moment...' Kendrick turned his head, muttering some kind of oath under his breath as she stood up, too, wondering why he was still so upset after she'd just reassured him. He seemed overwrought, as if her marriage had hurt him personally, but then maybe he was simply tired. He'd just said that he'd been in the south when he'd heard the rumours about her marriage and ridden straight here. No doubt that explained it.

Impulsively, she reached for his hands, trying to calm him. 'There's no need to worry about me, Kendrick, truly. My marriage to Fergus has nothing to do with caring, but it makes sense. I'm doing what's best for my son, that's all.'

'*Coira?*'

She jumped and then swung about to find Fergus

standing behind them, his eyes focused on her hands, still folded tight around Kendrick's.

'Oh.' She drew them away quickly and then berated herself for the action. It made her look more, not less, guilty. And how much had he just heard? She racked her brains to remember what it was she'd said to Kendrick, but the words were all jumbled. Judging by the flinty look on Fergus's face, however, none of it was good.

Kendrick, meanwhile, looked like he'd just fought a battle and emerged the victor.

Fergus let his gaze travel from his wife's now empty hands to a man who looked so uncannily like Nevin Barron that for a second he'd thought he'd been staring at a ghost. Another second had brought him back to his senses, although it was taking considerably longer to calm the anger that was still raging through his veins like wildfire. *Their marriage had nothing to do with caring. She was doing what was best for her son.* And she'd been holding the bastard's hands as she'd said it!

'Fergus.' Coira looked like a woman who was trying her hardest not to look guilty. 'You're back early.'

'Aye. I saw horses arriving from the top of the glen.' He arched an eyebrow interrogatively. 'Is that a problem?'

'Of course not. This is Kendrick MacWhinnie, Brody's youngest son. He came to…congratulate us on our marriage.'

'Did he?' Fergus walked slowly across the hall, keeping his eyes fixed on their guest. Her brief hesitation had been enough to tell him that there had been a *lot* more to their conversation than congratulations and the defiant way in which the man was returning his stare confirmed it. Whatever else he'd come for, it definitely hadn't been to congratulate them.

'Fergus MacMillan. So you're the man who's taken my cousin's place?' Kendrick tipped his chin up as Fergus halted an arm's length away. Like Nevin, he was exceptionally good-looking and looked like he knew it, with pale blond hair scraped back from his chiselled cheekbones and blue eyes that hundreds of women had probably swooned over. He was well dressed, too, as if he thought he might be summoned to court at any moment. No doubt he could write poetry and sing ballads, as well. Maybe *that* was why Coira had been holding his hands… Just the idea made Fergus see red again. He wanted to send him sprawling into the rushes and then rolling down the keep steps for good measure.

'Aye,' he answered calmly, resisting the urge to point out that if anyone had taken another person's place, it had been Nevin taking his six years ago. He had the distinct impression that this lookalike cousin was trying to goad him into anger and the last thing he was going to do was give him the satisfaction of knowing he'd succeeded.

'I hope that my visit doesn't inconvenience you too greatly?' Kendrick smiled insincerely. 'Given all the activity outside. Everything seems to have changed since I was last here.'

'We're making sure we're ready in case of an attack. I presume you know about the Campbells?'

'I do now.' Kendrick lifted one shoulder. 'I've been away to the south for a little while, but I heard about the situation a couple of days ago.'

'And your response was to come straight here? Will your father not be expecting you?'

'I'm sure he has everything well in hand. Besides, Coira and I are old friends.' There was a possessive edge to the other man's voice. 'I thought that perhaps I might be able to lend some assistance here instead.'

'That would explain the small army you've brought with you, then. The bailey's almost full to bursting.'

'I stopped to gather a few men, aye.'

'Very thoughtful of you, but we're managing well enough. On limited provisions.'

'I'm pleased to hear it.' Kendrick's expression had about as much warmth as a cornered polecat. 'None the less, I was going to ask whether I might stay for a couple of nights? I've been travelling a great deal of late and a little rest sounds very appealing. It would allow me to spend some time with Gregor, too. The lad needs a father figure.'

'Here's the wine.' Coira bustled between them, looking visibly relieved at the sight of a servant bearing a tray. 'Shall we sit?'

'The lad already has a father figure.' Fergus remained standing. 'A stepfather.'

'Ah, so he does.' Kendrick's smile didn't falter. 'But you know what I mean. A blood relation. He's a Mac-Whinnie as well as a Barron, after all, and as such I'm sure he wouldn't refuse hospitality to a member of his own clan...would he?'

'Of course not,' Coira interrupted smoothly. 'I'm sure that a couple of days is no inconvenience to us. Is it, Fergus?'

He folded his arms, looking from her to Kendrick

and back again. Given their clan ties, he knew it was impossible for her to refuse and yet he found himself wishing that she'd at least try. 'If that's what you want.'

'Then it's settled.' Kendrick's tone was more than a little gloating. 'I look forward to lending a hand about the place. Anything you need, just ask.'

Fergus gritted his teeth as the other man took a seat next to his wife. To her credit, Coira shifted sideways slightly, as if she were unsettled by such close proximity, but he wasn't prepared to give her any credit for this. Typical that she would be *friends* with a lookalike version of Nevin, if that was all the man really was to her! If she'd been trying to enrage him, she could hardly have found a better way. And just when his feelings towards her had begun to soften, too! Just when he'd been starting to wonder whether he'd been partly to blame for what had happened six years ago! Well, more fool him for that. Hadn't he known that she couldn't be trusted? Hadn't she proven it thoroughly enough?

He reached for a cup of wine and drank deeply, his old resentment flaring to life all over again. He was livid, he was furious, he was…jealous? The realisation stabbed him in the gut, although perhaps it was a good thing, a timely reminder that Coira was so incredibly dangerous to him. Despite all his best intentions, he was in danger of starting to care for her all over again. Maybe jealousy would stop him from doing something stupid. Something like reneging on his original intentions and staying with her even after the threat from the Campbells was gone.

'Fergus?' Coira's voice held a note of appeal. 'How was your ride?'

'Uneventful.' He slammed the cup back down on the tray. He might not be able to turn Kendrick MacWhinnie out of the castle, but he sure as hell wasn't going to sit there and make idle talk with him. He wasn't about to let Coira know how he felt either. 'Now if you'll excuse me, I have work to do. I'll leave the two of you *old friends* to get reacquainted.'

Chapter Twelve

Fergus stood up from his seat at the high table, glowering like he'd never glowered before. Beside him, Coira was laughing softly at something Kendrick had just said, which would have made him scowl even more if his brows hadn't already been clenched so fiercely that it was physically impossible to do so. She'd never laughed like that with him, although in all fairness he wasn't prone to making jokes either. Maybe he ought to start. Her laughter was a pleasant sound, like warm rain on a summer's afternoon. The fact that it was for another man, however, made him want to smash his trencher against the wall and storm as far away as possible.

He didn't bother to excuse himself, striding out of the hall, down the keep steps and across the bailey until the sounds of merriment had completely receded and he found himself standing in front of the east wall. Fortunately, the night was clear and surprisingly mild, with a waxing half-moon and sky full of stars to illuminate the recent building work.

'It's a pleasant evening, is it not?' Malcolm approached

from the other direction. 'I've just been for my evening walk, but don't let me disturb you.'

'You're not.' Fergus stilled him with a gesture when the old man would have moved on. 'Truth be told, I'd be glad of some company.'

'Then I'd be happy to provide it.'

'Why did you leave the hall so early?'

Malcolm made a sound like a snort. 'One of the few advantages of age is that people accept any excuse you choose to make for escaping such occasions. I can be tired or choleric or have an ache in my back and no one bats an eyelid.'

'So what's the real reason?'

'In this case, disgust. There are some sights I prefer not to watch. My lady having to suffer the company of Kendrick MacWhinnie for one.'

Fergus held the old man's shrewd gaze for several long seconds before glancing pointedly around the bailey. 'You have a room for your work, do you not? Somewhere we might speak in private?'

'Aye, beside the gatehouse. I have wine, too, if you'd care to join me?'

They made their way there in silence, closing the door firmly behind them. It was made of heavy oak, Fergus noted with approval, well nigh impossible to hear through, just in case any of Kendrick's men might be tempted to eavesdrop.

'So...' He took the cup Malcolm offered, sitting opposite him in front of a glowing fireplace. 'Tell me about MacWhinnie. You don't like him?'

'No.' The older man didn't hesitate to answer. 'He's visited often enough over the years, but more and more since Nevin's accident. He used to come every three or four months. Now, it's every few weeks.'

'Were he and Nevin close?'

'They were cousins.'

'But were they close?'

There was a momentary pause. 'That's how it appeared.'

Fergus quirked an eyebrow at the distinction. 'But you think differently?'

'Not necessarily.' Malcolm took a sip from his cup, as if he were taking a moment to consider. 'They were close enough as boys and as young men. Nevin and Kendrick were of a similar age and had a great deal in common, but after Nevin's marriage, after he eventually reconciled with Brody and Kendrick was free to visit again that is, things were different. Not obviously so, but there was something…a feeling, especially whenever my lady was in the room. Then there was some kind of terrible argument, about a year ago now.'

'Do you know what it was about?'

'No, they were alone in the solar at the time. All I know is that Kendrick rode away in a temper and Nevin was furious for days afterwards.'

'Then what happened?'

'They didn't speak for almost five months. Eventually, they made it up and Kendrick started visiting again, but then he was *too* much like his old self. It felt false, as if…' He stopped and frowned.

'As if?' Fergus prompted him.

'Perhaps I shouldn't say. I've no proof.'

'Then tell me your suspicions.'

Malcolm lifted a hand to his beard, stroking it

thoughtfully. 'As if his friendship was all a pretence and he was waiting for something to happen, biding his time almost. And the way that his eyes always followed my lady… It made me uncomfortable, though she never noticed, of course.'

'Why of course?'

'The way that Nevin treated her gave her a low opinion of herself, I think.'

Fergus swallowed a mouthful of ale too quickly, stifling a cough. 'What do you mean? How did he treat her?'

'As for that…' Malcolm's gaze shifted to one side evasively. 'It's not my place to tell.'

Fergus sat back in his chair, thinking. Malcolm had said something similar just after his arrival, he remembered. Something that had caused him to wonder whether Coira and Nevin had been as happy as he'd always assumed, although he'd pushed the thought aside at the time. *Had* they been happy? Now he wished that he'd forced Euan to tell him exactly what Coira had said about marriage. That might have revealed something. Although the fact that no one in the village, or even the castle, now that he thought of it, had ever said one positive thing about Nevin was surely revealing enough.

'All right, then. Tell me, how long before Nevin's accident were he and Kendrick reconciled?'

'Not long.'

'A month?'

'Less.'

'And what happened exactly? I heard that Nevin was gored in a hunting accident.'

'Aye, a boar. He was gashed in the side with one of the tusks.'

'Did anyone else see the boar attack?'

'There were other men around, but I'm told it happened very fast.'

'You saw the wound?'

'Aye, but that doesn't mean it was the only one.'

Fergus took a deep breath, the implication hanging in the air between them. 'That's a serious accusation.'

'I know.'

'What time of day did it happen?'

'Dusk. The light was fading.'

'Accidents happen.'

'So do other things.' Malcolm lowered his voice despite the size of the door. 'And another perk of age is that I've seen them all before.'

Fergus nodded slowly. 'How did Kendrick behave afterwards?'

'Convincingly distraught. He kept saying that he should have done something to save him. Nobody who trusted him would have ever suspected a thing.'

'And now he visits more often?'

'Aye. He claims that it's his duty to take care of Lady Coira and the bairns. It strikes me as a little too convenient.'

Fergus stared into his cup for a long moment before draining the rest of the contents and sitting forward, bracing his arms over his knees. 'Tell me truthfully, Malcolm—when Kendrick looks at my wife, what do you see?'

'A man who wants something. And I think we can both guess what.'

'Aye. That's what I see, too.'

He turned his head and stared into the fire, wondering how far he was letting Kendrick's resemblance to his cousin shape his judgement. How far he was letting jealousy affect him, too. On the other hand, it was clear that he wasn't the only person suffering from that particular emotion. Kendrick had obviously been outraged by the news of his wedding to Coira. He'd obviously wanted to take his cousin's place in her bed, though whether he'd been prepared to kill for it was another matter...

'It doesn't make sense.' He curled his empty hand into a fist. 'If Kendrick had wanted her so badly, then why didn't he simply ask for her hand after Nevin's death? He could have asked his father for the match.'

'Maybe he intended to, only he thought it was too soon.' Malcolm spoke hesitantly. 'Or maybe he thought that his father wouldn't approve. She wouldn't have received a second dowry.'

'Perhaps.' Fergus put his cup aside and stood up. 'Either way, I appreciate your honesty.'

Malcolm inclined his head. 'Perhaps I'm letting my imagination run away with me, but it seemed to me you had a right to know. I've thought several times of speaking to Lady Coira, but she appears to have no suspicions about him at all.'

'For the time being, it might be best to keep it that way.'

'Aye. Although you might want to be careful. If Kendrick did have some involvement in Nevin's accident...'

'Then I might be next?' Fergus laughed, feeling almost heartened by the prospect. Just let the man try to do anything to him and he'd take immense pleasure in fighting back, in imagining him as Nevin, too. First of all, however, he needed to speak to his wife.

He moved towards the door and then stopped with his fingers on the latch. 'Just one more question. My wife…do you think she's trustworthy?'

To his combined frustration and relief, Malcolm's response was swift and decided. 'Completely. I'd trust her with my life.'

'Where did you go?' Coira was sitting up in bed, cradling a grumbling Ailis in her arms, when he entered their bedchamber.

'I wanted some air.' He removed his plaid and set it beside the bed with a scowl. His temper had cooled somewhat, but he was still aware of an undercurrent of resentment and jealousy. He was surprised, too, to find her still awake. Going to bed at separate times, they'd both made a point of always being, or seeming to be, asleep by the time the other arrived. 'I didn't think it necessary to stay when you were doing such a good job of entertaining Kendrick on your own.'

'Only because you wouldn't. You've hardly spoken two words to him since he arrived.'

Fergus grunted, pulling his tunic over his head and tossing it on to a coffer. 'I don't recall him making much of an effort to talk to me either.'

'Maybe because it's so obvious that you don't want him to.' She sighed. 'I swear, I had no idea that he was coming. I wish he'd sent word ahead so that I could have explained matters to you first.'

'What matters?'

'That he's been a good friend to me over the past couple of years. A loyal one, too. I couldn't turn him away.'

'Friend.' He repeated the word as if he were testing it. '*Just* a friend?'

'Of course!' She jerked upright so violently that Ailis let out a wail of protest. 'What else are you suggesting?'

He held her gaze for the space of several tense heartbeats before sitting down on the edge of the bed, wondering whether he could trust the gleam of indignation in her eye. It looked real enough, but then she always *seemed* genuine. She always had and yet she'd already proven herself an excellent actress... What if she was acting again now? Pretending innocence to deceive him about the nature of her relationship with Kendrick? Despite himself, he didn't think so. What was it that Malcolm had said? Not just that she was trustworthy, but that he'd trust her with his life. And he'd lived alongside her for six years... Damn it. Every time he thought he came close to understanding his wife, she confused him some more.

'Nothing.' He looked over his shoulder. 'I shouldn't have said that.'

'No, you shouldn't have. I only wish that you could be friends with him, too.'

He bit back a snort. Whatever else he and Kendrick might be in the future, they definitely weren't going to be that... Instead, he clenched his jaw, gesturing towards Ailis. 'What's the matter with the bairn?'

'I think it's her teeth. See how red her cheeks are?' Coira bent a knuckle and rubbed it across her daughter's small mouth. 'She can't seem to settle tonight.'

'Here.' He held his arms out. 'Let me try.'

'You?' She stared at him blankly for a few seconds before leaning forward. 'All right… Here you go. Be careful, she's heavier than she looks.'

'She's light as a feather.' He wrapped his arms around the small girl and stood up, rocking her back and forth gently in his arms. 'Aren't you, lass?'

'I think she likes you. She's stopped grumbling already.'

'Aye.' He glanced back at the bed just in time to catch the strange expression on Coira's face. A combination of relief mixed with tenderness and outright amazement. 'What's the matter?'

'Nothing.' She gave her head a small shake. 'I just never thought to see you with a baby… She looks so tiny against you.'

'I *have* held a babe before.'

'Really?' She sounded dubious.

'Aye.' He smiled sheepishly. 'Of course it was Elspeth and I was only a wee bairn myself at the time, but you don't forget.'

'Obviously not. You seem to be a natural. Well…' Coira smiled brightly before flinging herself down on the mattress and rolling over. 'Goodnight, then.'

'What?'

'Only joking.' She rolled back again. 'Although it's extremely tempting.'

'I'm sure it is, but we haven't finished our talk yet.'

Her smile faded. 'You mean about Kendrick?'

'Aye. I still want to know what he's doing here. And don't tell me he came to congratulate us.'

'No.' She propped herself up on to an elbow and sighed. 'He came because he was concerned about me.

He'd heard a rumour about our marriage and he wanted to know if it was true. He seemed to think that I'd been forced into it against my will.'

'Which you were.'

'Which we *both* were.'

'Which is why it has "nothing to do with caring", I suppose?'

She winced. 'I didn't mean it like that, but you have to admit, our marriage *didn't* have anything to do with caring, not at first.'

He lifted an eyebrow, studying her face. *At first* seemed to imply that the situation had changed since. Her brow was slightly puckered, too, as if the words had surprised even her.

'The point is...' she coughed and went on '...that I was just trying to explain things to Kendrick, to make him understand that even though we were forced into it, I'm content being married to you and that he doesn't need to worry about me or the children any more. I know his manner was bad, but he's been very kind to me over the years, the only member of my husband's family who ever *was* kind.'

'What do you mean?'

A shadow passed over her face. 'Nevin married me without Brody's consent. And after all the trouble it caused... In the end, the MacWhinnies blamed me for "entrancing" him. That was the word they all used, as if I'd done something underhand to make him run away with me.'

'Why did they blame just you?'

'I suppose it was easier to blame an outsider, especially a woman, than one of their own. Maybe it made it easier for Brody to reconcile with Nevin, too, but they made me feel that I'd brought shame on the clan. All of them except Kendrick.'

'And Nevin? Surely he defended you?'

There was a momentary hesitation before she answered, 'Aye, of course.'

He studied her face again, trying to interpret that hesitation. 'Malcolm says that Kendrick's visited more frequently since your husband died.'

'Only because he feels guilty. He was with Nevin when the boar attacked and he thinks that he should have done something more to save him. He thinks it makes him responsible for me in some way, too. He and Nevin were like brothers.'

'That doesn't mean he thinks of you as a sister.' Fergus gave her a pointed look. Malcolm was right and she obviously had no suspicions about Kendrick at all. 'He objects to our marriage, doesn't he?'

'Only because he's worried about me.'

'What *exactly* did he say?'

She lifted her shoulders with a look of exasperation. 'That I should have sent for him and that he would have found a way to persuade his father against it.'

'So he could marry you instead?'

'What? No!' Her eyes widened. 'Don't be ridiculous. He didn't say anything of the kind!'

'Coira...' Fergus paused, lowering his voice as Ailis burbled. 'I've seen the way he looks at you. Trust me, it's not *just* as a friend. And definitely not as a sister.'

'You're imagining things.'

'No, I'm not.'

'Yes, you are! Kendrick would never look at me in

that way. No man—' She stopped, biting down hard on her lip as she turned her face to one side.

'No man what?'

She let out a soft sigh. 'You know what.'

He took a step closer, frowning. 'No, I really don't.'

'*No* man would look at me in that way, not any more.'

'What?' He looked from her to Ailis as if the babe might somehow be able to explain her own mother to him. 'What on earth makes you think that?'

'Because look at me!' She tossed the bed covers aside and leapt to her feet, abruptly flinging her arms out to the sides. 'Just look!'

'I'm looking.'

'I look like an old woman!'

He opened his mouth, tempted to say something unsuitable for any child's ears, and then closed it again, too stunned to get the words out. A week ago, he might have agreed with her, but now… Now he felt as though he was looking at her through new eyes. Eyes that seemed unable to drag themselves away from the lower part of her body where her cotton nightshift clung to her hips. She wasn't particularly slender or shapely, but the curves that she did have looked perfect to him. With the fire behind her, he could make out the long outline of her legs, too.

'You see!' She swung away again, obviously taking his silence for agreement.

'Coira.' He wasn't entirely sure where to start. 'You don't look like an old woman.'

'Well, I don't look like a maid any more.'

'No-o.'

'Exactly!'

'But all I can see is a beautiful woman.'

'Beautiful?' She jerked her head back around, her eyes even wider, repeating the word in a rough whisper.

'Aye. You always were. The first time I saw you...' He cleared his throat gruffly, wondering why the hell he was telling her this and yet strangely compelled to keep going. 'I thought you were the most beautiful woman I'd ever laid eyes on. I couldn't believe that you were going to be mine.'

'But...that was six years ago. I've had two children since then.'

'That doesn't mean you're not still beautiful.'

'It doesn't?' She gaped at him as if he'd just told her she was the Queen.

'So what I'm trying to say is that Kendrick might not look at you in quite the way you think.'

'What?' She blinked. 'Oh...no, I've never noticed anything like that.'

Fergus rolled his eyes, tempted to point out that with her apparent lack of confidence she probably wouldn't have noticed if Kendrick had started drooling in front of her. She was acting as if *no one* had ever told her she was beautiful before. Hadn't Nevin?

'Just think about it.' He sighed and nodded his head at the now sleeping baby. 'She seems settled.'

'She looks like she's smiling.' Coira gave him a swift, intense look before taking Ailis from his arms. 'I've brought her cot in here for the night so that I can tend to her if she needs me. I hope you don't mind?'

'You don't need to ask my permission.'

'No, but I thought...' Her voice faded. 'Thank you for not objecting.'

He climbed into bed finally, watching as she tucked Ailis into her cot, vaguely unsettled by the disparaging way she seemed to think of herself, not to mention the presumption that he might object to her keeping her teething daughter beside her. What kind of man would object to that? What kind of husband had Nevin been?

'Fergus…' She broke the silence again, sliding under the quilt beside him. 'Did you really mean it? What you said just now?'

'Aye.' He folded an arm behind his head, staring up at the canopy above. 'I might not say much, but I always mean what I say.'

'In that case, I appreciate it and…for what it's worth, I thought you were very handsome the first time I saw you, too.'

He twisted his face towards her. 'I thought you said I was too stern?'

'That doesn't mean you weren't handsome. Although I think I prefer you now.' Her gaze moved slowly over his face as if she were scrutinising every tiny detail. 'Especially when you stop frowning. Then you're *very* handsome.'

Their eyes locked and he shifted position. 'Aye, well, whatever I am, I'll make you a bargain. I'll mind my manners around Kendrick if you promise to be careful.'

'Careful?' Her expression clouded again. 'Why would I need to be careful?'

'I don't know yet. Maybe it's nothing, but just in case… I don't want you to get hurt.'

'All right, I'll be careful, but I really don't think there's any need.'

'Humour me.' He reached a hand out before he could

think better of it, touching his palm to her cheek and rubbing gently. Her skin felt velvety soft and warm. 'Sleep well, Coira.'

He heard the breath snag in her throat. 'You, too, Fergus.'

Chapter Thirteen

'Remember not to hold the quill too tightly. Just move it slowly and copy the shapes I've done for you… That's right. Perfect.'

All I can see is a beautiful woman.

Coira leaned over Gregor's shoulder, trying to focus her wavering attention on his lesson, but it was proving difficult to concentrate on letters when the words Fergus had said the night before kept echoing around her head like a tune that wouldn't go away. Nevin had only called her beautiful once, during their night-time flight from Sween Castle and then only because he'd wanted her to marry him, not because he'd truly meant it. Fergus, on the other hand, was a man who, by his own admission, only and always said what he meant… and he'd been cradling her daughter in his arms all the while. The memory of it made her heart flutter in a way that made it *very* difficult to focus on learning.

She sucked the inside of her cheek, remembering the way he'd touched it so tenderly after they'd lain down. His skin had felt rough, but his fingers had been infinitely gentle, causing her stomach to tie itself in several tight knots. Sleep had taken a long time to come afterwards, her body swirling and aching with a heady brew of sensations. And then when she'd woken up... She'd found herself wandering to their chamber window to watch when he'd left with the scouts, her eyes boring into his back as he'd ridden away, her pulse throbbing far too hard and too fast for a woman who was doing nothing more strenuous than standing beside a window. Just like it was doing now when all she was doing was thinking of him.

'Ah, there you are.' Kendrick's voice at her shoulder almost made her jump out of her skin. 'I was starting to think you were hiding from me.'

'Kendrick. Of course not.' She forced her lips into a smile at the sight of their guest. In all honesty, she *had* been hiding from him a little, irritated by the way he persisted in acting as if she needed his protection. It seemed that no matter how many times she told him there was no need to worry and that she was content with her marriage, he refused to believe it, only shaking his head and regarding her with a sad, baleful expression as if he thought she was simply putting a brave face on things. It set her nerves on edge, making her wonder if there might have been a small grain of truth in what Fergus had suggested, after all.

It was all so confusing. If Fergus was right and Kendrick *did* have feelings for her, then surely she ought to be bemoaning the fact that he hadn't told her himself and sooner? If she really *had* to marry, then he was exactly the kind of man she would have thought she might want. Most importantly, he was already a friend whereas Fergus… Well, their relationship was certainly better than it had been, but she could hardly describe him as *that*. And yet the idea of being married to Kendrick instead of Fergus felt completely, instinctively wrong. If she had to choose, there was no contest—a fact that confused her even more.

'How's my favourite cousin?' Kendrick bent down, allowing Gregor to climb on to his shoulders. 'What do you say about the three of us going out for a ride?'

'Not this morning,' Coira answered quickly, remembering Fergus's request. 'I'm afraid we have lessons to finish.'

'Can't we finish them later, Mama?' Gregor pouted. 'I want to go for a ride!'

'Your lessons are important.'

'Your mother's right.' Kendrick lowered him back to the floor, tousling Gregor's hair before turning reproachful eyes towards her. 'Although it's a shame. I would have liked for us to spend a little time together before I left.'

'You're leaving so soon?' She tried not to sound too pleased by the idea.

'Unfortunately, yes. I had intended to stay for a couple of days, but I'm afraid that my welcome here is already wearing thin. Your husband doesn't appreciate my visit, I think.'

'It's not that. He just has a lot on his mind with the threat from the Campbells. I'm sure that if the two of you were to get to know each other a little better…' She let the words trail away, aware of how unconvincing they sounded.

'Perhaps.' Kendrick rubbed a hand over his chin with

a sigh. 'I suppose I can understand why he resents my presence, but all I wanted was to make sure that you and Gregor were all right.'

'And Ailis,' she reminded him pointedly. Like his father, Kendrick had an irritating habit of forgetting about her daughter.

'Of course. Ailis, too. I care about all of you. I hope that *you* understand that, at least?'

'I do.' Coira smiled, struck with a pang of guilt for having doubted his motives, even for a second. Kendrick was the only person who'd cared enough about her and Gregor to come and see how they were and here she was, practically chomping at the bit for him to leave! It was ungrateful and unkind, especially when there was nothing in his face to suggest that he thought of her in *any* way beyond friendship. Fergus was obviously overreacting. She'd tell him so tonight and make him understand that his suspicions were unfounded. 'Thank you for coming, Kendrick. I do appreciate it, even if things have been difficult.'

'Then why not come for a ride with me to prove it?' He grinned, reaching for her wrists and circling his own hands around them. 'Surely you can spare an hour for me before I go? Just one?'

'Well…' She glanced towards the window high up on the far wall. The shutters were pulled back, revealing another bright, golden day, perfect for a ride. It *would* be a shame not to make the most of it when there was really no danger. It wasn't as if she *wasn't* being careful. And it was surely just her imagination that Kendrick's fingers were holding on to her a little too tightly, like iron manacles around her wrists. And it *definitely* wasn't his fault that when he smiled like that, he reminded her so very much of Nevin, sending a wary but unwarranted chill down her spine… 'Very well, but just a short one.'

'Fergus?' Euan came running across the bailey the moment he dismounted.

'What is it?' Fergus turned towards the keep, looking for some sign of trouble, but everything was just as he'd left it a few hours before.

'It's Lady Coira.' Euan's voice was tense. 'She and Gregor went for a ride out with Kendrick Barron.'

'What?' He felt as if all the air had just left his body, as if he'd been struck in the face by something cold and heavy. Had she run away from him again? No. The thought flitted away almost as soon as it arrived, a quick glance around the bailey showing that Kendrick had left the majority of his guards. That meant he'd be back for the others, not that it was a very great consolation. Even if Coira hadn't run away, she'd still ignored his warning and gone for a ride with a man who, if Malcolm was right, was capable of a lot more than bad temper. Still, he felt too fearful at that moment even to feel jealous.

'I tried to stop her, but she said not to worry and that she wouldn't be long.'

'Why didn't you go with her?'

'I tried to, but he dismissed me. He said that he was taking some of his own guards and that they were enough. I couldn't argue.'

Fergus swore violently and then put a hand on the younger man's shoulder as he winced. It wasn't Euan's fault, after all. 'How long ago did they leave?'

'Almost an hour, but at least that means they should be back soon.'

'Aye, they *should*.' He started up the steps to the ramparts and then stopped halfway, turning around again. 'The other day, when I found you and Grizel in the armoury, what were you going to say?'

'In the armoury?' Euan looked confused. 'I don't remember—'

'You were going to say something about Lady Coira objecting to the two of you getting married. What was the reason? Why wouldn't she approve?'

'Oh…' Euan glanced awkwardly over his shoulder as if he thought that Grizel might be standing behind him, ready to scold again. 'It's because of some of the things Lady Coira's said in the past.'

'Such as?'

'That love is for fools and marriage is a prison. That's what Grizel told me anyway. It was before you came, but it's why we can't ask for her permission to wed just yet. Grizel is afraid that she'll try to talk her out of it.'

'And Grizel is afraid of being swayed?'

'No. She just doesn't want to argue and upset her.' Euan lowered his voice. 'She says that Lady Coira has been through a lot and that she doesn't like to talk about such things, but Grizel's hopeful that now you're here and she seems happier, there's a chance she might change her mind.'

'I see… Thank you.' Fergus furrowed his brow before climbing the rest of the steps to the battlements two at a time. Heartened as he was by the fact that his wife *seemed* happier, apparently there were other things they needed to talk about. Things that he didn't want to ignore or put off any longer. They *had* to talk. Just as soon as she came home.

He narrowed his gaze into the distance. So where the hell was she?

'He's growing into a fine lad.' Kendrick gestured towards Gregor, riding ahead of them, as he nudged his horse sideways, bringing it so close to Coira's that she felt his leg touch against hers. 'Nevin would have been proud.'

'Aye, he would.' She pressed her knees subtly into her own mare's flanks, trying to edge ahead. The first part of their ride had been very pleasant, enough to convince her that she'd been right about Kendrick all along, but now they were out of sight of the castle walls she was beginning to feel uneasy. There was a growing atmosphere of tension in the air, making her feel uncharacteristically, and unpleasantly, vulnerable in his company. Now she wished that she'd insisted on bringing some of her own men along, too, but Kendrick had laughed the suggestion away, saying that his own were more than sufficient as guards, and there had been no way to insist without offending him. Now all she could do was let her gaze wander anxiously across the hills, willing Fergus to appear with his scouting party.

'Nevin was a good father,' Kendrick went on, 'despite his other faults.'

'What?' She turned her head sharply. 'What do you mean?'

'I think you know what I mean. As a husband—' his gaze intensified '—I fear that he left a great deal to be desired.'

She swallowed, glancing nervously over her shoulder to make sure his guards were far enough away not to overhear. Kendrick had witnessed first-hand the insulting way his cousin had treated her, of course, but she'd never complained to him and they'd never spoken of it directly before. She'd thought it was understood that the subject was out of bounds.

'That's all in the past now.'

'I thought so, too, and yet now I find you in the same position all over again.' Kendrick shook his head with a mournful expression. 'I miss my cousin, but I thought that at least with him gone, you would be free.'

'I don't think—'

'I know that you won't tell me the truth about MacMillan,' he interrupted her. 'You never complained to me about Nevin either, but I wish that you would. You can trust me, Coira. I *want* you to confide in me. If MacMillan mistreats you, too, then—'

'He doesn't!' She felt a rush of anger at the very suggestion. 'And I *am* telling you the truth! I might never have told you about Nevin, but I never defended him either. Whereas Fergus's behaviour has been nothing but honourable towards me. I told you, I'm content. I just wish that you would believe it!'

Kendrick sighed heavily. 'You're too good, but you should know that there are ways...if you wished to be free?'

'What do you mean?' She shivered, feeling her stomach start to roil. 'What kind of ways?'

'For a start, if the marriage hasn't been consummated then it can still be annulled.' He waved a hand to his men, bringing them to a halt behind them before reaching out and grasping hold of her bridle. 'Has it been consummated?'

'Kendrick!' She gasped, shocked by the intimacy of the question.

'Has it?'

'I won't answer that!' She tried to wrench the bridle out of his hand, but his grip was too strong. 'Let me go!'

'Not until you tell me the truth. I need to know, Coira.'

'Why? What does it matter to you?'

'Are you really so blind? Have you truly not guessed how I feel?' His gaze narrowed in on her face like a hawk. Unfortunately, it also gave the frightening impression that she was the prey. 'I love you, Coira, I've loved you since the first moment I saw you, more than Nevin ever did. The way he treated you drove me wild. I hated him for it. Hated him so much that—' He stopped mid-sentence, twisting his face to one side for a few seconds before turning back to her. 'He didn't deserve you.'

'I don't understand why you're telling me this now.' She shook her head, half horrified, half bewildered. Despite everything that Fergus had said, it was still hard to believe that Kendrick cared for her in that way. 'You never said anything before. I thought we were friends.'

'We were. *Are.*' He leaned closer, breathing hard. 'I knew you were too good and loyal to understand how I felt before, but now there's a chance for us, Coira. If your marriage can still be annulled, then tell me. We can be together! I'll go to my father and—'

'It cannot!' She lifted her chin, desperately hoping he wouldn't read the lie in her eyes. She could still hardly believe the words emerging from his lips, but she wanted them to stop. And not just the words either. His whole manner alarmed her. There was something too bright, too wild, about his eyes, as if he wasn't in control of his own emotions. 'I'm married in *every* sense. So it's no use talking like this or about annulments either. No matter what you think you might feel for me—'

'What I *might* feel?' His voice hardened. 'Then you think this is all just a whim for me? You think me incapable of love?'

'No, I didn't mean—'

'I would do anything for you, Coira. *Anything.*' A muscle leapt in his jaw. 'Run away with me.'

'What?'

'Run away. You did it once before. Do it again.'

'No! I wasn't already married before! I didn't have children! And even if I—'

'Mama!'

She jerked her head about, heart thumping with panic, as Gregor came trotting towards them on his pony, a broad grin on his face.

'What is it, darling?' She kept her voice calm with an effort, letting out a breath she hadn't known she'd been holding as Kendrick finally released her bridle.

'A white-tailed eagle! Look!'

'Oh! So it is.' She tipped her head back, thinking that she'd never been so relieved to see anything in her whole life as the mighty bird with vast brown wings and a white tail soaring above them. 'How beautiful.'

'Can we follow it?'

'Not today. It's time for us to be getting back. We still have lessons to finish, remember?' She pulled on her reins, turning her horse back in the direction of

Castle Barron and desperately hoping that Kendrick wouldn't argue. If he did, she knew there was little she could do to stop him.

The next few seconds seemed to drag on for ever before he eventually nodded. 'Aye. We'll head back.'

'There they are!' Euan pointed into the distance, somewhat unnecessarily since Fergus was standing beside him and looking in the same direction.

'Aye.' Fergus heaved a long, shuddering breath as he sighted Coira riding alongside Kendrick and Gregor at the front. He'd been on the verge of riding out to look for them, surprised by just how afraid he'd been, but now he could feel relief giving way to anger. He'd told her to be careful and instead she'd gone off with her son for a ride with the very man he'd warned her against! If that was taking care, then they needed to have a long discussion about what the words actually meant.

He forced himself to stand still, waiting until the small party were almost at the gates before descending the gatehouse steps to greet them, planting his feet firmly apart and standing with his arms folded.

'MacMillan.' Kendrick's tone was even more openly belligerent than before. 'Have you nothing better to do than wait around for us?'

Fergus ignored him, his first glimpse of Coira's face instantly defusing his anger and leaving only concern in its place. Her complexion was ashen and the skin across her forehead looked stretched, as if she was upset or shaken about something, but the swift look that she threw him was sharp as a knife. She wasn't just acknowledging him, he realised. She was appealing to him not to do anything. And, surprisingly, he was going to agree. For now.

'We saw a sea eagle!' Gregor jumped off his pony and came running eagerly towards him. 'It was so big, it looked like a dragon!'

'Then I'm glad it didnae breathe fire on you. You had a good ride, then?'

'Just to the far end of the glen and back,' Coira answered quietly as she dismounted. 'Kendrick wanted to say goodbye.'

'He's leaving?' He didn't bother to address the man himself.

'Aye, but I'll visit again soon.' Kendrick's gaze was unreadable as he stared at Coira. 'We haven't finished our conversation.'

'Actually, I think that we've both said enough.' She offered a tight, strained-looking smile in response. 'I appreciate your coming to check on us, Kendrick, but like I said, there's no need to worry any more.' To Fergus's surprise, she came to stand beside him, curling her fingers around his arm. 'There's no need for you to come back either. Now ride safely.'

There was a long, ominous-sounding silence before Kendrick finally inclined his head, beckoning for the rest of his men to follow as he thundered out through the gates without another word.

'What the—?' Fergus started, but Coira interrupted him, taking her hand away and placing it on Gregor's shoulder instead.

'You'd better go and find Duffy. I expect she's been missing you.'

As if the puppy had overheard the words, she

emerged from the keep at that very moment, scampering enthusiastically towards Gregor.

'Duffy!' The boy charged off to greet her.

'We can't talk here,' Coira murmured, taking a step towards the gatehouse. 'Come inside.'

'All right...' Fergus followed, scowling at the guards outside so eloquently that they scattered like a flock of surprised birds. Behind him, he could hear Kendrick's men hastily packing up and preparing to ride out after their master. Evidently, his sudden departure had taken them by surprise, as well.

'I shouldn't have gone.' Coira spun to face him the very moment the door closed behind them. 'Before you say anything, I know that now and I'm sorry, but Kendrick said he was leaving and it felt churlish not to go for a short ride before he departed. I thought that you were mistaken about his feelings and intentions towards me, but—'

'What did he do?' Fergus was beside her in two strides. 'Did he lay a hand on you?'

'No.' She looked faintly surprised at both the speed and strength of his reaction. 'He didn't touch me. He just said...things.'

'What things?'

She hesitated, wrapping her arms around herself as if she were chilled by the memory. 'He asked if it was possible for us to get an annulment.'

'An annulment?' Fergus gritted his teeth. 'So that he could marry you instead?'

'He didn't say so exactly, but...I think so.'

He turned aside, clamping his hands over the back of a chair and squeezing the wood tight.

'It's all right. I told him that it was too late, that we'd already consummated the marriage.'

'And he believed you?'

'Aye. Why wouldn't he?'

He grunted, reluctant to admit that their behaviour suggested anything *but* a consummated marriage. Her hand on his arm had been the first time she'd deliberately touched him since the night she'd tended to his cheek. Sometimes he still felt as if he could feel the press of her fingers on his jaw.

'What else did he say?'

'That he was in love with me. That he'd been in love with me for years.' She drew in an unsteady breath. 'I can't believe it. I honestly thought that you were imagining things last night, but then he asked me to run away with him and—'

'He *what*?' Fergus hastily released the chair as the wood made a loud cracking sound beneath his fingers.

'He asked me to run away with him,' she repeated, flinching as he unleashed a torrent of oaths. 'I refused, of course.'

'Why?'

'Why?' She looked surprised by the question. 'Because I'm already married to you and I have children to think of!'

'So if we weren't already married and you didn't have children, you would have agreed?' He couldn't keep the bitter edge out of his voice. 'You would have preferred him to me?'

'No!'

He lifted an eyebrow. 'Did you tell him that?'

Her gaze faltered beneath his and when she spoke

again her voice had a quaver in it. 'I was going to, but then Gregor interrupted us and I didn't get a chance to say any more, but I told him that I was content.'

'I see.' He clenched his jaw. *Content*. Nothing about caring for him or choosing him, only *content*. 'So then he just gave up?'

'Aye. I told him to stop talking that way.' A fearful expression crossed her face. 'I think he understood.'

'I doubt it. He said that your conversation wasn't over.'

'But I told him it was.'

'Not all men give up so easily.'

She heaved a sigh and then sank down on to the chair he'd almost destroyed. 'Maybe not. It was like he refused to believe anything I said. What a mess! I don't understand how this has happened, but I never gave him any encouragement, I swear. Or if I did, I never meant to. I really thought he felt sorry for me and that we were friends and that was all there was to it. He was kind to me at a time when I needed kindness.'

Fergus frowned, wondering whether to share his suspicions about Kendrick's involvement in her husband's death and then deciding against it. Suspicions were all he had at that moment and it struck him that she'd already had enough of a shock that morning. What good would another one do? Besides, there was something else she'd just said that interested him much more. Something that confirmed another of the suspicions gradually taking shape in his mind...

'Why would he have felt sorry for you?' He unclenched his jaw with an effort, coming to crouch down beside her instead. 'Why did you need kindness, Coira?'

'You know why.' She stared down at her hands. 'I can tell by your voice. You spoke to Malcolm about Nevin and me, didn't you?'

'Only a little. He said that it wasn't his place to tell me. Nobody here seems to want to talk about Nevin at all.'

'They wouldn't. He wasn't a very good laird and he didn't treat people well.' She laced her fingers together, swallowing visibly. 'But you've already guessed the truth, haven't you?'

'I think so, but I want to hear it from your own lips.'

She lifted her face again finally, her expression distraught. 'I needed kindness *because* of Nevin. He hated me.'

Chapter Fourteen

Coira squeezed her eyes shut, trying to steady her breathing, but it was almost impossible when her heart was racing like a hound after a rabbit and the air felt as if it were trapped in her lungs, unable to get out. Just thinking about the way Nevin had treated her made her feel as if the cold, stone walls of her marriage were closing in around her all over again, crushing her heart and spirit the way they had for more than five miserable years.

There was a heavy silence before Fergus picked up another chair and placed it in front of her, sitting down so that they were positioned knee to knee. 'I don't understand. I thought that you and Nevin were a love match. That's what they told me.'

'No.' She resorted to blowing air out between her lips. 'There was never any love between us. I tried. For a while, I even thought that it might be possible. I thought that if I tried hard enough then maybe he'd learn to love me as well, but...' She squirmed, trying to find a way to describe their relationship and settling on an understatement. 'We weren't suited.'

'But you ran away with him. You went willingly. There were witnesses who saw you.'

'And how many of them were paid?' She gave a humourless laugh. 'Maybe there were a few honest witnesses, but what actually happened…what people might have thought they saw…it didn't happen the way everyone thought.'

'Then what *did* happen?'

She arched her neck, staring hard at the ceiling for a few seconds. 'If I tell you, you need to promise never to share it with anyone else or to seek revenge.'

'That depends.'

'No, it doesn't. You have to promise me or I won't tell you.'

'That's not fair.' He made a rumbling sound in his throat before grunting assent. 'All right. I promise.'

'Thank you.' She lowered her eyes back to his, finally able to draw in a new breath. 'The truth is, I had every intention of marrying you. The night before our wedding, I was bathed and put to bed like a bride. Everything was ready for the next morning. The gown, all the arrangements… I was nervous, but I'd just managed to fall asleep when my brother came. He told me to get up and dressed and to meet Nevin outside the castle. They'd bribed a guard to let me out through a side door; no doubt he was one of those witnesses you mentioned. I didn't want to go. I barely knew Nevin. I'd danced with him two nights before, but my brother insisted. He thought that an alliance with a MacWhinnie would be more useful for our clan and he said that if I didn't go—' She stopped and clamped her lips together, biting back a swell of bitterness.

'If you didn't go?' Fergus prompted her, his voice harder than she'd ever heard it.

'He said that he'd tell you and everyone else that I wasn't a maid. He said that he'd spread false rumours about me and then disown me, as well. I didn't know if he meant it—I still don't—but I was young and frightened and it was the middle of the night. I didn't know what to do. If I'd cried out, then it would have brought guards running and there would have been bloodshed. I wasn't sure whether anyone would believe me either and I thought that you didn't like me anyway so…' She met his gaze briefly before looking away again. 'I did what he told me. I dressed and went down to the side door. After that, everything happened so quickly. Before I knew it, I was being bundled on to a horse and we were galloping for Castle Barron.'

'So your brother arranged it all?' Fergus's eyes were dark as obsidian stones. 'Why? If he wanted an alliance with the MacWhinnies, then why didn't he just arrange one in the first place?'

'He tried, but Brody thought our clan wasn't good enough and rejected the idea out of hand, even despite the size of my dowry. It was afterwards that Niall approached your uncle, but he was never satisfied, always wanting more. He met Nevin at Sween Castle right before our wedding and they came to an arrangement.'

'So he got a laird instead of a second son for a brother-in-law?'

'Aye.'

'Meanwhile Nevin got you?'

'Not me.' She laughed bitterly. 'It was all for my dowry and whatever other underhand schemes he and

my brother had cooked up between them. Our marriage
was all a trick—a trap. Oh, Nevin was charming enough
at first and I suppose I kept him entertained for a while,
until he decided that money wasn't enough compensa-
tion for such a low-born wife. He decided that taunting
me made much better sport.'

'What do you mean?'

Coira twisted her hands together in her lap. It was
strange. She'd thought that she hadn't wanted to talk
about it, not ever, but now that she'd started, she seemed
unable to hold anything back. It actually felt liberating
to let the words out finally. 'First it was little things.
Throwaway comments and criticisms in front of the ser-
vants. Then the comments got louder. If we had guests,
he made sure that they heard them, too. And after he
reconciled with Brody…he spoke as if *I'd* been the one
responsible for our marriage. That's what all the Mac-
Whinnies think, that I seduced and manipulated him.

'He did everything he could to belittle and demean
and insult me. He didn't like my voice, he said, so I
hardly dared speak and when he came to our bed…'
Her throat tightened. 'There was never any tenderness.
He even insulted me there, accusing me of lying with
other men, although he knew it wasn't true. He was a
monster who spent all of my dowry on himself, on food
and wine and often women, too. In the end, I felt like
I was living in a prison, as if he were trying to break
my spirit and drive me mad, or worse. I know that he
wanted to be rid of me. If it hadn't been for Gregor and
Ailis, I would have been utterly wretched.

'And then, one day, he went out hunting with Kendrick and never came back.' She shuddered and put a

hand to her chest. 'You'd think that I would have felt something after so many years, but there was nothing left inside of me, as if I couldn't feel anything any more. Even now…' She licked her lips, half-afraid to admit the truth. 'I love my children, but it's as if the rest of my heart has shrivelled. Or died. As if Nevin had actually taken up a dagger and cut part of it away. Now I don't think I'm capable of loving anyone else.'

Fergus leaned forward, his knees touching lightly against hers. 'When I saw you that first day by the loch, I thought you were still grieving for Nevin.'

'Because I looked so awful?'

'Tired.'

'That, too. It's been a long six years.'

'I wish that you'd told me all this sooner. I would have listened.'

'Would you?' She looked at him sceptically. 'Would you have believed me?'

He pressed his brows together, his tone sombre. 'I don't know. Maybe not at first, but once I got to know you…or had a little time to think about it…I hope so.'

'I didn't want to talk about it then anyway. I suppose I needed to get to know you, too. And part of me was embarrassed for having made such a terrible choice of husband.' She gave a brittle laugh. 'So there it is! The whole story. Yes, I ran away from you, but I paid for it. I ended up married to a man who only wanted my dowry and felt nothing for me but contempt. I was nothing more than a warm body in his bed when he couldn't find anyone else. I was utterly miserable with Nevin.'

There was a moment of absolute stillness before Fergus scraped his chair back, striding to the far side of the room and bracing his hands against the wall.

'Fergus?' She watched him, suddenly anxious about how much she'd just revealed.

'I should have come after you.' With his head lowered, his voice sounded strange, as if he was finding it hard to speak at all. 'I should have followed you here.'

'There was no point. Nevin and I were married almost as soon as we arrived.'

'I still should have come. If I'd known what had really happened, I would have broken down the gates. I would have torn down every stone. If I'd even suspected for one second...' He swung around again, his eyes blazing. 'I should have saved you, but instead I abandoned you with him and then I came here and acted like you were the villain. When all of it was my fault!'

'No!' She shook her head adamantly. 'I was the one who ran away.'

'Because you didn't know how I felt.' He came and dropped to one knee in front of her. 'I just didn't know how to talk to you back then. And you didn't think you could talk to me. If you had, then your brother would never have dared order you to run away with Nevin. You could have screamed and known that I'd come running.'

She dropped her gaze. That much was true. She hadn't wanted to run away. If she'd thought that she'd had any real alternative, then she would have seized it.

'I'm sorry, Coira.'

'You don't have to be. We were both young.'

'Not just for that. For being so angry and blaming you, too.' He made a face. 'I thought that the best way to forget was to let you go and never think about you again, but I should have insisted on finding out the whole truth at the time.' He pushed a hand through his hair. 'I just assumed that you thought I wasn't good enough for you.'

'Not good enough?' She stared at him blankly. 'Why on earth would you think such a thing?'

'Because that's what *I* thought.' There was a pained expression in his eyes, a vulnerability she'd never witnessed in him before. 'When our marriage was agreed on, I felt like the luckiest man alive. I thought you were everything I could ever want in a woman. That's one of the reasons I didn't know how to talk to you. I was afraid that you'd realise how one-sided the bargain was. My uncle always said that Ross was the one with the brains and I was the one with the fists. I knew from the start that I was getting the better part of the arrangement.'

'Fergus...' She reached her hands out, cupping his face inside them. 'I never thought such a thing. I never *could* think such a thing. I don't care what your uncle said. Of course you're good enough for me. You're a hundred times the man Nevin was.'

'But I let him have you. If I could only go back and do things differently...'

'But you can't. All we can do now is go forward.' She leaned closer, tipping her forehead against his, and then caught her breath, realising what she'd just done.

He seemed to go very still at the same moment, the warmth of his breath mingling with hers as they both pulled back slightly and gazed into each other's eyes. Their noses were almost touching and she was still holding on to him, she realised, her fingers still wrapped around his jaw, dangerously close to his mouth. If she moved her thumb just a little, it would scrape against his bottom lip. His skin felt rough, dotted with tiny bristles, and yet she wanted to rub her fingers across it, to stroke and rub and caress him. It was a heady feeling, as if she'd drunk too much wine, as if a small fire was being stoked inside her, the flames licking higher and higher, sending waves of heat pulsing through her body the longer she looked at him.

After Nevin, she'd never imagined that she'd want to touch another man ever again, but now she was almost desperate to touch Fergus, to do anything and everything her feverish mind could imagine, to chase away the words they'd both uttered and replace them with feeling. And then she was, or at least her fingers were, already moving, sliding across his cheeks and jaw and then down to his throat.

'Coira...' He pulled away, his hands coming up to cover hers.

'I'm sorry.' She swallowed, mortified by his reaction. 'I shouldn't have done that.'

'It's not that. I'm just not sure that we—'

Both of them jumped and swung around as the door to the guards' room was pushed inwards suddenly.

'Oh!' The guard in the doorway looked almost as horrified as she felt. 'My apologies. I'll—'

'Wait!' She leapt out of her chair as he started to turn away, seizing the opportunity to escape. 'It's all right. You can come back in now. We're finished here.'

'Coira—' One of Fergus's hands stretched out to catch her, but she evaded it, darting to one side and hoisting her skirts up as she hurtled across the room and out of the door.

* * *

Coira wasn't sure how she got past the guard, or how she crossed the bailey, and she had no memory at all of climbing the stairwell, or of traversing the solar or minstrels' gallery either, only somehow she must have since she found herself standing alone in the middle of her bedchamber a few minutes later, breathless, panting and yet still unable to outrun her embarrassment!

With a groan, she dropped her head into her hands, covering her eyes as she tried and failed to shut out the memory. It was all too much! After what Kendrick had told her that morning and what she and Fergus had told each other just now, there were so many thoughts and emotions swirling around inside her that she could barely think straight. All she knew was that she'd just made a terrible mistake. She'd *touched* Fergus, but in her defence, she'd thought that he'd wanted her to! What was it he'd said?

That he'd felt like the luckiest man alive, that he would have come after her, that he wished he could go back and do things differently, that he would have saved her...

And yet he'd still pushed her away.

'Coira?'

'No.' She dropped her hands from her face, holding them out instead at the sight of Fergus standing on the threshold. 'Please...not now. I need some time alone.'

'You didn't let me finish my sentence.'

'You don't need to. I understand. You wanted me six years ago, but you don't any more and you *really* don't want me touching you. I'm sorry for what happened just now and there's no more need for us to discuss it.'

'Will you not let a man speak?' He strode forward, closing the door behind him. 'I never said any of that.'

'But you think it's too late for us, don't you?' She shook her head helplessly. 'We've missed our opportunity.'

'Honestly, I don't know.' He came to a halt halfway across the room, his expression conflicted. 'The truth is, I wasn't just angry when you left. I was hurt, too, knowing how much I cared about you and how little you felt for me. I couldn't tell anyone, couldn't show it, but it hurt. It was just as you said, like a part of me had shrivelled and died, too. As if my heart were...' He stopped and drew his brows together. 'I don't want to risk going through that again.'

'But you wouldn't have to.' She stared at him in confusion. 'I would never run away again.'

'When I heard that you'd gone out with Kendrick this morning, I thought that maybe you already had.'

She sucked in a breath. 'I'm sorry. It never occurred to me that it might look that way.'

'I know, but it reminded me of how bad it felt.' He took another step forward. 'Coira, when I came here to marry you, I never intended to stay. I was planning to do my duty to my clan and then leave as soon as possible.'

'Leave?' She felt as if her heart had just plummeted down to her toes. 'You mean, all this time, that's what you were planning?'

'Aye. I intended to wed you, do whatever was necessary to defeat the Campbells and then go back to Sween Castle or wherever Ross had need of me.'

'I see.' She found herself swaying backwards. 'And now?'

'Now, I think that it would be hard to leave, but not

impossible. If we take things further, however, if we make this a real marriage...' He rubbed a hand over his jaw, his gaze sliding towards the bed. 'It's not that I don't want your touch. I want it more than ever, but just bedding you isn't enough for me. I want more than that.'

'You mean love?'

'Aye, or at least the possibility of it.' He kept a determined hold on her gaze. 'Coira, you were right, we can't go back, but I want us to put aside everything that's happened and try to care for each other the way we might have done six years ago if things had been different and your brother had never woken you that night. I'm not saying that it's possible, not for either of us. I'm not offering or asking for any promise, but I want us to try. I know there's a risk of being hurt again, but I want us to take that risk together. Otherwise I'd rather my heart stay shrivelled and we keep things the way they are now.' He closed the last step between them, looking deep into her eyes as if he were trying to see through them into her mind. 'What do you think? Could we try to care—truly care—for each other? Could we give us a second chance?'

Coira swallowed, baulking at the question. Could she? She'd tried to love Nevin and all she'd got in return was pain and heartache. She'd been completely wrong about him. *And* about Kendrick. What if she was wrong about Fergus, too? What if she was simply a terrible judge of men? No matter what her instincts might tell her about Fergus, she'd made so many mistakes. In which case, maybe it *would* be better for them to remain as they were. As companions with no touching allowed. Now that Fergus knew the whole truth, they had a good foundation for friendship. That was all she'd wanted when he'd arrived, except that now she knew she wanted more, too. She'd known it the moment he'd said it.

Slowly, she lifted her hands and laid them flat against his chest. Her emotions felt raw, as if talking about Nevin had opened up old wounds, yet, rather than shrink away and hide, keeping her pain to herself as she always had in the past, this time she wanted to lay herself open. To open her heart again.

'I don't know,' she answered at last, swaying closer as his face fell. 'I want to be honest with you. When you came, all I hoped for was friendship. I thought that was all I was capable of. All I'd ever want from a man, too. But now...' She flexed her fingers against his chest. 'I don't know if it's possible for me to care for a man again, but I think I'd like to find out. So, yes, if you're truly willing, then I'd like to take the risk, too. With you.'

He made a sound in the back of his throat like a growl and then crushed his lips against hers, kissing her so ruthlessly that she had to dig her feet into the floor to stop herself from staggering backwards. And then he folded her into his arms and she stopped worrying about falling or anything else, feeling as if she were being held up by steel bands.

Tentatively, she slid her fingers around the back of his neck, pushing them into his hair as his body heaved against hers. A rush of desire unspooled in her chest as his hands slid lower, pressing against the small of her back, pulling her against him so intimately that she moaned aloud, unable to contain herself.

* * *

'Coira?' He pulled back slightly, as if he thought she might be objecting, so she responded by reaching up on her tiptoes and pushing them back together, drawing his head down to hers and his body into the cradle of her hips until there wasn't as much as a breath of air between them, as if she were a trailing vine clinging to a tall tree. She could feel the heavy thud of his heartbeat through both sets of their clothes, the rhythm pulsing through her chest and echoing through her whole body, through her arms, her legs, her abdomen...

'Are you certain?' he murmured against her lips, his voice scraping against his throat as if he were afraid of his own question.

'More than certain.' She nodded, breaking the kiss so that he could see the sincerity in her eyes. She didn't know if she could love him, but she knew that she already cared enough for him to try.

He didn't hesitate any longer, seizing her mouth with renewed fervour, groaning as she kissed him back just as fiercely, digging her fingernails into his shoulder blades as she surrendered herself to the plethora of sensations rippling outwards along every nerve and limb, quivering, tingling and heating her blood to boiling point. At that moment, she hardly recognised her own body. She'd never felt this way before, as if she were both heavy and weightless at the same time.

'Come with me.' He reached for one of her hands, drawing her towards the bed, and she followed eagerly, catching her breath as he pulled his tunic over his head and then reached for her kirtle, untying the laces and peeling it away from her shoulders.

'You're so beautiful.' He nuzzled her throat in a way that caused her to emit a small keening sound she'd never heard herself make before. She hadn't even known such a sound was possible and, for some reason, it made him smile, too. She felt his lips curve as they moved lower, to the base of her throat and then across her shoulders, making her skin throb and causing a sharp, aching sensation low in her abdomen. Then slowly, with a tenderness she hadn't expected, but probably should have, he laid her down on the bed, somehow managing to draw her gown over her waist and hips at the same time.

'I've wanted you for so long.' He climbed over her, pressing kisses to her stomach through her cotton shift, his teeth catching hold of the fabric and lifting it gently away from her skin. 'I thought you were perfect from the very first moment I saw you.'

'Perfect?' She gasped, aware of a faint tremor of panic even through a haze of sensation. She wasn't afraid of what they were about to do, but she'd borne two children and there were parts of her body that showed it. What would he think when he saw them, as he seemed determined to do? He was already drawing her shift higher, his fingers brushing gently against her thighs. If he'd really desired her for so long then how could she *not* be a disappointment to him? How could anyone live up to being called perfect? Surely they could at least get under the blankets? Even though her temperature was already soaring...

'What is it?' He noticed the change in her mood immediately.

'What if it's not as good as you hoped?' She blurted

the words out before she could think twice about them. 'What if *I'm* not?'

He lifted his head, his eyes gleaming as he laid a hand on either side of her body and held himself over her. 'That works both ways. You might be disappointed in me.'

'Don't be ridiculous!' She stared up at him incredulously, letting her gaze roam over the solid expanse of his torso. The idea that he might disappoint her was ludicrous. A few kisses and he'd already given her a hundred times more pleasure than Nevin ever had.

'It's different.' She swallowed. 'My body isn't the same as it was six years ago.'

'And?' His brow wrinkled.

'And you should know, there are marks and…soft bits.'

'Do you really think that makes any difference to me?'

'It did to Nevin.'

'Ah.' He lowered his head again, kissing her for what was surely a full minute before breaking away to nuzzle at the corner of her lips. 'I'm not Nevin. If there are marks, then I'll enjoy finding them. As for soft bits…' another kiss '…as far as I'm concerned, the more, the better.'

'But maybe we could draw the shutters?'

'I will if you want me to, but I'd rather not.' He lifted a hand to stroke the curve of her cheek. 'Coira, you were the most beautiful woman in the whole of Scotland to me six years ago and you still are. Give me one hour to prove it and I promise that you'll believe it then, too. Trust me?'

Trust him? She inhaled sharply. Trust was a lot to ask for and yet, deep down, she knew that she already did, the tender look in his eyes convincing her and chasing away the last of her inhibitions.

She lifted a palm to his chest, catching her breath with anticipation. '*Just* one hour?'

His eyes flashed wickedly, making her insides tremble. 'Aye. To begin with.'

Fergus slid his fingers up over Coira's stomach, cupping one of her breasts in his hand, the feeling of her naked skin against his own making his blood pulse harder than ever before. For one terrible moment when she'd stiffened beneath him, he'd thought that she'd been about to change her mind and he was going to have to fling himself in the loch to cool down, but fortunately it had only been self-consciousness about her 'soft bits'. He'd almost laughed in relief at the words, though he'd known better than to actually do so.

She'd looked genuinely anxious and he'd done his best to allay her fears, telling her the truth: that she would only ever be perfect to him. Now he felt touched by her trust, although he knew he still had to be careful. After the years she'd spent with Nevin, the thought of which still filled him with a burning but futile sense of rage, he needed to be gentle and take things slowly, no matter how much he might want to hurry.

He brushed his thumb against her nipple, then buried his face in her neck as she gasped and arched beneath him, vaguely aware of a small voice at the back of his mind shouting a warning. She'd told him she didn't think herself capable of love any more, she'd told Grizel that she thought love was for fools…and yet here he was, offering to open his heart and risk having it broken into a thousand pieces all over again. He couldn't seem to help himself. He had the feeling that even if his brain *had* wanted to stop, which it didn't, the rest of him wanted her so badly that he might explode if he didn't make her his own soon.

Besides, it was a risk they were taking together. After all the misunderstandings and mistaken assumptions of the past, as well as everything they'd discovered about each other that evening, they surely owed one another that much. Just as long as he was careful, which he would be… That was the important part, to be prepared to admit the possibility of love, but not to actually fall into anything, not unless and until she loved him first. That point he was determined on.

He nudged her thighs apart, positioning himself between her legs, and then held his breath, giving her one last opportunity to stop if she wanted, before entering her. He moved slowly, trying not to cause any pain, moaning with satisfaction as he sheathed himself completely. Her body felt tight, her muscles tensing and contracting around him, but she felt even better than he'd imagined. For a moment, he almost didn't want to move, wanted to stay exactly where he was with their bodies joined together, holding on to the feeling for as long as possible. His mind felt completely content where he was. Then other parts of his body took over and he began to move, sliding gently back and forth in a steady rhythm.

'Fergus?' She murmured his name like a question, although she didn't seem to require a response, pushing and pulling and rocking against him as she mirrored his movements. Trying to maintain some restraint, he bent his head, catching a nipple in his mouth and suckling gently, but somehow the action caused her hips to convulse against him so he did the same to the other nipple, groaning as her movements grew wilder and more frantic, her fingers sliding down his back while her long legs wrapped around his in a way that almost made him lose control.

He felt as if every muscle in his body were straining, holding himself back with an effort. Judging by what she'd told him barely an hour before, Nevin had never given any thought to her pleasure and he wanted this to be good for her, but she was making it harder and harder for him to hold on.

He laid his head against her shoulder and clenched his teeth, willing her to hurry. And then she did, crying out at the same moment as he found his own release, his hips bucking one last time before he surged forward, shuddering as he spilled his seed inside her.

It was several minutes before he was able to think clearly enough to roll on to his side, feeling dazed and satiated and as if there were a heavy weight pressing down on his eyelids. It was all he could do to reach a hand out and grasp hold of hers, lacing their fingers together before tumbling heavily into sleep.

His last thought was that, despite everything, going to bed with Coira had been well worth the wait.

Chapter Fifteen

'Good morning.' Coira was perched on the edge of the bed, twisting her hair into braids, when Fergus finally opened his eyes.

'Morning?' He heaved himself up on one elbow, rubbing his other hand over his face as he looked towards the window, surprised to see yellow ribbons of sunlight already streaming into the room. He was usually one of the first in the castle to wake, getting up and about with the first flickers of dawn, but for once he appeared to have overslept. 'So it is. You wore me out, woman.'

'As I recall, the wearing out was mutual.' She gave him a shy smile, leaning across to drop a kiss on to his forehead. 'But if you're so exhausted, you'd better get some more rest. I'll see you later in the hall.'

'Oh, no, you don't.' He caught at the leather cord on one of her braids as she started to move away, causing the hair to unravel again.

'Fergus, I just did that!'

'I know.' He threaded his fingers through the tresses and then curved his other arm around her shoulders, pulling her down on top of him. 'Come back to bed.'

'I can't!' She let out a squeal, wriggling in a way that only made him hold tighter. 'I have errands to do!'

'So do I, but we've both worked hard enough of late. We can let others take the strain for one day.'

'Everyone will be wondering where I am.'

'Trust me, they won't. Not after yesterday. What time was it when we came up here? Not long after noon?'

'Yes, but—' Her eyes widened with an expression of shock and embarrassment. 'You don't think that *they* think—?'

He laughed and caught her waist in his hands, rolling them both over until she was pinned beneath him. 'Do you really care what anyone thinks?'

'No-o.' She scrunched her mouth up. 'Well, maybe a little. I'd prefer that everyone in the castle didn't know what we've been doing.'

'Something we ought to have been doing for the past six years. We have a lot of wasted days and nights to make up for.' He nuzzled closer, running his tongue along the shell of her ear. 'But if it helps, I'll make an effort to frown at everyone later.'

'You will not!' She batted a hand at him. 'Or they'll think you didn't enjoy it!'

'Then it seems I can't win.' He gave an exaggerated sigh, his fingers curving around one of her breasts as she caught her breath and stretched out beneath him.

'I like that.'

'So do I. Although I'd like it even more without this in the way.' His other hand plucked at her gown, tugging the fabric up. 'You didn't really think I'd let you get dressed and escape so easily, did you?'

'Later…'

'*Now.*'

'It's daylight! I've already opened the shutters.'

'It was daylight last time, too, so if you're objecting to me seeing you naked again then I really *will* start frowning...' He clamped his brows together, adopting an expression of such ferocity that she burst into giggles. 'Now stay still and let me undress you.'

'Wait.' She pressed her hands to his chest, pushing him backwards before rolling to her feet.

'Coira?' He frowned for real this time. 'I'm sorry. I didn't mean to upset you.'

'You haven't.' She smiled reassuringly as she slid her arms through the sleeves of her surcoat. 'But if you insist on my coming back to bed, then I'd rather not have another gown tossed in a heap on the floor...' She gave him an arch look. 'If men had to look after clothes, then they'd take a lot more care when it came to undressing.'

'I had other things on my mind yesterday,' he growled, his gaze following the movement of her fingers. 'But in that case, you'd better teach me how to undress you properly.'

'What do you think I'm doing?' She dug her teeth into her bottom lip, obviously trying not to smile as she removed the garment and folded it over a coffer. 'Now, my kirtle, as you can see, has laces up the sides. If you're too rough...' she lifted an eyebrow '...then I'll end up needing to thread them all again.'

'*Was* I too rough yesterday?' He felt a momentary anxiety.

'I said *if*. It's just for future reference.'

'Ah. Noted.'

He lay back, folding an arm behind his head as he

watched. In a few more moments, both her surcoat and
kirtle were lying side by side on the coffer, closely followed by her shift, leaving her almost completely naked.
Gorgeously, beautifully, stirringly naked. After yesterday and last night, he wouldn't have expected his body
to respond so quickly or convincingly, but apparently
his desire for her was undiminished.

'Wait.' He sat up as she bent to remove her hose. 'Let
me.'

She caught his gaze and then clambered on to the
bed beside him, lying absolutely still as he untied the
strings of her garters and smoothed the woollen fabric
down over her legs.

'That's better,' he murmured, wrapping a hand
around one of her ankles and lifting it to his lips, smiling to himself at the sound of her indrawn breath, followed by something like a purr. 'I take it this is allowed?
Or is there anything else you need to teach me about
undressing first?'

'No, I'm done. Oh!' She gasped raggedly as he trailed
his lips up her calf. 'I've never been kissed there before.'

'Something tells me you've never been kissed in a
lot of places before.' He continued upwards, touching
his tongue to the tender skin of her thigh. 'And I intend
to find each and every one of them.'

'What about you?' There was a half-teasing, half-
tense note to her voice. 'Or have you been kissed by so
many women?'

'Not so many, no.' He paused on his slow progress
upwards. 'There was only ever one woman in the world
for me. And now that she's mine...' He lifted his head,

looking at her intently. 'There'll never be another, I swear it.'

'Fergus...' She pressed a hand to his cheek as she whispered his name, her beautiful thistle-blue eyes misting over.

'Shh.' He lowered his head again. 'We can talk later. Right now, I have some more exploring to do.'

'Come for a walk with me.' Fergus held a hand out when they were both finally dressed.

'Now?' Coira finished tying a belt around her surcoat. 'After we've already spent most of the day in bed?'

'Aye. If we're going to take the day off work, then we might as well do it properly.' He adjusted his plaid and nodded his head towards the empty tray beside the bed. 'It was thoughtful of your maid to bring us some food. We might have wasted away otherwise.'

Coira felt her cheeks suffuse with colour. Grizel had tapped gently on the door around noon, murmuring a few words about food before scurrying away. As meals went, it had been basic, consisting mainly of bread and cheese, but they'd both worked up enough of an appetite to clear the lot. A hearty venison stew couldn't have been any more satisfying. Obviously her maid had guessed what they'd been doing for a large part of the past twenty-four hours, too.

'What's the matter?' Fergus touched her elbow. 'Are you really so embarrassed?'

'No, but I need to speak with Grizel. I've always been so against marriage and men, at least since she's known me anyway. I dread to imagine what she thinks of me now.'

'You might be surprised by what she thinks.'

'She's more to me than just my maid. She's a dear friend, as well. We've been through a lot together.'

He gave her a sharp look. 'Nevin?'

'Aye. He took an interest in her when she first came. It was four years ago and I found her crying in the solar one evening, although she wouldn't tell me why at first. She was afraid that I might blame her. Eventually it all came out, that he'd been trying to catch her alone, trying to force his attentions on her. It wasn't hard to believe. Nevin wasn't a very faithful husband. She begged me to help her so I did.'

'How?'

She lifted a shoulder. 'I simply told him that if he ever tried to touch her again then I'd cut off his manhood in his sleep.'

'That's some threat.' He looked impressed. 'Did it work?'

'Aye. To be honest, I wasn't quite sure how I'd actually go about doing such a thing, but he wasn't prepared to take the chance. He looked very nervous for several nights afterwards, but he left Grizel alone.' She smiled and then sighed. 'I admit I was half-afraid we were going to have the same situation with you.'

'What do you mean?' He seemed to go very still suddenly.

'It was just that you seemed to like her, too. I wouldn't have blamed you,' she added quickly as his gaze darkened. 'She's extremely pretty.'

'That's not the point. *You're* my wife.' He folded his arms, his expression growing increasingly belligerent. 'What on earth made you think such a thing?'

'Because you asked me about her on that first evening. And you played with her and Gregor and Duffy in the bailey that time...' She faltered, realising how weak her reasoning sounded.

'So you were jealous?' The furrow between his brows eased slightly.

'Maybe a little.'

The rest of his frown dropped away as he reached for one of her hands and tugged her forward. 'You have nothing to worry about. I told you, I've only ever had eyes for one woman. As for Grizel...there was a reason I asked you about her, only that's something you need to talk to her about yourself.' His lips twitched. 'Suffice to say, I wouldn't worry too much about what she'll think of you. Something tells me she'll be happier than you expect. Now—' He put a finger to her mouth when she was about to ask what he meant. 'Let's take that walk. The children will be wondering where you are.'

They collected Ailis from her maid before heading down the stairwell and out into the bailey. Gregor was already there, busy play-fighting with Euan as Duffy yapped and darted around their heels.

'Will you come for a walk, lad?' Fergus called out. 'That dog sounds like she needs a good stretch.'

'I've taught her to lie down!' Gregor came running towards them, grinning from ear to ear. 'Watch this! Lie down.' His face fell as the puppy only stared back, wagging her tail. 'She did it before.'

'I believe you, lad. It takes a little practice, that's all. Now, come for a walk. I've got two ladies here to protect...' Fergus tipped his head, indicating her and Ailis '...and I could do with another man to help.'

'Can I bring my wooden sword?' Gregor's chest puffed out with pride.

'I'm counting on it.'

The afternoon was bright with only a gentle breeze to disturb the smooth, green surface of the loch. Fergus drew in a deep breath, filling his lungs with crystal-clean air, before letting it out contentedly as they made their way down the well-trodden path to the beach. Given the threat from the Campbells, it seemed strange to feel so content, but there was no other word for it. With Ailis balanced on one arm and Coira's hand threaded through the other, he felt as if a bank of grey clouds he hadn't even realised hung over him had finally floated away. The idea lifted his spirits, warmed his soul and made him feel as if, at long last, he'd found the place where he was meant to be. Except that it wasn't as much a place as a person. It was Coira, the woman he'd been right to fall in love with all those years ago, the woman he might easily fall in love with again, only not yet.

He turned his head as Duffy bounded straight into the loch, spraying water all over Gregor as she romped about in canine delight. Beside him, he heard Coira laugh. It was a joyful sound, like sunshine itself. It seemed infectious, too, making him want to do something he hadn't done properly in a long time. It made him want to smile.

And then he did. Before he knew what his own features were doing, his lips had curved upwards and he was smiling.

'Fergus?' Coira stopped laughing at once, staring at him with a look of utter amazement.

'Aye?' He lifted an eyebrow, feigning innocence. 'Is something the matter?'

'No, it's just that you're—' She didn't finish, only returning his smile instead. 'Nothing. It doesn't matter. It suits you, that's all.'

'I've no idea what you're talking about.' He winked and then drew his arm away to take hold of her hand, threading their fingers together as he looked out over the water again. 'How long do you think it would take to walk around the whole thing?'

'The whole loch? Much too long. There isn't even a path in most places.'

'That's what I thought. It's a pity.'

'Are you in a walking mood?'

'Not particularly.' He tightened his grip on her fingers and tugged her closer. Even standing beside him, she seemed too far away. 'I just have the feeling I don't want this day to end.'

'I know what you mean.' She looked from him to Ailis, who, by the feel of it, was trying to remove some of his hair, and then back again, her smile widening. 'But tomorrow will be a good day, too. This is a whole new beginning for us.'

'Aye.' He rubbed his thumb gently over the backs of her knuckles. 'It's funny, but you even look like your old self again.'

'I feel like it.' She tipped her head sideways, resting it on his shoulder. 'It's like a burden has been lifted. Living with Nevin felt like a very heavy one. He made me dislike myself almost as much as I disliked him. When he first insulted me, I tried arguing back, but it only made him worse so I ended up cowed and silent.

Then, after he died, I told myself I was never going to be that way ever again. I decided that I would stand up for myself, no matter what it cost me.' Her voice hardened. 'Not that it helped me much with Brody. He always said I had a shrill tongue. It felt like I couldn't win with the MacWhinnie clan no matter what I did.'

'You can always stand up for yourself to me.' Fergus kissed the top of her head. 'And there'll be no more disliking yourself either. I want you to be exactly who you are. In fact, I need you to be. You're the clever one in this marriage.'

She twisted her neck, looking up at him quizzically. 'Why do you think so badly of yourself?'

'I'm just telling the truth. Ross is the one with the brains. I'm only grateful he was the eldest son and not me.'

'You shouldn't say such a thing. You're as intelligent as anyone.'

He felt his chest glow at her indignant tone. 'Maybe I have brains in a different way, but when it comes to learning…somehow I was never able to get very far. I can remember facts and details well enough, things said aloud that I can keep in my head, but reading was never easy for me. It wasn't for want of trying either. I had tutors enough, but whenever I tried to concentrate, the letters all seemed to move around before my eyes, as if my mind was resisting them.' He shrugged. 'Ross tried to help me, but it never worked. I could never manage words. I suppose that's why I was never very good at speaking them either.'

'I think you're perfectly good at speaking. Look at us now.'

'*Now*, yes. Six years ago, on the other hand...'

Her expression wavered. 'Did you really think I ran away because you weren't good with words?'

'Aye, it worried me. I told you, I thought I wasn't good enough, whereas I knew Nevin was clever.'

'Oh, Fergus, Nevin was *too* clever. You have something much more important.' She touched a hand to his chest, placing it over his heart. 'This. Not many men would have taken on two children the way you have, especially considering who their father was. You'll never know how much it means to me.'

He smiled, trying to wipe the sadness from her gaze. 'Hopefully it's good practice for when we have bairns of our own.'

She blinked. 'You've thought about that?'

'It occurred to me this morning. Seeing as we might only have another nine months to wait.'

A faint blush suffused her cheeks. 'I suppose so.'

'Not that I wouldn't like a little longer to practise making them.'

'Them?'

'Two boys and a girl.'

'Like you, Ross and Elspeth?'

'Aye. I wasn't close to my uncle, but I knew I could always rely on the pair of them.'

'That must have been nice. I only had Niall and he... well, you know.'

'I do now.' His brows lowered. 'And I'd like to have a wee word with him about that some time.'

'Except that you can't. You promised you wouldn't, remember?' She gave him a swift jab in the ribs. 'What would be the point anyway? My brother might have acted badly, but he probably thought it didn't matter who I married. I doubt he ever intended to hurt me.'

'Did he ever bother to find out how you were faring?'

'No.' She shook her head sadly. 'He and Nevin had a falling-out just after Gregor was born. Nevin wanted more money to make up for the trial of being married to me and Niall refused. I haven't seen him since.'

'Hmm.' Fergus gritted his teeth. 'All right, since I promised, I won't go seeking him out, but if we ever cross paths...'

'Then I'll be sure to step in front of you. I don't believe in revenge.'

'Even after he married you off to a monster?'

'Plenty of fathers do the same to their daughters. Not many women get to choose their own husbands.' She sighed. 'I don't want to hold on to the past. I need to move on.'

'If that's what you want, but if you ever change your mind, just say the word.'

'I won't, but it's reassuring to know.'

He squeezed her hand, turning to look at the track leading south. 'That's the spot where we met. The second time, I mean.'

'Maybe we should just think of it as the first time? Then all of those other things that happened... Well, let's just say they weren't us. They were two other people who misunderstood each other and made a lot of mistakes.'

'That sounds like a good idea.' He felt an unfamiliar lump in his throat. 'Just as long as things come right for them eventually.'

* * *

'There you are.' Coira found Grizel sweeping up old rushes in the hall when they returned. 'I wondered if I might speak to you for a moment?'

'Of course, my lady. Is something the matter?'

'No, I just wanted to talk about Fergus and…our marriage.' She hesitated, not quite knowing how to explain. 'You might be wondering why I…that is, why we…yesterday and…this morning…' She cleared her throat heavily. 'The fact is, I've decided that some of my previous ideas about marriage were…maybe not wrong, but…dependent on the person involved. My relationship with Fergus has changed…obviously…and after everything I said before about only wanting friendship… well, I suppose I feel a little foolish now. And I wouldn't want you to think too badly of me.' She winced. '*Do* you think badly of me?'

'Never!' She'd barely finished the question before Grizel rushed to embrace her. 'I could never think badly of you! I was hoping that you and he would come to like each other.'

'We do!' She hugged her maid back, heaving a sigh of relief. 'We're going to try to put the past behind us and move on. I don't know if it can ever be love…' she paused, swallowing a tremor of panic at the idea '…but I feel ten times better already.'

'I'm glad. You deserve to, my lady.'

'And there was something else I wanted to talk to you about.' Coira took a step back, lifting her eyebrows expectantly. 'Fergus thought there might be another reason you would be pleased for us, only he wouldn't tell me what.'

'Oh.' Grizel's expression looked guilty all of a sudden. 'The truth is that Euan and I wish to wed.'

'Wed?' Coira blinked in astonishment. 'But I had no idea that you and he even liked each other!'

'I know, my lady. We kept it a secret. I felt terrible keeping the truth from you, but I knew what you thought about love and marriage and I didn't want to upset you.'

'You mean you thought that I'd disapprove?' Coira shook her head regretfully. 'Oh, Grizel, I'm so sorry. I never meant to make you feel that way. I'm happy for you both, truly. You and Euan can be married as soon as you wish.'

'Really?' Grizel's face burst into a wide smile. 'Oh, thank you. He said that I should just tell you.'

'Euan?'

'Fergus. He found Euan and me together in the armoury the other day and he said that you'd understand.'

'He did?' She felt touched and surprised at the same time. 'Well, that's— Wait, what were you doing in the armoury with Euan?'

Grizel's cheeks flamed bright red. 'If it's all the same to you, my lady, I'd rather not say. It was a little embarrassing.'

'Oh.' Coira felt her own cheeks blossom in reply. 'In that case, it seems we have another wedding to prepare for.'

Chapter Sixteen

'Ahem.' Malcolm's shaggy beard appeared around the top of the stairwell one day when Coira was busy mending clothes in the solar. 'There's a guest just arrived for you, my lady.'

'Oh, no.' She looked up from her sewing with a sinking feeling. It had been more than a week since Kendrick had ridden away in a temper, time during which she and Fergus had grown closer than she would ever have imagined possible, but surely her unwanted suitor hadn't returned again so soon? She thought that she'd made her feelings for him abundantly clear.

'It's a woman.' Malcolm anticipated her next question. 'She wanted to speak with Fergus, but since he's still at the village, she asked for you.'

'Did she give a name?'

'No, my lady. She wouldn't tell me who she was, but she showed me a ring. It has the mark of the MacMillans.' He threw a swift glance over his shoulder and lowered his voice. 'She also asked if she could speak with you alone. Her escort are all still outside, but there are some of our men in the hall so...'

'Of course, send her up.' Coira got to her feet, her mind whirling as she waited for their mysterious guest to emerge from the top of the stairwell. It had been raining heavily all day, turning the roads into boggy, slippery quagmires, making the arrival of a visitor even more surprising. Fergus had insisted on making the short trip to the village anyway, but surely no one else would attempt a journey unless it was really important? As for a woman…she had no idea who it could be, but fortunately, she didn't have to wait long to find out. Barely a minute had passed before there were new footsteps in the stairwell, followed by a tall, slender figure, dressed in a long, grey cloak with a hood drawn over her head.

'Welcome to Castle Barron.' She smiled and took a step forward. 'I'm Coira Barron. I understand that you wish to speak with me?'

'Coira…' a woman's voice repeated before she drew back her hood, revealing a pair of bright green eyes and a waist-length red braid drawn over one shoulder. 'Aye, I remember you.'

'Elspeth!' Coira thought it was a good thing her jaw was firmly attached to her face or it might have dropped all the way to the floor. Fergus's little sister had been a pretty girl the last time she'd seen her, but she'd grown into a truly stunning young woman. 'How wonderful to see you again!' Instinctively, she moved forward to embrace her and then stopped, frozen in place by the glacial look on the other woman's face. 'What brings you to Castle Barron?'

'I came to see my brother.' Elspeth's voice was a

lot harder than she remembered, too. 'But they tell me he's not here.'

'Not at the moment, no.' Coira averted her gaze, feeling self-conscious beneath such a quelling stare. Elspeth might have been a sweet, spirited girl, one whom she'd looked forward to having as a sister-in-law, but any reciprocal affection she might once have felt for Coira was all gone. Clearly, Fergus wasn't the only MacMillan who'd resented her for running away. 'But he'll be back soon. Please…' She gestured towards a bench by the fireside. 'Take a seat. Would you care for some refreshment?'

'No…thank you.'

'Very well.' Coira took her seat again opposite, lifting her chin to veil her discomfort. Given the situation with the Campbells, there was obviously a lot more to Elspeth's arrival than simply a desire to pay a social call on her brother, but her demeanour discouraged any direct questions. There was a strange tension about her, too, an over-brightness in her eyes combined with a brittleness that suggested something more than dislike. 'So…how was your journey?'

'Wet.'

'Aye. It hardly seems to have stopped raining for the past week.'

'Mmm.'

'Do you wish to change your clothes? You're welcome to make use of my bedchamber if you wish?'

'No, thank you. My cloak was quite sufficient for the journey, but don't let me keep you. I'm quite happy to wait here for Fergus on my own.'

Coira bit down on her tongue, recognising the tone

of dismissal. She supposed she could hardly have expected Elspeth to be pleased to see her, but this woman was so cold she could almost feel icicles forming in the air around them.

The initial pleasure she'd felt at seeing her again was rapidly fading and being replaced by acceptance. Her first husband's family had resented her and now it was obvious that her second husband's did, too. She ought to have expected it. No doubt Elspeth wouldn't hesitate to remind Fergus of all the reasons why he ought to resent her, as well. The timing could hardly have been any worse.

'I was just mending a shirt for Fergus.' She reached for her thread instead. If they were going to sit in silence, then at least she could keep her hands occupied. 'So we can wait together.'

'As you wish.' There was a momentary pause. 'Do you know how long he'll be?'

'I'm afraid not, but if it's urgent, I could send someone out to look for him?'

Elspeth's expression seemed conflicted as her foot started to tap on the floorboards. 'No. I can wait.'

It was funny, Coira thought, peering at her sister-in-law from under her lashes. Appearance-wise, Fergus and Elspeth could hardly have looked any more different. She was willowy and red-haired where he was broad-shouldered and dark and yet the frown the sister was wearing now was almost identical to the one he'd worn when he'd first arrived. Not that commenting upon the likeness would do her any favours. She doubted there was anything she could say that would do that. And why did some silences have to feel so awkward?

'Elspeth?'

They both looked around at the sound of her husband's voice.

'Fergus!' Elspeth's whole demeanour transformed at once, her voice full of relief as she leapt to her feet and ran across the solar into his arms.

'They told me in the village that a small band of riders had arrived,' he explained, throwing Coira a quizzical look over his sister's shoulder. 'But I never would have guessed it was you. What are you doing here? What made you travel in such terrible weather?'

'I had to come—' Elspeth said and then stopped, throwing a suspicious glance in Coira's direction before lowering her voice. 'Perhaps we ought to talk alone?'

'No need. There's nothing you can say to me that you can't say in front of Coira.'

'But—'

'But nothing.' Fergus took hold of his sister's arm and led her back towards the fireplace, his voice firm. 'She's a MacMillan now, too.'

'Oh.' Elspeth's forehead crinkled. 'Oh, very well, then.' She sat back down though she kept her face turned firmly towards Fergus so that Coira could only see her profile. 'I decided it would be safer here than at the Abbey.'

'Why? I thought the plan was for you to stay there until Leith MacLachlan got back from Edinburgh and you could be wed?'

'Aye, I was supposed to.' There was a strange tremor in her voice. 'But there were rumours about the Campbells moving closer so it seemed safer to leave and hide here for a few days before travelling on to MacLachlan territory.'

'Hide?' Fergus moved from his position in front of the fire to behind Coira's chair, forcing Elspeth to look in her direction, too. 'So no one else knows that you're here?'

'Hopefully not. Unless we were followed, but we saw no sign of it.' Her gaze slid to one side. 'We came in such a hurry, I didn't even bring a maid.'

'What about Sween? Does Ross need me?'

'No. In fact, before I left he said that if I saw you, I was to remind you of your promise to stay put, no matter what, and that if you even think about disobeying his orders then he'll push you off the ramparts of Sween Castle himself.'

'How brotherly of him.'

'Aye, I thought it was quite touching.'

'But isn't there anything we can do to help?' Coira spoke up. 'If the danger is so very great?'

'Such as?' Elspeth's eyes turned cold again. 'Do you have any suggestions?'

'No, I just…' She let her voice trail away, chilled by the antipathy in the other woman's voice. 'No.'

'I thought not.'

'We can discuss it later.' Fergus's hands came to rest on Coira's shoulders, kneading her muscles lightly. 'In the meantime, we'll do as Ross commands.'

Coira twisted her neck to look up at him, simultaneously touched by the gesture and gratified to catch Elspeth's shocked expression out of the corner of her eye. 'In that case, I'll go and prepare the children's bedchamber for Elspeth. They can sleep out here in the solar tonight.'

'No.' To her surprise, Fergus contradicted her. 'Elspeth can sleep here.'

'But she's a guest!'

'She'll be perfectly comfortable on the daybed.' He turned his gaze interrogatively towards his sister. 'Won't you?'

'Honestly, I'd rath—' Elspeth caught his eye and then folded her arms. 'Aye, perfectly comfortable. Apparently.'

'Good. Then it's settled.'

'Well…' Coira looked between the two of them, deciding to make herself scarce anyway. 'I'll go and see to your men. I'm sure they must be hungry after such a journey.'

'Thank you.' Fergus reached for her hand as she stood, closing his fingers around her knuckles and lifting them to his mouth. His *smiling* mouth. 'We'll talk about the rest later.'

'Fergus…?' Elspeth waited until Coira had left before saying his name slowly, as if she thought he might actually be somebody else. 'What's going on?'

'What do you mean?' He sat down in his wife's now vacant chair, stretching his long legs out in front of him and crossing his ankles.

'The two of you. You just… I mean, you almost just smiled.'

'*Almost?*'

'You smiled!'

'Aye.'

'And you rubbed her shoulders!'

'So I did.'

'*And* you kissed her hand!'

'I'm aware.'

'Is that *all* you've done?'

'In front of company, aye...' He quirked an eyebrow. 'But if you're asking what I think you're asking then it's none of your damned business. However, I warn you, one more question like that and ye'll be sleeping in a pile of hay in the stables tonight instead of the solar, sister or not.'

'I don't believe it!' Elspeth thrust a foot out, catching him in the shin. 'I don't know how you can even bear to be in the same room as that woman after what she did to you!'

'I felt the same way at first, you know that, but as it turns out, things weren't exactly the way they seemed.'

'Oh, really? And *she* told you that, I suppose?'

'Aye.'

'And you believe her?'

'I do.'

'Urgh.' Elspeth rolled her eyes sceptically. 'She's manipulating you.'

'You think me so easily taken in?'

'No-o.'

'Then you think that I'm wilfully deluding myself?'

'Of course not.'

'In that case, you ought to trust my judgement.'

'I *do*, generally speaking, but you're still a man and no matter how clever a man thinks he is, often all it takes is—'

'I've never thought I was clever, you ought to know

that.' Fergus pushed himself back to his feet. 'But I believe Coira. More than that, I trust her. Now, you're welcome to stay here as long as you need, but if you do then I expect you to treat my wife with respect.'

'*Respect?*'

'Aye. It's not like you to behave so shrilly anyway. What's the matter?'

For a moment, he thought his little sister was about to tell him something. Her lips parted and there was a flash of vulnerability in her eyes before she twisted her face away sharply. 'It's nothing. I'm tired from the ride, that's all.'

'If you say so.' He nodded dubiously. 'Now I've let it pass once, but if you call Coira "that woman" or talk to her so rudely again then you'll find me a lot less pleasant about it. Do ye understand?'

'Very well.' Elspeth thrust her jaw out mutinously. 'I'll be polite to her, if it means so much to you, but that's all. Don't expect us to become friends.'

'You ought to give her a chance.'

'And you ought to understand that I'm only saying all of this because I care about you and I don't want you to be hurt again.'

'I do understand that.' He made a humourless sound. 'Trust me, if I didn't, you'd be halfway back to Ross by now, Campbells or no Campbells.'

'What did you say to your sister?' Coira regarded Fergus suspiciously as she climbed into bed beside him a few hours later. 'She could have turned me to ice with her looks when she first arrived, but she hasn't glared at me once all evening. She even thanked me for passing her the salt cellar.'

'Good.'

'I suppose so, but what did you say to her?'

'Nothing that you need to know about.' He reached for her waist, pulling her down to him. 'And definitely nothing I want to talk about at this moment. There are far more interesting things we could be doing.'

'Such as sleeping?' Coira batted her eyelashes. 'You're right. I'm exhausted.'

'Then I'll be quick.' He grinned, sliding his hands down until they came to rest on her hips. 'If that's what you really want?'

'Oh, I didn't say *that*.' She stretched out on top of him, propping her chin on his chest so that she could stare straight down into his gorgeous brown eyes. 'And I suppose I ought to be grateful for whatever it was you *did* say.'

'Good point. Feel free to thank me in whatever way you see fit.'

'Whatever way I see fit...' she repeated the words, pursing her lips thoughtfully for several seconds before wriggling downwards, touching her tongue to the edge of his nipple and then licking the skin around it. 'How's that?'

He groaned. 'It's an excellent start.'

'Good.' She slid across to the other side and did the same thing. 'Is there really nothing we can do to help your brother?'

He lifted his head, his expression incredulous. 'You're asking me about that *now*?'

'You said that we'd talk about it later.'

'I still say that. Much later. Tomorrow.'

'But what if he's in real danger?'

'He is, but Ross ordered me to stay here so that's what I'm doing. He'd also want me to protect Elspeth, so I'm doing that, too. Trust me, he knows what he's about. Now have some pity and go back to what you were doing before I have to beg.'

She smiled and placed a hand on his stomach, feeling the muscles beneath contract beneath her fingertips. 'Somehow I can't imagine you begging.'

'There's a first time for everything.'

'I quite like the idea.' She raised herself over him, straddling his hips with her thighs, feeling strangely powerful all of a sudden. 'Isn't that odd?'

'I thought you were supposed to be thanking me?'

'Maybe we can do both.' She lowered her body just enough to brush the tips of her breasts across his chest. 'Thank you.' She kissed his neck, lowering her bottom half this time and skimming herself gently against him. 'Thank you.' She wriggled, darting away again as he pushed upwards. 'Thank y—'

'You're welcome.' His hands gripped her bottom, his voice guttural as he pulled her back down. 'Now, come here. *Please.*'

She moaned as he entered her, revelling in the sensation. His shaft seemed to fill her completely, hard and hot and strong. When she moved, it felt even better, rubbing against her in a way that sent tiny vibrations pulsing out through her body.

'Wait… Let me.' She put her hands on his chest as he made to roll them both over, drawing herself up and then sliding downwards again, starting to rock back and forth on top of him. She wasn't entirely sure what she was doing, simply following her instincts as the vibrations grew stronger, building in intensity until she thought that she couldn't bear the tension any longer. And then finally it peaked, erupting in a hot burst of sensation that seemed to spiral outwards along every nerve ending, wrenching a cry of pleasure from her throat as all her muscles seemed to contract at once.

'Ah...' She collapsed on top of him at the same moment as his arms came around her, holding her tight as he thrust upwards a few more times and then found his own release.

'Fergus...' She murmured his name in a daze, unable to move as the last quivers of sensation rippled outwards. 'That was...'

'Aye.' He already sounded half-asleep. 'If that's you being grateful, then remind me to have words with my sister more often.'

Chapter Seventeen

As nights went, it had certainly been memorable, Coira thought, humming a melody to herself as she tidied up the children's bedchamber. Not to mention incredibly, unbelievably, spine-tinglingly pleasurable. Several hours later and she was still basking in the afterglow of so many sensations. As for her mind, it was hard to focus on any specific task when her thoughts persisted in wandering back to certain events. Four separate events in fact, each better than the last. It made her wonder what the next night would bring. If only they could hurry up and get through the day. The hours had never dragged so badly before. Even after a sennight of making up for lost time, she felt greedy for another sight of Fergus, but he was somewhere outside, keeping himself busy as usual. She wondered if he ever had trouble concentrating like this…

'You have a baby?'

She spun around to find Elspeth standing just inside the room, her shocked stare focused on the cot where Ailis was fast asleep.

'Aye.' Coira nodded, surprised that Elspeth actually

looked interested. 'Although she's not such a babe any more. She's almost a year old now.'

'May I take a closer look? I promise I won't disturb her.'

'Of course. She'll probably be waking for something to eat soon anyway.'

'She's lovely.' Elspeth's expression softened as she peered down into the cot. 'What's her name?'

'Ailis. After my mother.'

'That's bonny. A bonny name for a bonny girl. I sometimes wish I'd been named after my mother. I lost her when I was so young, it would have been something to hold on to.'

'That's why I chose it, to keep that bond, and my husband didn't care about naming a girl.' Coira bowed her head. 'How did you lose your mother?'

'Some kind of sickness, the pestilence that swept through the land years ago.'

'I remember. I lost my parents the same way. Myself and my brother survived, but so many people were lost... It was a horrible time.'

'Aye.' Elspeth swallowed. 'But Ailis here is a delight. I didn't know that you had a baby.'

'Neither did Fergus when he arrived.'

Elspeth looked up again, her mouth forming an O-shape. 'That must have been quite a shock for him.'

'It was, but he's wonderful with her.'

'Fergus? My brother Fergus?'

'The very same.' She laughed at the other woman's doubtful expression. 'I was surprised, too, but trust me, he's a natural with bairns. I'm actually starting to fear Ailis favours him over me.'

'Well, that's certainly unexpected, but as for you and he...' Elspeth paused as if she were choosing her words with care. 'You seem happy?'

'Aye.' Coira busied herself with tidying again, aware of her cheeks flaming as she wondered what exactly her sister-in-law meant by 'happy' and whether she'd overheard them in bed the previous night. At the time, she'd been so wrapped up in the moment that she hadn't taken a great deal of care to muffle her cries. And there had been one particularly long, drawn-out cry during that last time... More of a scream really.

'I admit it took us a wee while to get to know each other, but now...' She straightened her shoulders, put her embarrassment aside and looked her new sister-in-law straight in the eye. 'Now I realise what a huge mistake I made six years ago. I misjudged him.'

'You did. Badly.' Elspeth's steely gaze flickered. 'Although I suppose to someone who hadn't grown up with him he might have come across as a little intimidating. And grumpy. And terse. Maybe it was an easy mistake to make.'

'Thank you.'

'Just don't do anything like it ever again. Fergus thinks that Ross and I don't know how he felt about you back then, but we could tell. You broke his heart.'

Coira swallowed, her own heart aching at the idea. 'I know that now. Would it help to know that I was miserable afterwards, too?'

'A little,' Elspeth answered honestly. 'So your first husband wasn't kind to you?'

'That's one way of putting it.'

'Then I'm sorry for that. Truly. Still, if you ever hurt Fergus again—'

'I won't. We both want to put the past behind us.'

'Well then, it seems that we understand each other.' Elspeth lifted her shoulders as if the matter were over and done with. 'Anyway, he'll make me sleep in the stables if I hurt your feelings again so I suppose I should start being nice to you.'

'Well, in that case...' Coira sniffed the air and then glanced towards the cot. Her daughter's eyes were wide open as if she'd been eavesdropping on their conversation, but the look of mild concentration on her face suggested she was now busy attending to other, more pressing concerns. 'How good are you at tending to bairns?'

'Me? I don't think I've ever...'

'Then here's your chance.' Coira bent over and lifted her daughter on to the floor. 'You can help me to clear up the mess. Ailis, meet your new Aunt Elspeth.'

'What happened to you?' Fergus lifted both of his eyebrows as he entered the solar around noon to find his sister sprawled inelegantly on the daybed, her arms flung out to the sides with her legs dangling off the end.

'I had no idea that babies were so exhausting.' Elspeth sounded dazed. 'They're relentless.'

'You've been tending to Ailis?'

'Tending to her, playing with her, cleaning her...' She wrinkled her nose in distaste. 'I can't get the smell out of my nostrils. You wouldn't believe the number of times a baby can soil itself in just one morning.'

'I'm starting to get a rough idea.' His lips twitched

in amusement. 'It's good to see you taking your duties as an aunt seriously.'

'If that's you trying to be funny then you can go and—'

'Fergus!' His wife interrupted whatever insult his sister was about to hurl at him, smiling a welcome as she came in through the minstrels' gallery, rubbing her hands on a piece of linen. 'I didn't expect to see you back here so soon.'

'I hope that's not a complaint.' He closed the distance between them in two strides, gathering her into his arms and kissing her as if they hadn't seen each other in a month. Even spending a morning away from her now felt like a trial. Whatever power it was she had over him seemed to be growing stronger by the day.

'All right, you've made your point.' Elspeth sounded exasperated. 'Either let her go or take her somewhere more private because I'm too tired to move and I really don't want to sit here and watch *that*.'

'Mmm? I'd forgotten you were still here,' Fergus murmured against Coira's lips, grinning as his sister let out a squeak of indignation.

'This is where I sleep!'

'Fair enough.' He let go of his wife reluctantly, although the idea of going somewhere more private was extremely tempting at that moment. 'I just came to see how the two of you were getting along.'

'Oh, we've had a lovely morning.' Coira's tone was a little too enthusiastic, enough to tell him that she'd had her own form of revenge for his sister's rudeness the day before. 'Haven't we, Elspeth?'

'Aye, if you ignore all the…you know.' His sister

shook her head. 'I'm starting to think I may need to call off my wedding to MacLachlan. He'll probably want an heir and I'm not sure I'm cut out for motherhood.'

'You did very well for your first day.'

'I still feel like I need wine. A whole barrel, if you have any spare ones lying around?'

'I'll check the cellar.' Fergus laughed before turning back to Coira. 'I actually had another reason for coming to see you. Iver's gone.'

She blinked. 'What do you mean, gone?'

'Malcolm says he left the castle yesterday evening, claiming he had something to do in the village, only it seems he rode off in the other direction.'

'Oh...' She puckered her brow thoughtfully. 'Well, I can't say I'm sorry.'

'Neither am I, but the question is where he went and why.'

'Does it matter?'

'Hopefully not. It's just a feeling.' He reached for her hands, smoothing his fingers along hers. He wasn't entirely certain what he was worried about, but now that it was too late, he wished that he'd kept a closer watch on the disgruntled guard. Elspeth had stayed in the solar out of sight ever since her arrival, but people still knew that a woman had arrived and, given the circumstances, it wouldn't be too hard to guess her identity. 'Anyway, he's gone and it's too late to go after him now. Whatever happens, we'll deal with it.'

'Whatever happens?' Coira's gaze clouded. 'Now you're really making me worry.'

'Don't. I'm probably being overcautious. I thought you should know, but he's probably just gone to make a nuisance of himself somewhere else. No doubt the prospect of real fighting scared him away.'

'I hope you're right. It sounds terrible, but I honestly hope I never set eyes on him again.' She glanced across the room just in time to catch the stricken expression on her sister-in-law's face. 'Elspeth? What's the matter?'

'It's nothing. I…' Her sister-in-law turned her face away, her cheeks paling.

'It's not nothing.' Fergus went to crouch down in front of her. 'Tell us.'

Elspeth sniffed. 'It's just what you said about dealing with whatever happens. I don't want to bring any trouble on you, too.'

'Too?'

'Aye.' She twisted her hands together. 'I know that I should have told you yesterday, but I couldn't bear the thought of talking about it then. The truth is, the Abbey was attacked. The Campbells must have found out where I was hiding. Thankfully, it was just a skirmish and no one was badly hurt, but it felt like a warning. That's why I came straight here despite the rain. I left my women behind for their own safety.'

'A warning?' Fergus rubbed a hand over his jaw. 'That doesn't make any sense. If the Campbells knew where you were, why would they warn you about their intentions? They could have captured you there and then.'

'I don't know what they were thinking, I'm just glad I got away.' Elspeth curled her hands into fists. 'I sent a messenger to Ross and then rode straight here. I've tried not to think about it since, but every time I close my eyes, I remember. It was horrible, seeing so many men charging towards us and feeling so defenceless.' Her eyes flashed. 'If only I knew how to fight! Then I could have done something.'

'Women are no match for warriors.'

'So Uncle always said, but you don't *know* that until you give us a chance. I want to learn how to fight!'

'She's right,' Coira interceded. 'A woman ought to know how to defend herself and those she loves.'

'Aye, and if it were just up to me, I'd agree, but Mac-Lachlan might have other ideas.'

'Probably.' Elspeth's mouth twisted. 'He'll probably want me to sew his shirts, too.' She glanced across at Coira. 'No offence.'

'None taken.'

'In any case, I should ride on to his castle. If he's not back from Edinburgh already, then he will be soon. I need to get away from here before the Campbells find out where I am again.'

'Not until the weather improves.' Fergus shook his head. 'The roads aren't fit for travel after so much rain. You were lucky you reached here without any accidents.'

'In the meantime, you shouldn't be alone, not after what you've been through.' Coira put a hand on Elspeth's shoulder. 'Come down to the hall for the meal this evening. Let us entertain you properly as our guest.'

'Our *secret* guest.' Fergus threw her a warning look.

'There are no secrets in a castle, you ought to know that, and now Iver's gone, I can honestly say that I trust everyone here. Please, Elspeth, let me look after you like a sister.'

'A sister?' Elspeth's expression warmed again. 'Aye, I'd like that.'

* * *

'You didn't have to do all of this.' Fergus edged his chair closer to Coira's at the high table, lifting his gaze as the minstrels on the gallery struck up a jig. 'We ought to be saving food.'

'We're still saving plenty.' She tipped her head towards him, smiling. 'But Elspeth needs to have her mind taken off what happened to her. It must have been terrible and, besides, everyone here is on edge, too, waiting to see what's going to happen with the Campbells. Tonight gives them a chance to put their worries aside for a few hours and enjoy themselves.'

He knitted his brows, unable to resist one last glower. 'I suppose you might be right.'

'I know I am.' She touched a finger to the middle of his forehead before sliding it slowly across his eyebrow and down the side of his face. 'So you can stop frowning. There are still plenty of guards outside, aren't there?'

'Aye.'

'And they'll call out if they see or hear anything suspicious?'

'Aye.'

'Then what good would it do if we all just sat around being anxious?'

'I never had any intention of sitting around. I was planning to be lying down with you.'

She laughed and blushed at the same time. 'Much as I'd enjoy that, Elspeth is still our guest and she needs some distraction. We couldn't just go to bed and neglect her.'

'We did last night.'

'Last night she was exhausted. Anyway, today is different. She's accepted me as a sister. That's something to be celebrated, don't you think?'

'I suppose so,' he relented, allowing himself a smile as he watched his little sister hurling herself around the dance floor. Even as a child, she'd always thrown herself into whatever she was doing. After everything that she'd been through over the past few days, it was impossible not to admire that kind of resilient spirit. She probably *would* have made a good warrior, given the chance. 'At least she seems to be enjoying herself.'

'So is Grizel.' Coira pointed discreetly. 'I can't believe I never guessed there was something going on between her and Euan. Looking at them now, it's so obvious.'

'Aye.' Fergus chuckled. Euan in particular was making the most of the opportunity to touch his dance partner in public. If there had been anyone else in the castle who hadn't known about their relationship before, they certainly did now.

'What about you?' Coira's hand slipped into his under the table. 'Do *you* dance?'

He gave a snort. 'What do you think?'

'You must know how to.'

'Aye, I've just never done it willingly before.'

'But you wouldn't refuse your own wife?'

'Coira…'

'Especially if she promises to make it up to you later?' She batted her lashes. 'At least twice.'

He stood up and made a bow. 'Will ye do me the honour of a dance, my lady?'

'I'd be delighted.' She curtsied sedately before tightening her fingers around his and dragging him determinedly around the edge of the table.

'This is the first and last time, do ye understand?' He curved one of his arms behind her back and then reached the other across her stomach, ignoring Elspeth's amazed expression as they joined the line of dancers. If he wasn't mistaken, she'd just almost tripped over in surprise. 'I'm not making a habit of it.'

'That's what you think.' Coira smiled smugly. 'Because I happen to enjoy dancing.'

'There's always Malcolm.'

'Hush!' She laughed, twirling in a circle beneath his arm. 'I don't want any other man. I only want you.'

'Then you're in luck.' He pulled her against him, somewhat harder than the dance demanded. 'Because you already have me.'

She stared into his face for a long moment before twirling away again, leaving him to ponder his own words with a vague sense of surprise and a stronger one of alarm. He'd said them without thinking, but they were true. There was no point in pretending otherwise any more. No matter how much he'd intended to guard his heart, it was too late. He loved her. He was in love with her all over again and there was no going back now.

He didn't know whether to dance or cry.

Chapter Eighteen

'**G**ood morning, Malcolm.' Coira smiled a greeting to the steward as she passed him on her way into the hall a few days later, Ailis balanced on her hip. 'Are you feeling well? You look a little pale.'

'It's nothing, my lady. A touch of rheum, that's all.' Malcolm tugged on his beard before hurrying past, his head bent. 'I'll be well again soon enough, I'm sure.'

She watched him go with concern before walking across to Fergus. He was leaning back against one of the tables while staring hard at the floor, his hands gripping the wood so tightly that she could see the silvery gleam of his knuckles beneath his skin.

'Fergus?' She touched his shoulder. 'What is it? What's happened? I just passed Malcolm and he didn't seem himself at all.'

'Hmm?' He seemed to come back to himself abruptly. 'Oh, some of our scouts have returned.'

'Have they seen something?'

'No, but they've heard rumours about Castle Sween. You know Ross sent word of a skirmish a couple of weeks ago? Well, it sounds as if the Campbells have attacked again.'

'Oh, no.' She put a hand to her throat. 'Are they—?'

'As far as I know, everyone's all right, even though it was more of a concerted effort than last time.'

She slumped in relief. 'What can we do?'

'Not a damn thing. Ross ordered me to stay put.'

'But—'

'He must have known that this was likely to happen or he wouldn't have sent Elspeth away in the first place,' Fergus interrupted her. 'That means he must have a plan, but I wish I knew what it was. I hate the thought of sitting here doing nothing while he might be in danger.' He slid one hand around her waist and touched the other to Ailis's chin, tickling her when she giggled.

'I'm sorry.' Coira moved closer, leaning into his shoulder. 'I wish there was something else I could say.'

'Unfortunately, that's not all the scouts told us. We already knew from Ross's message that he thought the Campbells had split their forces. Now there's another rumour about part of Campbell's army heading north.'

'After so much rain? Surely that's unlikely.'

'But not impossible, especially if Alexander Campbell thinks we won't be expecting it. He's relentless and brutal and he won't care about any hardship to his men either. If he wants his army to march, then they'll march.'

'But why would they have divided their forces like that?'

'They might not have thought they needed their whole army for Sween. Or they might have been planning a siege and intending to catch us by surprise at the same time, but the rain's slowed them down. It would make sense for them to pick a smaller target like here. It's almost October and if they can't break into either Barron or Sween before the weather worsens, then they'll need somewhere else to garrison their men over the winter. That's if they don't return to Ireland.'

'So what do we do? And what about Elspeth? She's planning on leaving tomorrow.'

'It might be a good idea for her to go as planned. We don't want her to end up trapped here with us. On the other hand…' His frown deepened. 'Campbell's men might just as easily be heading for MacLachlan territory. Which means that she would be riding directly into harm's way. I'd want to go with her just in case, but I dare not risk leaving you and the children. Either way, it's a risk.'

'Maybe you should let Elspeth decide?'

'I already have and I'm going.' The woman in question appeared in the doorway. 'Yes, I was listening and, yes, it's dangerous, but we need as many allies against the Campbells as we can get, which means me marrying MacLachlan as soon as possible. I've stayed here too long already. I only meant to stay for a couple of nights and it's been almost a week.'

'That doesn't matter.' Fergus sounded sombre. 'The point is, I can't take you there safely and guard Castle Barron at the same time.'

'Then I'll go with the escort Ross gave me.'

'That's not enough men.' He put a hand up when she was about to argue. 'I'll think about it, and about how many men I can spare, but first of all, I need to send a messenger to Brody. If the Campbells are coming, then we need him to be ready to help us. It might be our only hope.'

Afternoon had turned to evening and the shadows were beginning to lengthen by the time Fergus finally returned to the solar.

'All right.' His eyes fixed straight upon Elspeth. 'You can leave first thing in the morning, but you'll take some of my scouts with you. They'll ride ahead and make sure the track is safe. If there's any sign of trouble or anything that looks remotely suspicious, I want you to turn around and come straight back here. Is that understood?'

'Completely.' Elspeth nodded firmly.

'Are you certain about this?' Coira put her sewing aside and went to put her arms around him.

'No. I don't like it, but Elspeth's right, we need the alliance with the MacLachlans.'

'Well then, perhaps... What's that?' She twisted her head at the sound of running footsteps in the stairwell. 'Euan?'

'You'd better come and see this!' The guard burst into the room, barely pausing to draw breath. 'All of you!'

'The Campbells?' Fergus didn't hesitate, grabbing Coira's hand and pulling her behind him.

'An army of them!'

'What?' She gasped, her whole body engulfed by a cold sweat of fear as they hurried down the stairs, out of the keep, across the bailey and up on to the gatehouse roof. Unfortunately, Euan hadn't exaggerated. 'Army' was the only way to describe the large gathering of men in the distance, too many to count, marching around the edge of the loch towards them.

'It seems the Campbells have chosen their target.' Fergus's voice was hard. 'We need to send another messenger to Brody and tell him to come now.'

'One of the men is already preparing.' Euan was still panting.

'Good.' Fergus squeezed her hand. 'I'll be back in a few minutes.'

Coira swallowed painfully as she looked out over the battlements, watching the slow, but inexorable, approach of the army towards them, their steel weapons glittering dangerously in the fading sunlight. There was no mistaking their purpose.

'There's so many of them...' she whispered to Elspeth. 'Too many to fight.'

'It's not always about numbers, but I'm afraid you might be right.'

'What do we do?'

'We listen to what they have to say for themselves.' Fergus returned at the same moment as a rider galloped out of the gates beneath their feet, riding as if a whole pack of wolves were on his tail. 'Then we defend ourselves as best we can and hope that Brody comes to our aid in time.'

'Oh, no!' Coira sucked in a breath, struck with a fresh sense of horror. 'It can't be!'

'What is it?' He was at her side in a moment.

'I don't believe it. Kendrick!'

'What? Where?'

'At the front beside that man with the black hair.'

'That's Alexander Campbell.' Fergus narrowed his eyes, peering closer. 'I'd recognise the bastard anywhere, although I don't see any sign of his son Calum.'

'But Kendrick and Campbell? Why would they be together? How would they even have met?' She gasped as a new idea struck her. 'Could it be at Brody's command? Do you think he's changed sides?'

Fergus drew his brows together, considering the idea, before shaking his head. 'I doubt it. A large part of Brody's territory is former Campbell land. He stands to lose as much as the rest of us if the Campbells aren't defeated.'

'But maybe he's made a deal with them?'

'No, he's too canny for that. He knows he can count on the support of the MacMillans and MacLachlans so long as he stands firm. Why risk all that to side with an untrustworthy madman like Campbell?'

'Then why is Kendrick here? It doesn't make any sense.'

'No, it doesn't, but I intend to find out the reason.' Fergus took a step backwards as the first enemy soldiers began to line up in front of the castle walls. 'I'm going out there to talk.'

'I'm coming with you.'

'No.' He put a hand on her shoulder. 'It's too dangerous. If Kendrick's made some kind of a deal with Campbell against his father's orders, then he can't be trusted. I'm not letting him within ten paces of you.'

She clamped her teeth together and then nodded, common sense overcoming her desire to stay with him. 'All right, but you're not going alone.'

'Agreed. Euan?'

'I'm willing.'

'Good. Keep your hand on your sword hilt, but stay behind me. Elspeth, stay out of sight. As for the rest of you...' Fergus looked along the line of guards standing with their bows at the ready. 'Keep your arrows nocked, but don't shoot unless I give the order. The last thing we want is to start a fight too soon. We need to stall for as long as possible.'

'Wait!' Coira grabbed at his arm as he started to turn away, trying to think of something to say to him and failing. Her thoughts were swirling, her emotions all convoluted, and she couldn't find the right words. She didn't know what she wanted to say and, besides, they had too many witnesses and too little time. All she knew for certain was that she was terrified of him being hurt. 'Be careful, Fergus. *Please*.'

'I will.' He touched a hand to her cheek, his face softening just for her. 'Trust me.'

Fergus waited until the gates of Castle Barron were firmly closed behind him before striding forward to meet Campbell and Kendrick. They were standing side by side, though it was obvious even from a distance who was in charge. Alexander Campbell wasn't particularly tall and yet somehow he gave the impression of being a giant, drawing all eyes towards him through sheer force of personality. If he hadn't known better, Fergus might have felt sorry for Kendrick. The younger man was several leagues out of his depth and sinking fast.

'MacMillan!' Campbell was the first to speak, greeting him as if they were old friends.

'Campbell. It's been a while.'

'Aye. How long has it been?' Campbell rubbed his chin, pretending to think. 'A couple of months now?'

'Since the day you killed my uncle, that's right.'

'These things happen in battle. I'm sure a warrior like yourself doesn't take it personally.'

'Then you'd be wrong.' Fergus shifted his gaze towards the other man. 'Kendrick. Was it something I said? Or was our hospitality not good enough for you?'

'You know why I'm here.' Kendrick thrust his chin out as if he were trying to assert his own dominance. 'I've come to rescue Coira. She deserves better than you.'

'She doesn't want rescuing.' He clamped down hard on an instinctive rush of anger. It was even greater than he would have expected, but he needed to remain calm. 'She already told you that.'

'Only because she's scared of you. Any fool can see that.'

'Then I must be a fool. You're wrong, Kendrick. She doesn't want you. She never did.'

'I love her!' Kendrick's eyes flashed with temper. 'More than you ever possibly could. She doesn't understand yet, but there's nothing I wouldn't do for her.'

'Such as murdering her first husband, you mean?'

'What?' Kendrick's expression froze as if an icy breeze had just swept through the glen. 'Nevin was attacked by a boar. Everyone knows that.'

'Aye, but was that all that happened?' Fergus made his tone deliberately taunting. 'From what I've heard, you were the closest man to him when he died.'

'That doesn't mean I killed him!'

'But you have to admit, his accident was very convenient for a man in love with his cousin's wife. Or maybe it wasn't so calculated. Maybe you simply took your chance and pushed him in the way of the boar when nobody else was looking.' He lifted a brow at the guilty flicker in Kendrick's eyes. 'That's the truth, isn't it? You pushed him into its path.'

'No! I just…'

'What?'

'Aye, what?' Campbell's eyes lit up with a look of gleeful interest, as if he were enjoying the exchange. 'I'd hate to think that you've been keeping information from me, MacWhinnie.'

Kendrick's jaw tightened. 'There was no pushing. Nevin mistimed his attack and the boar knocked him down. He was injured and couldn't move so he called to me for help.' His eyes glazed over as if he were watching the scene in his mind. 'He reached a hand out, but then the boar charged again.'

'And you did nothing? You made it look like you were trying to help, but actually left him to be gored?'

'For Coira. Anything I did was for her. You never saw the way he treated her! I did!'

'Then you should have challenged him honourably. Like a man, not a coward.'

'I don't answer to you.' Kendrick's expression hardened and then wavered again. 'How did you find out?'

'I didn't. I just suspected, that's all. Until now.' Fergus didn't bother to hide his disgust. 'You're not as clever as you seem to think, Kendrick. Just like your cousin.'

'Does Coira know?'

'Not yet. I thought I'd spare her that part.'

'It doesn't matter anyway.' Kendrick tossed his head defiantly. 'She loathed him.'

'Aye. Then again, I loathe you, but that doesn't mean I necessarily want you dead. Not yet anyway.' Fergus jerked his head towards the ramparts behind him. 'If it comes to a fight, however, you'll be the first man I look for.'

'Enough of this!' Campbell interrupted finally. 'I didn't come here to argue. I came for the woman. Hand her over.'

Fergus levelled a cold glare in his direction. 'You think I'll give up my wife to you?'

'Not her, the other one.' Campbell leered. 'Your sister.'

'Elspeth?' He made his face studiously blank. 'I don't know what you're talking about.'

'Come now, let's not play games. We both know that she's here. She arrived a few days ago and there's no point in pretending otherwise.'

Fergus ground his teeth. If Campbell wanted Elspeth, then it was because he knew he could use her as a weapon against both him *and* Ross. The question was how he'd found out where she was hiding and how he and Kendrick had come to join forces? Kendrick had left long before Elspeth's arrival and the only person who'd left the castle since had been...

'Iver!' he roared over the heads of the soldiers. 'Show yourself!'

Campbell laughed. 'And they told me you were the stupid one. You're smarter than they say, MacMillan. Unfortunately, that won't help you today. Hand over your sister and we'll leave you in peace.'

'Tell your spy that when I'm finished with you, I'll be coming for him next.' Fergus threw a contemptuous look at Kendrick before turning back to face Campbell. 'You expect me to believe that you'd just leave?'

'Aye. No offence to your home, but I'd rather have Sween and she's the perfect way to get it.'

'If you want her so badly, then why didn't you just take her from the Abbey?'

'Abbey?' Campbell looked genuinely confused. 'I've no idea what you're talking about.'

'Didn't you attack the Abbey?'

'Contrary to some people's opinions, I do have some standards. Now stop stalling and hand her over.'

Fergus clenched his jaw. Unlikely as it seemed, he actually believed that, in this case, Alexander Campbell was telling the truth, which meant that someone else must have attacked the Abbey... Not that he had time to wonder about that now, he reminded himself, dragging his thoughts back to the matter in hand.

'You're too late. My sister was here, it's true, but she left. Just this morning, as it happens.'

'Is that so?' Campbell's gaze flickered suspiciously. 'Where did she go?'

'MacLachlan territory. To wed.'

'You're lying.'

'And you're wasting time.'

'If there was any chance of us catching up with her, then you wouldn't have told me.' Campbell's tone was smug. 'Besides, I'm not in the mood to ride any more today. I've a mind to tear this place down stone by stone instead, just to find out whether or not you're lying.'

'Then you'll lose men.'

'Men are expendable. It might be worth it just to watch you and MacWhinnie fight over this bride of yours. She must be quite special.' His lips curved lasciviously. 'Maybe I'll let you kill each other and then take her for myself, eh?'

'She's mine.' Kendrick's expression contorted. 'We had a deal.'

'Aye, so we did. In that case, this conversation is over.' Campbell put his hands up. 'You're fortunate that I'm feeling so tired, MacMillan. You have until tomorrow morning to change your mind about your sister. Open your gates at dawn or we'll find another way to come in and look for her, whether she's really there or not.'

He threw one last appraising glance at the battlements before turning away, leaving Fergus and Kendrick alone.

'I take it your father has no idea you're here?' Fergus speared the other man with a look. 'Betraying your own clan?'

'My father doesn't understand how I feel.'

'*He* doesn't understand… *She* doesn't understand… You cause a lot of misunderstandings, it seems.' Fergus jerked his head towards Campbell's retreating back. 'I suppose you know he can't be trusted? He'll turn on you, as well, once you're no longer useful to him.'

'In that case, maybe *we* ought to come to some arrangement.' Kendrick glanced over his shoulder, his voice turning crafty. 'Give Coira to me now and you could save us from fighting at all.'

'You think that Campbell will just let you withdraw?'

'No, but I could change sides once the battle starts, strike from the rear while you repel him from the walls.

Then I'll tell my father it was all a scheme to help you and no one will be any the wiser.'

'Very clever, but if you think that I'll just hand Coira over to you then you're mad. Maybe it's down to the company you've been keeping.'

'MacWhinnie!' Campbell bellowed in the distance. 'Enough talking!'

'Just think about it,' Kendrick muttered, turning away. 'It's the only hope you have of saving yourselves. Otherwise, I'll see you at dawn.'

'What did they say?'

Coira and Elspeth came sprinting out of the gate-house the moment the gates closed behind Fergus. Briefly, he thought about lying, but it would do no good. Neither of them was likely to accept that Alexander Campbell's sudden arrival so soon after Elspeth's was just a coincidence. As for Kendrick's presence, there was only one possible explanation. A single glimpse of Coira's face showed that she knew it, too.

'Campbell's looking for you.' He turned to his sister first.

'What?' Elspeth pressed her hands to her mouth, horrified. 'You mean, they've come here to capture me?'

'I told them you'd already left.'

'Did they believe you?'

'No.'

'But how did they find out Elspeth was here?' Coira put a hand on his arm. 'And so quickly, too?'

'Iver.' He muttered an oath. 'He must have ridden straight to find Kendrick. I wouldn't be surprised if he's been spying on you for a while.'

'That deceitful, underhand bastard.' She glared at the gates as if she could spear Iver through them. 'So what do we do now?'

'They've given us until dawn to surrender Elspeth. Otherwise, we fight.'

'Over me?' Elspeth's face blanched. 'No, you can't.'

'Yes, we can. The men are ready and the walls are strong.'

'But—'

'No buts.' Fergus clenched his jaw. 'You're my sister and if you're about to say what I think you're about to say, then you can put it out of your mind right now.'

'I don't want people to die because of me.'

'Neither do I, but I'm not handing you over to a monster like Campbell, not for any reason. Now I need to speak to the men.' He threw a look of appeal towards Coira as Elspeth stormed away. 'Look after her. Don't let her do anything stupid.'

'I won't.' She held his gaze sombrely. 'Kendrick's here for me, isn't he? He's betraying his own clan for me?'

'Aye.' He reached for her wrists, wrapping his fingers around them before kissing each in turn, feeling the flicker of her pulse beneath his lips. 'But I won't let him have you, I promise.'

'I know that.' She moved forward, pressing her cheek against his chest so that he couldn't see her face. 'You're a good husband, Fergus.'

Chapter Nineteen

'I have to surrender to Campbell!'

'No.' Coira closed the door to the solar firmly behind them as Elspeth started to pace up and down. 'You heard Fergus. That's not going to happen.'

'Campbell only wants me as a pawn against Ross. He won't hurt me.'

'Maybe not to begin with, but who knows what he might do to convince your brother to give up Sween Castle?'

'Ross won't give up Sween…not ever.'

'And *then* what might Campbell do to you?' Coira started pacing, too. 'You'd be putting Ross in an impossible situation, having to choose between you and his home and people.'

'Fergus is in an impossible situation right now!'

'I know, but neither of your brothers would want you to sacrifice yourself.'

Elspeth opened her mouth to argue some more, closed it again, and then flung her arms out, clenching her fists. 'I *hate* feeling so powerless when I'm the only person who can do something about it! You've seen the size of their army. We're outnumbered twice over. If they attack—'

'Fergus knows what he's doing. If anyone can defeat them, it's him.' Coira clasped both of her hands over her forehead. 'I just can't believe that Kendrick has sided with Campbell.'

Elspeth stopped pacing to look at her enquiringly. 'Who is this Kendrick anyway?'

'My first husband's cousin. He claims he's in love with me.'

'No!' Elspeth's eyes widened. 'Do you think he's come for you?'

'Aye. I told him a while ago that I don't share his feelings and I'm happy with Fergus, but he refused to believe me. He refused to believe anything I told him! It's like he thinks I don't know my own mind.'

'Men!' Elspeth started marching up and down again. 'Most of them are like that. My brothers are better than most, but they still think they know best. So Campbell wants me, Kendrick wants you and my stupid brother is prepared to let good men die to defend us.'

'Don't call him that.' Coira put her hands on her hips. 'He's not stupid.'

Contrary to her expectations, Elspeth's face softened. 'You're right, he's not. I meant honourable. Stupid and honourable.'

'Unfortunately, there doesn't seem to be anything we can do about it.'

'We'll see about that.' Elspeth caught her bottom lip between her teeth and chewed thoughtfully for a few seconds. 'First, we need to know exactly what was said. They were talking for long enough, which means there might be some way out of this that Fergus isn't telling us. Who was that guard who went with him? He would know.'

'Euan. He won't tell us anything…' Coira smiled slowly. 'Although there's someone else he might talk to…'

'I found out, my lady.' Grizel crept into the solar, speaking in a whisper. 'You were right. We have until dawn to hand over Lady Elspeth or they'll attack.'

'Isn't there any room for negotiation?'

'There's only one chance.'

'What?'

'You.' Grizel's gaze darted from Coira to Elspeth and then back again. 'Euan was a few feet away, but he overheard what Kendrick said to your husband after Campbell stalked off. He admitted that he was only here for you and he said…' She lowered her voice even further. 'He said that if we hand you over to him then he'll change sides once the fighting starts and attack Campbell from the rear.'

Coira sank down on to a chair. 'Kendrick said that?'

'Aye.'

'So if I go to him then we'll be the larger army? Or equal, at least.'

'It doesn't make any difference.' Elspeth waved a hand dismissively. 'You can't go.'

'Why not?'

'Because if Fergus won't let *me* go, then he definitely won't let you.'

'Maybe it's not up to him.' She lifted her chin resolutely. 'Maybe you're not the only person who can do something to prevent bloodshed.'

'Oh, no.' Elspeth started to shake her head. 'You can't tell me not to sacrifice myself and then do it yourself.'

'It's not the same situation. There's one huge difference between Campbell and Kendrick.'

'Which is?'

'Kendrick isn't planning to use me to manipulate anyone else. He won't hurt me either.'

'You don't know that for certain, my lady.' Grizel sounded anxious. 'Euan said there was also some talk about Kendrick doing something to Nevin. He said Fergus accused him and he looked guilty.'

'Does he have any idea what it was?'

'No. Euan couldn't make it all out because he was standing behind, but it must have been serious because even Campbell looked surprised.'

Coira scrunched her mouth up, considering. Fergus had probably been referring to him falling in love with his cousin's wife, but it didn't matter anyway. Kendrick still wouldn't hurt her and it made a lot more sense for her to go than Elspeth.

She pushed herself back to her feet and walked across to the window. The sun was almost over the horizon now, bathing the world in a deep orange glow that belied the deadly situation they found themselves in. The soldiers in the camp outside looked so small and harmless at a distance, too, their metal pikes seeming more like toys than weapons, but it was just an illusion. If she didn't do something, then dawn would reveal the terrible truth.

'I don't know why we're even discussing this.' Elspeth came to join her. 'I admit that it sounds like a safer option, but Fergus is hardly likely to let you just walk out through the gates.'

'He doesn't need to.' Coira turned around again, filled with a new sense of resolve. 'He doesn't need to know anything about it. There's another way out. A tunnel that comes out into the woods on the hillside.'

'Really?' Elspeth looked impressed. 'But what about that man who already betrayed you? If he knows about it, then there could be men waiting at the other end. They could capture you and then use it to get into the castle.'

'I doubt Iver is aware of its existence. Malcolm showed me the door once, but he said that it hadn't been opened for years and I don't remember anyone else ever talking about it. Besides, it's locked at this end. Once I'm through, you can turn the key behind me as a precaution.'

'I don't like the sound of that.' Grizel exchanged a wary look with Elspeth. 'What if the tunnel's collapsed in the middle? You could find yourself trapped.'

'It's a risk I'll have to take.' Coira stiffened her shoulders. 'It's the only other way out of the castle and if I go to Kendrick tonight then Fergus won't find out anything about it until dawn.'

'At which point he'll kill me.' Elspeth rolled her eyes. 'So it'll all have been for nothing anyway.'

'You know perfectly well he won't lay a finger on you. He'll be angry, but he won't hurt anyone. Whereas, if I don't go, we're outnumbered.'

'What if Kendrick doesn't keep his word?' Grizel asked quietly.

'He might not,' Coira admitted after a few tense seconds. 'He'll know that Fergus won't just let the matter rest if he changes sides, but once he has me then even if he doesn't attack Campbell like he promised, he'll have no more reason to stay and fight either. He can head for MacWhinnie lands and rely on his father's protection.'

'But he's disobeyed his father's orders. What if Brody refuses to help him?'

'It'll be his word against Fergus's and Kendrick will probably claim it was all a ploy to rescue me. The important thing is that if he abandons Campbell's army at dawn then you'll have fewer men to defend against. Then, when it's all over, Fergus can come for me.'

'*If* Fergus wins.' Elspeth looked solemn.

'He will. He has to.'

'And what might happen to you in the meantime? If Kendrick says he's in love with you and you go to him...' Elspeth made a face. 'If you really want to persuade him to abandon Campbell then you'll need to pretend you feel the same way about him.'

'I know. I don't like the idea either, but I'll handle it somehow.' Coira swallowed heavily. 'Whichever way you look at the situation, this seems like our only chance.'

'You might be right, my lady.' Grizel nodded though she still sounded dubious. 'It's the best of all our horrible choices, but don't leave straight away. We've sent two messengers to Brody MacWhinnie today and news travels fast through the glens. It's still possible that he'll send men to help us in time.'

'I hope so, but it's a good eight hours' ride to his fortress and it's almost dark now.'

'But it's still possible.'

'All right,' Coira agreed. 'I won't leave until an hour before dawn, but right now, we have to go down to the hall and behave completely normally. Or as normally as possible under the circumstances.'

'No.' Elspeth clamped a hand around her arm. 'I can't let you do this. I can't let you sacrifice yourself for me, especially after I was so horrible to you to begin with. Now that I've seen you with Fergus, I can see how much you care for him.'

'I love him.' She smiled as she spoke, feeling as if all the confused and confusing thoughts and emotions that had been swirling inside her before had finally coalesced into one true statement. She loved him. She wanted to stay where she was and grow old with him, but if she didn't go to Kendrick then Castle Barron would be overrun for certain and Fergus would most likely be killed. Which meant that she had no choice but to run away with another man all over again, the one thing that would hurt her husband the most. She only hoped that this time he would understand why she was doing it.

'You do?' Elspeth's eyes looked misty.

'With all my heart.' She unpeeled her sister-in-law's fingers from around her arm. 'Which is why I can't allow you to be dragged away to be used as a weapon against his brother.'

'I still think...'

'*And* I love my children. I need them to be safe. If

there's any way for me to reduce the number of men Campbell can use against us, then I have to do it.'

Elspeth seemed to hold her breath for an unnaturally long time before nodding. 'Very well. Then I promise you this. If we're overrun or our defences fail, then I'll give myself up. I won't let anything happen to your children, I swear.'

'I'll take them out through the tunnel myself if it comes to it, my lady,' Grizel added.

'Thank you.' Coira looked between them both gratefully. 'Then we're agreed. This is the best way. Or at least we have to hope so.'

Tucking the children into bed that night was even worse than Coira had expected. Ailis had seemed to cling to her more than usual and Gregor had smiled so sweetly as she'd stroked his hair, waiting for him to fall asleep. She'd stayed until they were both snoring lightly before creeping away, squeezing her eyes shut against the tears that threatened to course down her cheeks. She knew she had no choice but to leave them behind. It was for their own safety, for everyone at Castle Barron's safety, but it made her feel as if her heart were splintering into a thousand pieces.

Elspeth nodded to her silently as she passed through the solar. Some clothes and shoes were hidden inside one of the coffers, ready for the morning, and her sister-in-law had insisted on staying awake to help her. All they had to do now was wait.

Taking a deep breath, she opened the door to the bedchamber and stepped inside to find Fergus sitting beside the fireplace, head in his hands, though he sat up quickly when she entered.

'Can I fetch you anything?' She headed straight towards him, her heart aching at the tortured expression on his face.

'No.' He pulled her down into his lap. 'Just you.'

'I'm here.' She curled up against him, tucking her head into the gap between his neck and shoulder and breathing in the musky scent of his skin. 'This is like the calm before the storm, isn't it?'

'Aye. This is always the worst part.' He tightened his arms around her body, gathering her closer.

'But we're ready. The east wall is propped up, the men are prepared.' She repeated the words she'd heard so often, trying to reassure him.

'It's still not enough.' His tone was bleak. 'Campbell's men are experienced warriors. Mercenaries. I wouldn't say this to anyone else, but the best we can hope for is to hold them back long enough for Brody to come to our rescue.' He lifted his hands to her face, brushing aside a lock of hair that had fallen across her forehead. 'Coira, if anything happens to me—'

'Don't.' She tensed. 'Don't say it.'

'I have to. If Campbell gets past the gate—'

'No!' She pulled away, raising her voice this time. 'We're *not* discussing it.'

'All right. I know that you'll do the right thing anyway.'

'You do?'

'Aye. I trust you.' He leaned back in the chair, one corner of his mouth curving upwards. 'Although to be honest, I was hoping you might have thought of a way out of this.'

'I'm afraid not.' She dropped her gaze, wriggling out of his lap and holding a hand out. 'Come and lie down. You need to rest.'

'Something tells me I won't be getting much sleep tonight.'

'Then let me hold you instead.'

'Ah.' He took her hand, rubbing his thumb gently over the backs of her fingers. 'That sounds better anyway.'

They walked to the bed and climbed on top of the covers without undressing. Coira lay down first, curving her body around his as he settled on his back beside her.

'No matter what happens, I'm glad we had this time together, however brief.' His voice sounded hoarse.

'So am I.'

'Right here and now, I'm happy. You make me happy, Coira.'

'You make me happy, too. More than I ever expected.' She pressed her face into his chest to muffle a sob. 'Remember that, tomorrow.'

'As long as I have breath. You remember it, too.' He placed a finger beneath her chin, tilting it up and kissing her tenderly.

'Fergus…'

It was on the tip of her tongue to say that she loved him. She *wanted* to tell him, but she forced the words down again. If she told him now and then he awoke to find her gone in the morning, it would make him feel even worse. Even if he understood why she'd done it, which she desperately hoped that he would, he'd be beside himself with worry at a time when he needed to focus on defending the castle. Defending her children, too. And if anything happened to her…her stomach churned at the thought…it would be easier for him to recover if he never knew how much she'd truly cared. She'd already caused him enough anguish in the past and she couldn't bear to do it again. If they survived and were reunited, *then* she'd tell him. In the meantime, all she could do was show him how she felt.

She lifted her mouth back to his and kissed him, rougher and harder this time, opening his lips with her tongue and sliding it inside as she climbed over him, straddling his waist and pulling at the ties on his braies.

'Coira…' he breathed her name and then his hands were beneath her clothes, grasping hold of her waist as she lowered herself on to him.

They each let out a groan of satisfaction at the same moment and then she started to move, heaving herself upright and holding a hand to his chest to stop him from moving. Slowly, she rolled her hips, trying to hold back the oncoming tide of sensation and failing completely. She tipped her head back as wave upon wave of pleasure rolled over her and then she was on her back and Fergus was on top of her, thrusting so deeply that she felt as though their two bodies were becoming one. She cried out as a fresh burst of feeling exploded inside of her, barely hearing his echoing cry as she felt the warmth of his seed deep inside.

'Fergus…' She wrapped her arms and legs around

him as he withdrew, holding tight. She didn't want to let him go, not now or ever.

'I love you, Coira.' He murmured the words into her hair as he lay beside her and she closed her eyes, feeling tears slide out from beneath the lids, pretending not to hear, hoping that he would think she'd already fallen asleep.

There was a long silence before gradually his breathing slowed and he slept.

And then she waited.

Chapter Twenty

'I was starting to fear you'd fallen asleep.' Elspeth was wide awake and waiting, Grizel seated beside her, when Coira finally crept across the minstrels' gallery and tiptoed into the solar.

She shook her head, unable to say anything in return. Now that the moment of leaving had come, she felt heartsore and sick with anxiety and guilt.

'Coira?' Elspeth peered into her face. 'If you've changed your mind about this, then you can turn around and go back to bed. You only have to say.'

'I haven't. I just…' She threw a cautious glance over her shoulder and then towards the door of the children's room, steeling herself to keep going. 'It hurts, that's all, but this is the only way.'

'Come on, then.' Elspeth passed her the clothes from the coffer and helped her to dress. 'Do you have the key?'

'No need. It's kept in the cellar for emergencies. Malcolm showed me the hiding place.' She pulled on her shoes. 'There. I'm ready, but the two of you should stay here.'

'And what makes you think we'll agree to that?' Elspeth lifted her eyes to the ceiling. 'Besides, there'll be more guards around tonight. You might need us to cause a distraction.' She shrugged when Coira looked at her enquiringly. 'I could faint or something. That's probably what they'll expect from a woman.'

Coira smiled despite herself as they set off down the stairs. A quick peek around the edge of the stairwell and through the door to the hall showed that most of the household were sleeping, but there were still a couple of guards by the main door. There would be no way to slip past them and carry on down the stairwell to the cellars without being noticed.

'I'll deal with them,' Elspeth whispered, handing her lamp to Grizel. 'Then the two of you hurry past.'

'Thank you.' Coira touched her shoulder.

'Just don't get yourself hurt.' To her surprise, Elspeth gave her a quick hug. 'Or Fergus will never forgive me.'

'I'll do my best.'

Coira held her breath, exchanging a swift glance with Grizel as Elspeth stepped out into the hall and immediately struck up a conversation with the guards.

'I can't sleep.' She sounded every inch the haughty lady. 'I need some air.'

'That might not be a good idea tonight, my lady.'

'It'll be light soon enough and I'll be safe with you, won't I?'

'Aye, my lady, but...'

'Come on.' Coira tugged on Grizel's arm, creeping around the edge of the stairwell and scampering down the next set of steps as the still protesting guards followed Elspeth towards the main door.

'I don't think they saw us.' She heaved open the door to the cellar and squeezed through, pausing to lift a small flagstone on the left and retrieve the hidden key. 'But we need to hurry. Elspeth won't be able to distract them for long and you need to get back to the children's room before Fergus wakes.' She made her way hurriedly past row upon row of barrels and casks towards the far wall, moving aside a pile of old boxes to reveal a small door, half her height, covered in dirt and cobwebs. 'There it is.'

'That's it?' Grizel sounded dismayed. 'It's not very big.'

'No-o.' Coira couldn't deny that. It had seemed significantly bigger when Malcolm had first shown it to her. Carefully, she pushed the key into the lock and then twisted, or tried to, feeling a sudden burst of panic. 'Oh, no, I can't turn it.'

'Here, let me try.' Grizel reached forward, wincing as she tried. 'Maybe it's rusted?'

'One more try.' Coira put both hands on the key this time. This was it, the only way to save her husband and children and everyone else she cared about. If she could only turn this key. She was *going* to turn this key, even if she broke all her fingers trying.

She closed her eyes, clenched her teeth and felt it click in the lock. 'I did it!'

'Here.' Grizel helped her to prise the door halfway open before passing her the lamp. 'Don't forget this.'

'Thank you. Now lock the door behind me and get back upstairs.'

'No.' Grizel shook her head determinedly. 'I'm not

locking anything until you've had time to get away. The tunnel could have collapsed in the middle or anything.'

'What about Elspeth?'

'She already knows. We decided this part between us.' Grizel smiled as she plucked at the large cloak around her shoulders. 'Why do you think I'm wearing this? I'll stay down here in the cold for as long as it takes. I'm not risking you getting trapped inside there.'

'You're a good friend.' Coira wrapped her arms around the maid's shoulders, holding her close for a few seconds. 'Good luck and…' She bit her tongue. 'I don't want to say goodbye.'

'I know. Good luck to you, too. Let's just hope this works.'

Coira nodded and hunched over, making her way tentatively into the darkness. The air inside the tunnel was cold and stale-smelling, like dirt and ice and mould all mixed together. Meanwhile, the roof was held up by two rows of wooden beams, though they were cracked and partially collapsed in places, some so rotten-looking that she didn't dare to touch them in case they crumbled away beneath her fingers. No doubt there were worms and worse all around her, she thought with a shudder, pulling her gown up to her waist and crawling on her hands and knees through the dirt, but she had no choice but to keep going. There was no other way out.

She carried on for what felt like hours, but was probably just a few minutes, until the lamp spluttered and she froze, terrified that the flame was about to go out. The tunnel was low and narrow enough, but the thought of being plunged into total darkness made her feel as though the walls were already collapsing in around her, burying her alive. She clenched her fists, trying to maintain some control over her terrified body until, fortunately, the light flared and steadied and she twisted her head to one side, exhaling with relief. Slow, steady movements were what was needed, she told herself sternly, shuffling forward again. She had to remember that. That and the fact that Grizel was still there at the other end. Grizel who wouldn't abandon her. Not as long as—

She stopped abruptly, confronted by a dead end of soil. A dead end? A cold sweat broke out on her forehead. Where was the door? There *had* to be a door! What was the point of a tunnel without a door? Desperately, she placed both her hands against the wall of soil in front of her, but it refused to budge. There were fewer wooden beams here, too, she noticed, as if the tunnel had simply petered out, as if it were unfinished or had been filled in from the opposite end. Her heart began thumping a heavy tattoo on her ribcage and she closed her eyes, beginning to despair, when a memory came back to her. Coming out into woodland meant that the way out was more of a trapdoor, Malcolm had told her, which surely meant... She lifted her hands over her head, bracing them against what felt like leather, and pushed.

For a moment, nothing happened. Then there was a long creak followed by a whooshing sound as she felt the leather give way. It was heavy, but if she used her shoulders... Achingly slowly, she pushed herself to her feet, feeling a rush of triumph as the trapdoor finally thumped on to the ground behind her.

She shook her head, sending a shower of dirt flying

in all directions, and looked around. She was in woodland, just as Malcolm had said, with the first faint glimmers of dawn visible through the trees. Quickly, she extinguished her lamp and closed the trapdoor again, making sure to hide all the evidence of its existence with some branches, although it looked filthy enough as it was. She wasn't even sure that she'd be able to find it again if necessary. Then she brushed herself down and made her way in the direction of the enemy camp. She'd made certain to note the position of Kendrick's tents from the window the evening before since the last thing she wanted was to be taken to Campbell instead. Kendrick was in love with her and could hopefully be persuaded to do what she wanted, whereas Campbell... From what she'd heard, love wasn't a word in his vocabulary. The idea of either herself or Elspeth meeting him face to face sent chills down her spine. Now all she had to do was put on an act for Kendrick and be very, *very* convincing.

'Coira?' Kendrick's jaw dropped as she was hustled into his tent a few minutes later. He looked bleary-eyed, as if he'd just woken up, though his eyes brightened immediately at the sight of her. 'Let her go!' he snapped at his guards, clasping hold of her shoulders and pulling her into his arms. 'Am I dreaming?'

'You're not dreaming.' She forced herself not to tense at the contact.

'Did he send you?'

'Fergus? No, I came by myself.'

'You mean you escaped?' A wondering smile spread over his face. 'You came to me.'

'Aye.' She felt a sharp stab of guilt at the lie. She'd lain awake all night wondering about how to behave with Kendrick and, as horrible as it seemed, playing along seemed the only option. If she berated or condemned him or, worse, told him how much she loved Fergus, then he might attack Castle Barron out of spite. No, she had to make him believe that she'd chosen him despite what she'd said the month before and come willingly. It was the only way she could get him to abandon the fight. 'There's a secret door Fergus doesn't know about. I used that.'

'My love.' Kendrick smoothed cold fingers across her cheeks. 'I should have known you'd find a way. I'm only sorry it's taken me so long to come and claim you.'

She leaned forward, avoiding his eyes. The look in them frightened her. It was too fierce, too intense. It made her want to run.

'Come.' He pressed his lips into her hair and then bent down, lifting her into his arms.

'Wh-what are you doing?' she gasped as he moved towards the camp bed. 'We need to make ready. The attack… It's almost dawn.'

'We have time.'

'But we can't. It's too soon.'

'I've waited for years.'

'But…' She strove to look demure. 'It's all happening so fast. That's why I didn't respond when you first told me how you felt. It took me a while to realise the strength of my own feelings. And now that we're together… I want you, too, but I need a little time to adjust.'

'Of course. I understand.' He set her back on her feet

again. 'Forgive me, my love. I don't want to rush you, but I can't wait for long either.'

'Neither can I.' She forced herself to lift a hand to his face. 'But now you need to make ready. The attack will be starting soon.'

He nodded grimly. 'It pains me that it's come to this. I don't want to destroy your home. It's Gregor's birthright.'

'But surely you won't be destroying it?' She blinked in surprise. 'Not now. You'll be fighting for Castle Barron.'

'Fight *with* your husband? Why would I do that?'

'Because you told him you'd change sides if he gave me up.'

'But he didn't give you up, did he?' Kendrick gave a harsh laugh. 'Besides, I'm not foolish enough to betray Campbell. He'd cut me down where I stood.'

'Then let's run away.' She clutched at the front of his shirt. Their conversation wasn't going remotely the way that she'd hoped. 'Let's leave them to fight it out together. Your father will protect us.'

'Nay, my love. Whichever of them survives will come after me. This way, when the castle falls, so will MacMillan. Then we'll be truly free to be together, as man and wife.'

She stared at him in growing horror, all her plans unravelling. 'So you'll betray your clan twice over? Disobey your father's orders and break your word, too?'

'For you. Because I love you. Coira, you're the only reason I'm here.'

'What kind of a man are you?' She shoved at his chest. 'You're mad!'

'Mad?' His face twisted angrily. 'Is that why you really came? To persuade me to change sides?' He grabbed the back of her neck, hoisting her against him. 'MacMillan did send you, didn't he? He sent you to persuade me to run away!'

'No.' She struggled in his grip. 'He doesn't know anything about it.'

'You still came to deceive me. After everything I've done for you, you were trying to trick me.'

'What do you mean, everything you've done for me?' She aimed a hard kick at his ankles. 'I thought you were my friend and instead you're trying to destroy my son's inheritance!'

'Ungrateful bitch!' He tugged her closer again. 'If it hadn't been for me, you'd still be living with Nevin, being humiliated and mocked and insulted every day! I got rid of him for you!'

'What?' She felt as though her blood had just frozen in her veins. 'You killed Nevin?'

'I saved you! And in return, you attempt to betray me! Pretend to care for me, get me to do what you want and then rejoin your husband, was that your plan? You really prefer that dolt?'

She threw her fist forward instinctively, hitting him in the face hard enough to send him toppling backwards and giving herself time to run towards the tent flap. She was almost there when his fingers caught at her dress, dragging her down to the floor with him.

'Ah!' she cried out, her head hitting the ground so heavily that a shimmer of sparks flared and danced before her eyes.

'He's turned you against me.' Kendrick clambered

over her, his breath hot and damp against her ear. 'But you'll come round, I'll make sure of that. I'll enjoy it, too. In the meantime, I have a castle to attack and you're going to watch.'

Coira closed her eyes in dismay, but the sparks were still there, like shooting stars across her vision. Her whole plan had gone wrong. Kendrick wasn't going anywhere and she'd left Fergus for nothing. Running away from him had been an even bigger mistake the second time than the first.

Her stomach clenched painfully. What was he going to think?

Fergus blinked his way to consciousness. He'd slept fitfully at first, tossing and turning as he'd tried to think of a way to avoid bloodshed, soothed each time by Coira's comforting hand on his forehead or her voice in his ear. Sleep had finally overcome him in the early hours, though his dreams had been so troubled that he'd almost wished it hadn't. Now his head felt marginally clearer and yet something felt wrong, something he couldn't quite identify, like a shadow across his mind. He reached an arm out for Coira, only to find the space beside him empty and cold, as if no one had lain there for hours. He sat up, but the chamber was empty, too. Quickly, he dressed, rushing out into the solar to find his sister waiting for him.

'Elspeth?' He stopped dead, seized by a sense of foreboding. She was standing in the centre of the room, her hands clasped in front of her, her expression far too tense for his liking. 'What is it?'

'You need to stay calm.'

'What is it?'

'Just stay calm.'

'What is it?'

She took a deep breath. 'We only did what we thought was best.'

'Coira!' he bellowed, a bolt of fear shooting through him as he headed for the children's room.

'She's gone to Kendrick.' Elspeth stepped sideways, blocking the way as he made to go around her.

'What?' He stiffened as if an icy wind had just blown into the room, freezing him to the core. It was all he could do to move his lips. 'She's run away?'

'Yes. No! Not like that.' Elspeth shook her head quickly. 'It's nothing like last time.'

'She's run away in the middle of the night to be with another man!' He rounded on her. 'How is that *not* like last time?'

'Because— Wait!'

He ignored her, storming past and barrelling down the stairwell. Coira had done exactly what he'd feared and run away again! Leaving him for another man a second time! After they'd made love so passionately the night before! And just when he'd thought that she'd been starting to care for him. Just when he'd realised how much he cared for her, too! Somehow she'd got past all his defences and into his heart, making him trust her when he'd known that he shouldn't and now she'd abandoned him again just like she had six years ago! And not just him this time, but her children, as well…

He stopped at the bottom of the stairwell so abruptly that Elspeth ran into the back of him, letting out a small yelp as her chin bumped into his shoulders.

'She would never abandon her children.' He turned around slowly.

'Of course not!' Elspeth placed restraining hands on his tunic despite the fact that he was no longer moving. 'And she wouldn't leave you either, you fool! She loves *you*, anyone with eyes can see that! Just like you love her and don't you dare tell me you don't! She's done this to save you! Us. Everyone!'

'I don't understand.' He stared at her, hardly daring to hope. 'Why would she leave me to save me?'

'Because she's gone to persuade Kendrick to change sides like he promised he would!'

'What?' He drew a hand over his brow as the words started to make sense. Half of him felt relieved and elated while the other half... The other half wanted to pound his fists into the wall and start roaring. 'How do you know about that?'

'It doesn't matter how we found out. The point is that Kendrick said he'd change sides if we—'

'He's a murderer!' Fergus exploded. 'You can't trust his word!'

'What?' Elspeth's fingers dropped from his tunic. 'What do you mean? Coira never said—'

'Coira doesn't know.' He raked both hands through his hair. 'I didn't want to tell her. Not yet anyway.'

'Oh, no.' Elspeth staggered backwards against the wall. 'She thought she could trust him not to hurt her.'

He swore so roundly and fluently that she flinched. 'How did she get out?'

'There's an old tunnel in the cellars. She left about an hour ago.' Elspeth spoke through bloodless lips. 'She thought that even if he was lying about changing sides and attacking the Campbells himself, then he'd at least abandon the fight and ride for MacWhinnie territory.'

'He won't.'

'Why not?'

'Because he knows that whoever wins here today will kill him if he flees.' Fergus clenched his jaw as several images darted through his mind, images of what Kendrick might do to Coira once he got hold of her, what he might already have done…

'But his father…?'

'Brody won't be able to protect him from me. I'll make Campbell look like a mewling kitten.'

'So what do we do now?' Elspeth stared at him helplessly.

'There's only one thing to do.' He wrenched his shoulders back, angling his neck from one side to the other. The last time Coira had run away, he'd done nothing. He'd assumed the worst and failed to protect her, making her life miserable as a consequence. This time, he wasn't going to rest until he got her back. He would fight an entire army single-handed if he had to. 'I'm going out there and I'm not coming back without her.'

Chapter Twenty-One

‘**M**acMillan! This is a welcome surprise. I thought I'd have to summon you.' Campbell walked slowly up from the camp to meet Fergus outside the castle gates, his eyes narrowed suspiciously despite the cheerfulness of his greeting. ‘You've made your decision, then?'

‘Not yet.' Fergus folded his arms. ‘I have business with your *ally* first.' He looked past Campbell to where Kendrick was pushing his way through a group of soldiers. ‘He has my wife.'

‘What?' Campbell looked equal parts surprised and amused, spinning around to face Kendrick. ‘How did that happen? You seem to like keeping secrets from me, MacWhinnie.'

‘I hadn't had a chance to inform you, that's all.' Kendrick answered defensively. ‘She came to my tent in the early hours.'

‘Lucky man.' Campbell smirked. ‘Though it seems her husband wants her back.'

‘Too late. She's mine now.' Kendrick's lip curled. ‘In *every* way.'

Fergus dug his heels into the dirt, battling the urge to charge and start pummelling. 'I don't believe you, but if you want to keep her then you're going to have to fight me. Honourably, this time. I'm sure that left to your own devices, you'd prefer to plunge a dagger into my back or abandon me to be trampled, but in the absence of a boar...' He lifted his shoulders, letting the insult hang in the air. 'You may think I'm as bad as your cousin, but I would never lay a finger on Coira. Or belittle her either.' He raised his chin. 'But that doesn't really matter to you, does it? You'd kill me anyway.'

'Because she should have been mine!' Kendrick practically hissed. 'I was going to ask my father for the match after a year had passed. After what I did for her, she should have been mine!'

'But she's not. Even if I die today, she'll never be yours.'

'Come on, MacWhinnie!' Campbell jeered. 'The man just challenged you. Are you brave enough to fight or are you as much of a coward as he says?'

Kendrick's expression wavered. 'It's a trick, a way of stalling. He thinks that if he injures me, my men won't fight.'

'Oh, but I assure you, they will.' Campbell's eyes glittered. 'No matter who wins, they'll fight, but let's make this interesting.' He waved a hand to one of his men. 'Go and fetch this woman. Let's see who she favours. The lady should be allowed to choose her own champion, after all.'

'What?' Kendrick swung around, but the guard was already moving towards his tent.

'I want to see what's so special about her anyway.'

Campbell grinned, obviously enjoying himself. 'There must be something since you're both willing to fight over her.'

Fergus sucked in a breath at the sight of Coira being dragged through a crowd of soldiers. Her clothes were dishevelled and dirty, her hair was falling around her shoulders in dark disarray and there were red marks on her cheek and forehead as if she'd fallen, but she was still fighting defiantly against her captor. Fergus clenched his fingers around his sword hilt, struggling to restrain his temper.

'My lady.' Campbell made an exaggerated bow. 'We're honoured that you saw fit to join us this morning.'

She lifted her head to answer, though whatever she was about to say froze on her lips as she saw Fergus. Instead she simply mouthed his name, her expression stricken.

'Now, perhaps you can settle an argument for us?' Campbell continued, his tone still incongruously cheerful. 'Which of these men do you favour?'

'Fergus.' She didn't hesitate, wrenching herself free from the guard's grasp and taking a few steps towards him. 'I'm sorry I ran away again. I was trying to help. I never meant to hurt you!'

'I know.'

'You do?' She drew herself up short. 'I was afraid that you might think—'

'I did,' he interrupted her. 'But only briefly. I told you last night, I trust you, Coira.'

Her expression transformed with relief as she turned

back to face Campbell. 'I choose my husband, Fergus MacMillan. I love him.'

Despite everything, he felt a warm glow in his chest. She loved him. Somehow, when Elspeth had told him that part, he hadn't completely believed it, but here and now, looking into Coira's face, he knew it was the truth.

'No!' Kendrick's eyes looked wild. 'You can't love him.'

'But I do. With every part of my being. I'm sorry, Kendrick. I never meant to make you care for me, but I never asked you to hurt Nevin either.'

'If I can't have you, then neither can he!'

'Coira!' Fergus charged forward, wrenching his sword from his belt as Kendrick drew a dagger and swung it towards her, but it was too late. There was too much distance between them and too little between her and Kendrick. He was never going to reach her in time. He was going to see her struck down in cold blood... And then Kendrick's arm faltered in mid-air, his body jerking violently before it crumpled abruptly to the ground, Campbell's knife stuck beneath his ribs.

'Kendrick?' Coira's eyes widened in horror as Fergus grasped hold of her arm, pulling her safely behind him.

'You killed him?' Fergus's gaze shot to Campbell.

'He was becoming unpredictable.' Campbell shrugged, bending over to retrieve his knife. 'And a man who lets his own cousin die in cold blood? It takes an untrustworthy man to know who to trust. Besides, I had a wife once. I would have fought anyone who tried to take her from me.' A flicker of some tender emotion crossed his face before his jaw hardened again. 'She was a lady, too, but she died a peasant's death. Thanks to you and your family. And his.'

'You were exiled for your crimes. Anything that happened afterwards was down to you.' Fergus lifted his sword a little higher. 'So what now?'

'Now you hand over your sister. Nothing's changed.' Campbell nudged Kendrick's body with his boot. 'Nothing of any importance anyway.'

'I told you, she's not here. And even if she was, I wouldn't let you have her.'

'Her either?' Campbell laughed mirthlessly. 'We're going around in circles, MacMillan. You can't have it all your own way. How many women do you want?'

'I would never give up anyone under my protection.'

Campbell drew in a deep breath and then let it out loudly, his dark gaze flickering up to the ramparts, taking in each and every one of the arrows trained on his chest. 'Then you leave me no choice. I'll count to one hundred and then you and your wife and your sister and everyone else behind those walls had better hope that help is on its way. One hundred seconds and then your time's up, MacMillan. I won't ask nicely again.'

'I wouldn't expect you to. Although I have another idea. You could fight me instead.'

'What?' he heard Coira gasp behind him.

'Trust me,' he murmured, looking around into her horrified, questioning face before turning back towards Campbell. 'I challenge you!' He raised his voice so that it carried over the whole camp. 'Let's settle this matter between the two of us.'

Campbell put his hands on his hips, his expression

quizzical. 'Now explain to me why exactly I would want do that.'

'Because you just called Kendrick a coward for attempting to refuse a challenge. Is that what you are, too? Would you let your men die just so that you could avoid fighting yourself?'

He bit back a smile as Campbell threw a swift glance over his shoulder. Enough of his men were gathered now, watching and listening with interest.

'You're craftier than I gave you credit for, MacMillan.' The other man's voice was almost approving. 'All right. If it's a fight you want then you can have it, but if I win then she...' he lifted the bloodied knife still in his hand and pointed it towards Coira '...she opens the castle gates and lets me in.'

'Agreed. On condition that if *I* win, you and your men leave.'

'That sounds reasonable.' Campbell nodded slowly. 'You have a bargain. Fortunately for me, I never lose.'

'Only because you've never fought me before.' Fergus flexed his fingers around his sword hilt. Campbell was grinning confidently now, trying to undermine his nerve, but it only strengthened Fergus's resolve. He wouldn't lose today. He had too much at stake. 'Get back inside the castle.' He stretched his other arm out, turning his head slightly to address Coira.

'No.' She didn't move. 'I'm staying by your side from now on, no matter what.'

'This is different. I don't trust him.'

'Neither do I, but I won't leave you, Fergus.'

'This is the one time I want you to.' He took a few steps backwards to join her. 'Please, Coira. He'll fight dirty and I don't want to give him an opportunity to use you against me.'

She hesitated, looking conflicted, before nodding quickly. 'All right, but I meant what I said before. I love you.'

'I know. I love you, too.' He pressed one last kiss to her forehead before pushing her away. 'That's why I'm going to win.'

'How much more time do you need?' Coira heard Campbell shout as she ran towards the castle gates. 'Perhaps you'd like to recite her a poem while we wait?'

'I'm ready. Swords and shields only?'

'Where's the fun in that?' Campbell was already circling. 'I don't like rules.'

'Fine. No rules.'

Coira belted through the gate as it opened, barely pausing to acknowledge the guards behind it before hurtling up the steps to the ramparts. The walkway was already crowded with archers, along with Malcolm and Elspeth, crouching low enough not to be seen, but listening to every word. Not that there was any more talking. The only sounds now were the clash and clamour of metal accompanied by grunts and raucous jeering from Campbell's men.

Holding her breath, she peeked over the top of the wall, just in time to see Fergus land a punishing blow on Campbell's shield, knocking him off balance long enough for him to aim a powerful kick at his knees. As she watched, Campbell let out a roar and dropped to the ground, though he swept his sword in a wide arc at the same time, forcing Fergus to relinquish the advantage and jump backwards. Another second and he was surging forward again, but somehow Campbell was already back on his feet and fighting furiously, as if the moment of weakness had given him a fresh burst of energy.

'What's happening?' Elspeth whispered urgently. 'Who's winning?'

'I don't know.' Coira shook her head in despair. It was impossible to tell. Both men were bleeding in several places and panting heavily with the exertion. Fergus seemed to be limping slightly, while Campbell's left arm seemed to have lost some of its force, but neither appeared to be gaining an advantage. Fergus had the benefit of youth while Campbell had twenty years' worth of battle experience. They looked perfectly, terrifyingly, matched.

'Mama?'

She swung around, aghast to find Gregor running up the rampart steps.

'What are you doing here?' She gathered him against her, pulling him low against the wall so that he couldn't see what was happening outside.

'I ran away from Grizel. She said that you had to go away for a little while, but you're back already!'

'Aye, I am.' She embraced him tightly before holding him out at arm's length. 'But you need to go back to the keep. It's not safe here.'

'Is there fighting? Can I watch?'

She opened her mouth to refuse and then stiffened, aware that the men outside the castle walls had all fallen silent. She jerked her head up and saw that her own men had gone completely still, too, their expressions tense and expectant. Malcolm looked as if he'd turned completely to stone.

'Stay down.' She pushed Gregor towards Elspeth and stood up, her pulse racing frantically as she stared at the scene below. Fergus was still on his feet, looming over Campbell, who was now crouched on the ground, one side of his face gushing blood. She swallowed as time seemed to stand still for several seconds. There was no movement, no sound, not so much as a breath of air, before Campbell's body wavered and then toppled sideways into the dirt.

'He won!' She flung her arms around Malcolm's shoulders. 'Everything's going to be all right!'

'Not yet, my lady.'

'What?' She looked back around in dismay. But it was all over, wasn't it? It ought to be over. The fight was finished and Campbell was dead. He'd promised that his men would leave if he lost, but judging by the angry faces now lining up to confront Fergus, she had a horrible feeling there might be worse to come.

'Keep your arrows ready!' she heard Euan call out, though to her horror, Fergus took a step forward instead of retreating.

'Are we done here?' He lifted his voice along with his sword as if he were challenging the entirety of Campbell's army. 'Your leader is dead. You can take his body back to his son, but you've nothing to gain by staying here now.'

There was another heart-stopping moment of silence while everyone on the ramparts held their breaths, followed by a low rumble, as if a wave were passing through the enemy army, before they all lowered their hands from their sword hilts and turned away.

Chapter Twenty-Two

'You did it!'

Fergus staggered backwards under the combined weight of his wife, sister and stepson, all embracing him at once.

'Are you hurt?'

'That was a stupid thing to do!'

'They wouldn't let me watch!'

'One at a time!' He laughed, trying to wrap his arms around each of them in turn. 'I have a sore leg and a few cuts, but nothing that won't mend, Coira. Aye, it was stupid, Elspeth, but it worked. And they were absolutely right, Gregor. You're too young to watch such things.'

'But you won!'

'No.' He grinned down at his stepson. '*We* won.'

'So the Campbells are defeated?'

'One of them is. I'll have to write to Ross and tell him. As for the other, hopefully it won't be long before he meets the same fate but, until then, we'll all have to be on our guard.'

'That's enough of the Campbells. Come with me so

I can take a look at those injuries.' Coira caught hold of his hand, pulling him towards the keep. 'Your face is a mess.'

'Not yet. I need to make sure that Campbell's men are really leaving.'

'Malcolm and Euan can do that.'

'I need to find Iver, too. I'm going to make him wish—'

'No, you're not.' She stopped and stared hard into his face. 'I understand why you'd want to, but there's been enough violence this morning.'

'Don't I get a say in this?' He lifted an eyebrow at her imperious tone.

'None at all. Besides, if I know Iver, he's long gone already. As for the rest of you...' she looked around the bailey, narrowing her eyes in warning '...no one, and I mean *no one*, is to disturb us unless absolutely necessary.'

Half an hour later, Fergus folded an arm behind his head and made a solemn promise never to dispute his wife's orders ever again.

'If I'd known that was what you meant by "take a look at those injuries", I would have agreed to come with you a lot sooner.'

'I *didn't* mean that.' She rubbed a hand lazily across his chest. 'Or at least, not just that. And I had a good look at you first.'

'I noticed. You were very thorough. I almost wished I had more cuts for you to tend.'

'Don't joke about it.' She shuddered. 'I was so scared.'

'*You* were scared?' He wrapped an arm around her

shoulders, manoeuvring them so that he was lying on his side, peering down into her face. 'When I found out where you'd gone this morning...' He sucked air between his teeth. 'I've never been so frightened in my whole life. Don't do anything like that to me ever again.'

'I'm sorry. I honestly thought I was helping.'

'As it turned out, you did help. Everything worked out, even if I don't quite understand how.'

'In that case, it was all deliberate and my plan worked perfectly.'

'I always said you were the smart one.' He laughed softly. 'However, I'll be looking after the key to that tunnel from now on.'

'I don't have it.' She pushed herself up on one elbow when he looked sceptical. 'I really don't! Grizel was the one who locked me out.'

'Then I'll ask Euan to get the key from her. He'll enjoy the task, I'm sure.'

'Probably a little too much. We should really hurry up and arrange their wedding.'

'One thing at a time. We might have won today, but the fight with the Campbells isn't over yet. Alexander still has a son and, if he's anything like his father, it won't be long before he comes looking for revenge.'

'Do you think he might attack us, too?'

'I don't know what he'll do, but whatever it is, he'll be facing the MacMillans, the MacWhinnies and the MacLachlans all together.' He touched a finger to her brow, trying to uncrease it. 'And we've just proven that we're not easy to defeat. We're more than a match for his army.'

'I'm not so certain about Brody's support. We'll have

to go and tell him about Kendrick, which means telling him what Kendrick did to Nevin, too.' She sighed, her expression turning even more anxious. 'Poor Nevin. I didn't love him, but I would never have wished such a terrible thing on him either. As for Kendrick, I can still hardly believe he was capable of something so wicked. He was always so kind and thoughtful and he seemed genuinely upset after Nevin's death. I never suspected a thing. Neither of them was what they seemed.' She lifted a hand to cradle the back of his head. 'I was completely wrong about you, too. You were far better than you seemed. I've been a terrible judge of character.'

'Some people are good at deceiving and some of us are good at giving the wrong impression. Both Nevin and Kendrick were talented actors.'

'Kendrick didn't deceive you.'

'No, but I was prepared to be jealous of any man who spoke to you.' He gave her a nudge, trying to lighten the mood. 'If Malcolm had been ten years younger, I might have been wary of him, as well.'

'Aye, he's a good-looking man underneath all that beard.'

'Hush or he'll find himself banished to the village.' He smiled. 'The point is that none of this was your fault.'

'I wish I could be sure of that.' Coira rolled away on to her stomach, shaking her head as if she were trying to chase away her own thoughts. 'I can't help but worry that I encouraged Kendrick somehow. Why else would he have felt so strongly? I never intended to make him care for me, but maybe I was too friendly towards him or—'

'Or maybe Kendrick simply chose to see what he wanted to see,' he interrupted her. 'If you never intended it then it wasn't your fault.' He smoothed a hand gently over her hair and then down to her waist, rolling her back over again. 'Thinking that way won't do any good. You can't blame yourself for other people's feelings. Kendrick was responsible for his own actions.'

'But what if Brody doesn't believe that? He already dislikes me. He might think that we're lying.'

'Brody has eyes in more places than you think. He probably already knows that his son sided with the enemy and if by some small chance he doesn't, then Kendrick's men will tell him. They'll be on their way to his fortress by now. They were probably reluctant to attack Castle Barron in the first place since Gregor's their clansman. In any case, I'll ride there tomorrow and make sure that Brody knows the truth.'

'No. *We'll* ride there tomorrow.'

'Coira…'

'*We* will,' she repeated more firmly. 'And you won't persuade me otherwise this time. We'll face him together and tell him the truth together.' Her brow furrowed. 'Although you might be right about him having eyes everywhere. I wonder now if he suspected something about Kendrick's feelings for me. That would explain why he was so determined to marry the pair of us off so quickly while Kendrick was away, too. Maybe he was afraid of his son making the same mistake as his nephew.'

'Don't do that.'

'What?'

'Don't call yourself a mistake. Nevin was too much

of a fool to know how lucky he was.' He kissed the tip of her nose. 'However, if you're right about Brody suspecting, then it'll make explaining things a whole lot easier.'

'What if he punishes you for challenging his son to combat?'

'He won't. It was a reasonable challenge given the circumstances and it was Campbell who dug the blade in.'

'Don't remind me. It's not a sight I'm likely to forget in a hurry.' She shuddered and put a hand on his shoulder, smoothing her fingers across his collar bone. 'Do you think it's really necessary to tell him what Kendrick did to Nevin? I've no liking for Brody, but I've no wish to hurt him either. Maybe we can just keep that part between ourselves?'

'If that's what you want.'

She nodded firmly. 'Yes. Unless it becomes absolutely necessary, it should remain our secret.'

'Agreed. The important thing now is that we're together and Castle Barron and the children are safe.'

'Aye.' She drew his face back down to hers again. 'Now just how recovered are you?'

'Recovered enough.' His lips curved as he slid a hand over her hip. 'I thought you were never going to stop talking.'

'Goodbye again.' Elspeth embraced Coira on the steps of the keep, taking several seconds longer than she had on the previous occasion. 'I'd tell you to take care of my brother, but I have a feeling I don't need to.'

'I promise to do it anyway.' Coira hugged her back. The morning was bright and golden, sunshine warming her face for the first time in weeks. 'Are you sure you want to leave so soon? Some of Campbell's men might still be around.'

'It's probably safer to go now than to wait. Once Calum Campbell finds out what's happened, there's likely to be more trouble, which means that the sooner I reach the MacLachlans, the better. You've already done your part in this fight. Now it's my turn.'

'As long as you're certain. Ride safely.'

'And goodbye to you, too, big Brother.' Elspeth smiled affectionately as Fergus approached with her horse. 'No more fighting for a while, d'ye hear? That face needs a chance to recover.'

'And here I was, expecting you to tell me it was an improvement.'

'It crossed my mind, but I thought my new sister might not appreciate the comment. She's quite defensive in regard to you, you know.' Elspeth looked between the two of them with a bemused smile before mounting her palfrey. 'Do you know what the most annoying part of all this is? Ross was right about the two of you being well suited.'

'I'm sure he'll come and make the point himself before long.' Fergus rolled his eyes. 'I hope that things work out between you and MacLachlan, too.'

Elspeth's smile wavered. 'Hopefully, my marriage will be enough to scare Calum Campbell from our shores permanently. With any luck, this will be the last we ever hear of the name Campbell.'

Coira tipped her head on to her husband's shoulder as Elspeth and her escort rode away. 'I hope that she finds happiness.'

'So do I.' He slipped an arm around her waist, turning his head sideways so that his cheek rested against her hair. 'I just can't quite imagine it with Leith Mac-Lachlan.'

'You don't like him?'

'I don't *dis*like him. I just don't think they're a good match.'

'Not like us?'

'No.' He tightened his grip. 'Not like us.'

'What a pity.'

'You know, there's still one thing that bothers me.'

'Oh? What's that?'

'Campbell claimed he wasn't involved in the attack on the Abbey where Elspeth was hiding before she came here.'

'And you believed him?'

'Aye, that's the strange part. It was really as if he didn't know anything about it. If it had been Calum, wouldn't he have told his father? But I can't think who else it could have been or what possible motive they might have had. I can't help feeling that I'm missing something.'

'Mama!' Gregor came scampering across the bailey at that moment, Duffy hard at his heels.

'What is it?' She greeted him with a smile, glad of the distraction. She'd had enough talk of fighting for a while.

'Watch. *Lie down!*' Gregor pointed a finger at the dog, who obediently lay down in the dirt. 'I kept giving her treats, like Fergus said, and then all of a sudden, she just did it.' He beamed up at them. 'She'll give me her paw, too, if I ask her. *Paw!*'

'Well done, lad.' Fergus patted him on the shoulder as the dog obeyed. 'I'm glad there's one female around here who does what she's told.'

'Excuse me?' Coira pulled away from him in protest.

'Running away with another man, going for rides against my advice, crawling through tunnels in the dead of night…' He grinned as he tugged her back again. 'Fortunately, after due consideration, I've decided I wouldn't want you any other way.'

Chapter Twenty-Three

'How dare you!' Brody MacWhinnie braced his hands on the arms of his chair and pushed his massive bulk to his feet, looming above Fergus like a red-faced mountain. 'How dare you come to my hall and spread lies about my son!'

'They're not lies.' Fergus stood his ground without flinching. 'Kendrick's men must have returned here by now. Ask them and they'll tell you that he sided with Campbell. He led him to Castle Barron to capture *my* sister.'

A muscle twitched in Brody's jaw, confirming that he already knew. 'They also told me you challenged him to combat.'

'What choice did I have? I challenged Kendrick honourably, but Campbell was the one who killed him.'

'Only because he got to him before you did!'

'Perhaps, but we'll never know now.'

Brody advanced a step closer, his pale eyes narrowing. 'Do you really expect me to believe that my son was in love with your wife?'

'I do.' Fergus lifted his chin. 'Because I think you know it already. That's why you jumped at the chance of an alliance between Coira and me. Then you sent him south so that he wouldn't hear anything about it until it was too late.'

Brody's gaze flickered guiltily, darting sideways as if making sure that nobody else was in earshot. 'It wasn't the only reason. I also knew you were the best man to defend Castle Barron until Gregor came of age, but I admit that getting her away from Kendrick played a part, too.' His brows lowered into a scowl. 'I saw how she was getting her talons into him, just like she did with Nevin. *He* told me how she seduced him, how she led him to betray his own family and elope with her that night before your wedding. All because she wanted to be a laird's wife. And after she was done with him, she thought herself good enough for *my son!*'

'As opposed to good enough for me?' Fergus raised his chin a notch higher. 'You're wrong about Coira. She never seduced anyone and she's never had any talons. Nevin ran away with her because he came to an arrangement with her brother, not her. He was a liar, a coward and a bully and he betrayed his family for money. As for Kendrick, she thought he was a friend, that's all. She never even suspected how he felt about her.'

'Pah!' Brody's lips twisted into a sneer. 'I thought it would be a good way to avenge my nephew, forcing her to marry you after everything that's passed, but now I see you've fallen for her snares, as well.'

'See what you like, but say it out loud one more time and I'll be challenging you to combat next.'

Brody held his stare for a few seconds before lowering his shoulders, his belligerent expression fading. 'I ordered Kendrick to stay away from Castle Barron. I threatened to disown him if he went near her again, but I never imagined he'd go against my orders and join forces with Campbell. My own son...' His voice broke before he jerked himself upright again. 'I want it said that he died in combat with Campbell, that he was fighting on the side of Castle Barron at *my* command. I want everyone who was there to understand that, no matter what they might think they saw.'

'As you wish.' Fergus nodded solemnly. 'On one condition. That you and your family treat my wife with the respect she deserves as Nevin's widow and Gregor's mother. I want it known that anyone who speaks against her will answer to me and I *won't* be reasonable.'

'No, I don't suppose you will be,' Brody snorted. 'Very well. If that's your price then we have an agreement.'

'Good. In that case, you can start as you mean to go on.' Fergus half turned his head to where Coira was standing alone on one side of the hall, an isolated but defiant figure in a room brimming with unfriendly eyes. 'She's waiting to see which of us is going to kill the other first.'

A flash of grim amusement crossed Brody's features before he opened his mouth and bellowed loudly enough to draw shocked stares from everyone in the hall. *'Niece!'*

Coira gave a jolt of alarm, even glancing over her shoulder as he beckoned to her, as if she thought he might be calling to somebody else.

'Come!' Brody called again, reaching a hand out to

enfold hers as she moved haltingly towards him. 'Your husband and I have come to an understanding.'

'You have?' Her eyes darted between them, anxious and hopeful at the same time.

'Aye. He argues well on your behalf. It appears there have been matters about which I *might…*' he paused meaningfully '…have been misinformed. If so, then I ask your forgiveness.'

'My forgiveness?' Coira gaped at him, looking as surprised as if he'd just offered to give her his hall. 'I mean, of course.'

'Then I thank you.' Brody bowed over her hand. 'Now tell me, how is my great-nephew?'

'Gregor's well.' She pressed her lips together as if she were trying to stop herself from saying something else and then couldn't resist. 'So is Ailis.'

'Ailis?'

'My stepdaughter,' Fergus answered as he saw her eyes flash. 'A bonny lass. She's going to be just as beautiful as her mother one day.'

'Is that so?' Brody lifted an eyebrow. 'Then you must bring them both for a visit here soon.'

'Does that mean we're free to go home?' Coira sounded a little too hopeful.

'Aye, in the morning.' Brody almost smiled. 'Tonight, however, I'd like you to stay and dine as my honoured guests.'

'*Honoured?*' She repeated the word as if it were too much for her.

'Honoured,' Fergus confirmed, grabbing hold of her hand before she fell over from shock. 'And we'd be *honoured* to accept.'

* * *

'How much longer?' Fergus leaned sideways to murmur in Coira's ear, using the opportunity to slide a hand up her thigh at the same time.

'Fergus!' she gasped, squirming as his fingers moved higher. 'How much longer until what?'

'Until we can escape from this table and I can get you out of that gown.'

'Shh.' She batted his hand away, feeling her cheeks flush and her pulse accelerate anyway. 'Someone will hear!'

'I don't care. We're honoured guests, remember?'

'That's why we can't leave. This is the first time I've been treated with anything other than contempt and disdain in this hall and I want to enjoy the experience. It might not last very long.'

'Trust me, it will. No one's going to treat you badly ever again, not if I have anything to say about it.'

'Fergus…' She cast him a sidelong look. 'Please tell me you didn't threaten Brody.'

'Not directly.'

'Fergus?'

'I'm telling the truth. Sometimes the way you say something is enough. As long as it's accompanied by a frown, of course.' He clenched his brows together. 'I'm very good at those.'

'So fierce!' She laughed. 'But wasted on me, I'm afraid. I'm not intimidated by them any more.'

'I'm glad to hear it.'

'I'm actually coming to love your frowns. They're so quintessentially you.' She tipped her head to one side. 'And I love *you*.'

'I love you, too.'

'But we still can't leave. It might cause offence.'

'All right.' He sighed heavily. 'But I warn you, I have plans for later.'

'Is that so?' She reached for a sweetmeat, lifting it slowly and deliberately to her lips. 'And what plans would those be exactly?'

'Well…' He leaned closer, whispering in her ear until she felt her temperature soar.

'Oh…' She felt positively breathless by the time he'd finished speaking. 'That does sound…time-consuming.'

'Aye, when it's done properly it is…' His lips skimmed the shell of her ear. 'And I don't care how late we get to bed. You won't be able to escape me this time.'

'Then it seems we won't be getting much sleep tonight.' She met his gaze, her own warming. 'Fortunately, I don't want to escape you. Never ever again.'

'Is that a promise?'

'Aye.' She reached for his hand as it caressed its way back up her thigh, clasping it between both of hers. 'It is.'

'Good. Because running away from me twice is enough.' He pressed his lips against hers before getting to his feet and raising his goblet, his eyes never leaving hers for a second. 'To Coira MacMillan! The finest lady and best wife in all of Scotland!'

'To Coira MacMillan!'

She smiled and squeezed her eyes shut, aware of moisture gathering behind them as her name echoed around the hall. Some of the cheers might have sounded reluctant, but she didn't care. Fergus was looking at her with love and that was all that mattered. She was Coira MacMillan now and, for the first time in six long years, she was finally and truly happy.

* * * * *

*If you enjoyed this story
be sure to read the first book in
the Highland Alliances collection*

The Highlander's Substitute Wife
by Terri Brisbin

*Look out for the next book
in the Highland Alliances collection*

The Highlander's Stolen Bride
*by Madeline Martin
Coming soon!*

*And while you're waiting for the next book
why not check out Jenni Fletcher's
other great reads?*

The Duke's Runaway Bride
A Marriage Made in Secret
"The Christmas Runaway" in Snow-Kissed Proposals

*Read on for a teaser of the final instalment in
the Highland Alliances collection,*

The Highlander's Stolen Bride
by Madeline Martin.

A roar sounded from the trees and five men rushed from the foliage, their deep blue gambesons similar to the shade of the surrounding forest. The insignia stitched on their clothing was one Elspeth immediately recognised as it had been the same as those worn by the curs who had attacked the abbey she'd previously been sent to for her safety.

They had come for her then, attacking the nuns in their effort to steal her away.

And now, they were here for her again.

The marauders clashed with her remaining guards in a clang of metal on metal and grunts as each man struggled to not only kill their opponent, but also emerge alive and unscathed.

Elspeth had once harboured grandiose ideas of bravery in a scenario such as the one in which she now found herself. The idea of lifting a sword and wielding it expertly, cutting her own way to freedom. Now she remained in place where she hid behind the guards, uncertain what she could possibly do with only her simple dagger.

The guard to her left was knocked from his horse.

His beast tore off at the first opportunity of freedom, leaving a gap in her wall of protection.

One of the marauders filled the gap immediately and reached for her. 'I have her.'

She lashed out with her foot, thrusting it towards the man with all her might.

Her shoe was a dainty leather thing, meant more for traipsing about a castle as mistress than for fighting in a battle, but she put every bit of her strength into that kick. Whether it was the force of the blow or the surprise that a lady would so readily attack, the man fell back.

But the man's determination to claim her only confirmed what she suspected. They wanted her. To use her against her brothers, knowing full well she was Ross MacMillan's weakness.

On the road between Castle Barron and Castle Lachlan, she was vulnerable.

'Run!' the young guard said as he fended off the attacker. 'Run!'

Though fleeing went against everything in Elspeth's spirit, she knew the best thing for her people would be to avoid capture, to keep from becoming their enemy's pawn. She snapped her reins and did exactly as the guard ordered, running from a battle she knew they could not win. Rain stung at her face and left her hair clinging to her skin like cobwebs, but she ignored it all as she hugged her body to the horse's powerful neck and fled.

No sooner had she departed from the two remaining

guards, than another horse thundered behind her. Her heart caught in her chest, but she didn't dare look back.

She didn't have to…not when she already knew exactly who was there.

A man rumoured to be immeasurably cruel, one who took innocent lives and burned the homes of peasants, the son of the very man who had killed Elspeth's own father.

As the ominous pounding of horse hooves rumbled closer, she gripped the reins with one hand and slid free the dagger with the other, locking it in her fist. For she would rather die than be taken by the likes of Calum Campbell.